Eternal Road

- The final stop

By John W. Howell

Keewaydin Lane Books

ISBN: 978-1733571-0-8
Editor: Harmony Kent
Printed in the United States of America
Keewaydin Lane Books

Dedication

Eternal Road - The final stop I am dedicating to my father, John A. Howell (1911-1951). Although he left this earth at the young age of forty, his influence and love remain with me. He was a man who also lost his father at a young age. He persevered where others would have used this excuse to fail. The larger than life lesson he taught me was we all have challenges in our lives, and those that can succeed in reaching their goals despite them will find happiness. This book is about reaching a goal and achieving personal satisfaction as a result. I think my dad would have liked this story, and like James, the protagonist, I will enjoy his reaction someday.

Acknowledgments

Eternal Road – The last stop is a piece of fiction written out of the author's imagination. The events described and places are purely fictional, with no intent to depict reality. Big thanks to Harmony Kent for her editorial professionalism. I also want to acknowledge my beta readers whose suggestions and comments enhanced this story. Finally, thank you, Molly, for your continued support.

Prologue

The little girl skips from the schoolyard while singing a song she's heard but can't remember the name. The lyrics reflect her mood, and the rhythm matches her gait. She's finished her first-grade reading assignment and can't wait to show her mother the note from her teacher. The thought of rushing in the door and announcing her perfect grade causes her mouth to spread widely while she sings. There will be cookies and milk and laughter after her mother reads what the teacher has to say.

Her dad will come home, and her mother will tell him the good news. Since the weather has grown warmer, maybe she can convince her parents that a great way to celebrate her fab news is going out for ice-cream after dinner. Next, her thoughts turn to the different flavors that she'll need to review until she can settle on one. The last time, she had pure chocolate with sprinkles. Who knows what she'll have this time? Not chocolate, because she wants to try something new. Maybe something with nuts, but then she can almost feel them as she bites the cold hard meat. No, she'll have to go for a flavor without nuts.

***

The man squats low in the woods. The little girl will come to the curve in the sidewalk soon. For the past month, he's watched her walk home. She always takes this way. He chooses to squat so that he won't get his pants dirty while he waits. It wouldn't do to go back to the office with dirt on his knees. That would give folks a tip-off for sure. Someone would remember him walking in with dirt on his fine gabardine pants, and the police would put two and two together.

He's planned this snatch and grab for weeks. Has lain awake nights thinking of how he will need to take utmost care.

And he must make sure that the girl makes no noise. Though the dense woods muffle a lot of sounds, enough people use the area that one cry could bring down disaster. After a series of deep, calming breaths, he believes he is ready.

The sound of skipping comes to his ears. He looks toward the sidewalk. Through the brush, the girl approaches, singing as she skips. A few seconds more, and she will be his forever.

He calls her name, and she stops.

"Samantha, come here."

"Where are you?" comes back her little voice.

"In the bush."

"Are you a troll?"

"No, sweet thing. Your mother sent me to bring you home. Come here. We'll play a game."

The youngster edges nearer to the bush. When she bends a little to see beyond the foliage, he grabs her hand and pulls her into the trees. At the same time, he yanks a black cloth bag over her head. Then he clamps his hand over her mouth and drags her deeper into the woods to a small clearing. Weeds cover the dirt here, so he can allow himself to not worry about muck on his pants.

He whispers to her, "Nothing will happen as long as you keep quiet. I'll take my hand away if you promise not to make any noise. Do you understand?"

She nods, and he releases her mouth. The girl shakes. Her fear makes him smile—little girls afraid will do pretty much everything he asks. "I want to kiss you, Samantha. Is that okay?"

Samantha begins to cry.

"Shut up."

But she can't help herself, so he takes her by the head, yanks the bag up above her mouth, and pulls her to his face. He pushes her lips open with his tongue and shoves it deep into her

7

mouth. Samantha struggles, so he holds her head tighter in a one-handed grip while he rips off her clothes with the other. The girl fights and kicks at him, but her weak blows do little. Finally, he pulls away, and—immediately—she yells. In a panic, he hits her full in the face, which makes her go limp and quiet.

"I told you not to make any noise. Now look what you made me do." The man feels for a pulse. A weak, but steady beat taps against his searching fingers. Oh hell. He places his hands around her throat and listens for her breathing to stop.

After all signs of life have left her, he lets her go. He will have to come back for her later. Because his evidence is all over her, he can't afford for anyone to find her like this, and he'll need to hide her where no one will ever discover her body. Later, though, when the woods have quietened down.

Adrenaline pumping, he lifts himself from the grassy ground and duck-walks to the edge of the woods. With no one in sight, he exits the brush at speed, stands straight, and walks back toward the office. When he rounds the next curve, two people walking on the sidewalk startle him. The man and a woman block the walk. He puts his head down and continues toward them. They pull over to the side and make room for him to pass. To make this encounter as unmemorable as possible, he avoids eye-contact.

After a few more steps, he takes a moment to stop and look back. Sure enough, the woman has also glanced back at him. His heart races—he'll need to move his little Samantha tonight. In no way can he risk anyone coming forward and putting him anywhere near the spot where someone has murdered a child. Glad to see the couple walk on, he does the same.

Chapter One

In just a couple more hours, I'll be able to rest my eyes. Been on this damn highway for what seems like forever. I must stay awake. James nods slowly until the cacophony from the rumble-strip jerks him awake. "Shit. I fell asleep," he yells and yanks the wheel. The tires screech in protest when he swerves back onto the highway. His heart hammers at the walls of his chest, and his eyes feel like they could explode. Scared alert, he regrets being so weak as to give in to the physical need for sleep. Also, it alarms him to realize that sleep could overtake him without any warning. One second, his eyes could be open, and the next closed. Thank God for the jarring and noise of the rumble strips. Without their alarm, he would surely have ended up piled into a tree.

As his heart settles down, he concentrates on the road ahead. Someone stands on the shoulder about a half-mile away. A hitchhiker by the looks of the backpack. A sign in the person's hand proves unreadable at this distance. *It would be a good thing to have someone else in the car to help me stay awake.* Of course, picking up a stranger brings its own dangers. When he gets closer, he can see that the hitchhiker is not a guy like he at first thought. It's a young woman, who looks to be about his age. She wears overalls, but the distinctive female form still comes through. James slows down and assesses the situation. A girl makes all the difference in trying to reach a decision for or against a pickup. After all, who knows where this could lead? He does. She isn't as likely to stick a knife in his ribs and demand his wallet.

James eases the 1956 Oldsmobile sedan to the shoulder and can't help kicking up some dust in the process. The sign is facing him even as the person turns away to avoid the dust storm he has created. Kansas City in black marker on cardboard is all it says.

He opens the passenger door and waves her over. "I'm going to Kansas City. Want a ride?"

The young woman looks back at him, and he can tell she is doing an evaluation of the safety prospects of accepting a lift. She slowly hoists her backpack on to her shoulder and walks with hesitant steps toward the car. She puts her hand above her eyes to cut the glare of the sun and stops short of the door. She leans in. "Did you say you're going to Kansas City?"

"Yes. Yes, I did. I also asked if you would like a ride."

"That all depends on your intentions?"

"My intentions?"

"Yeah. You are offering a ride. How much will it cost me?"

"Cost you? I'm going to Kansas City. Your sign says Kansas City. Why would it cost you anything?"

"Just want to make sure is all."

"No charge. I've been on the road forever, it seems, and I would welcome the company. My name is James."

"Sorry, James. I know I sounded a little ungrateful, but I have also been on the road and have met several guys that think I owe them something for a ride."

"I can understand that. Let's just say you can ride or not. It's your choice. No other decisions to be made."

"Fair enough. I accept your offer. My name is Samantha." She slides in and slams the door.

"Nice to meet you, Samantha. You want to put your backpack in the rear?"

"No, I'll just keep it here in the front with me. You can never tell."

"Tell what?"

"When I'll have to bail. Everything I own is in this pack, and I sure wouldn't want to leave it behind."

"I get it. No use trusting someone just 'cause they say you can."

"Right. I think I like you, James."

"Wainwright. My last name's Wainwright. How about you?"

"Not sure I have a last name. I go by Samantha, but you can call me Sam."

"No last name? How can that be?"

"You going to start this car, or is my fear well-founded?"

James flushes as he turns the ignition. "Yeah, here we go." He looks in the side mirror and signals as he pulls back on the highway.

"You are a cautious one. There's no one for miles."

"I guess it's a habit from city driving." He keeps checking in the mirror until he gets up to highway speed.

Samantha asks, "Where you from?"

"New York. You?"

"I think I was originally from down south somewhere."

"You don't know?"

"Well, it's been a long time."

James glances at her and sees that she is lost in thought. Her fair skin covers the high cheekbones and lips of a runway model. She seems vaguely familiar to him—a bit like Joni Mitchell. Samantha has an innocent, fragile look that makes him want to take care of her.

Samantha blinks. "I'm sorry. What did you say?"

"I didn't say anything. I'm amazed you don't know where you come from."

"Well, do you remember where you're from, or is it someone told you?"

11

She has a point. James only knows he was born in Chicago because his parents told him so. He lived in New York for twenty years, so unless clued in, he would have thought he'd lived there his whole life. "I guess I should rephrase the question. ... Where did you last live?"

A grin stretches her lips. "That makes more sense. I lived in New York, too."

"What a coincidence. Do you believe that?"

"I can believe that. Someone once said there are only six degrees of separation of everyone on Earth. You and I traveling this road at the same time certainly falls into that realm."

"Aw, come on. We're both on this road going to Kansas City. That has to be more than a coincidence."

"I never said I was going to Kansas City."

"Wait. You've that sign that says so."

"Doesn't mean I'm going there."

"So, what does it mean?"

"You think I know?"

"I'm getting a weird feeling here. Like you aren't telling me something."

"Do you remember swerving after you ran off the highway?"

"What? Back there. Yeah, I remember almost falling asleep. Hey, wait a minute. How'd you know about that?"

"Think a minute. How do you think I could ever know about that moment?"

"I'm too tired for guessing games. What's this all about?"

"Do you feel okay?"

"Yeah, just tired."

"Look around. Do you see any other vehicles?"

"No, but I haven't for a while. What're you trying to tell me?"

"You fell asleep."

"When did I fall asleep? I know I nodded off, but when did I go out completely?"

"Just before your car went off the road, and you hit a cement culvert."

James looks at Sam, trying to get a hint from the look on her face. Seeing nothing helpful, he looks away. "Now, you are joking. Right?" He looks at her again. "Right, Sam?"

She shakes her head. "No joke, James." She nods at the windshield. "Look ahead. What do you see?"

"Uh, up the road, you mean?"

"Yes, up the road."

"Nothing but what looks like a sandstorm."

"It's no storm. It's nothing."

James takes his eyes off the road and tries to figure out who is sitting in his car. "Who are you anyway?"

"Do you remember that little girl who went missing in the second grade?"

"Yeah, what does that have to do with you?"

"Does the nickname Jimmy Jeans mean anything?"

"That's what Samantha called me in the second grade."

"How'd I know that?"

"You wouldn't, unless ..."

"Unless I'm Samantha."

James pulls off to the side of the road. He puts the car in park and turns to face Sam. "Oh, my God. Sam. It's you. Where have you been?"

"That's not important. What's important is you were broken-hearted when I vanished. You prayed for my return and made promises to God if only I would come back."

13

"I never got over that either. I know I was just a kid, but you never left my mind. I think of that little gir–I mean, I thought of you almost every day. Why didn't I recognize you?" Sam puts her hand on James's arm. "Because I'm all grown up. There would be no way."

James stares down at Sam's hand. Tears well up in his eyes. "Where have you been? I missed you so much." His eyes overflow.

"Don't cry. I'm here with you now." She squeezes his arm, and he places his hand on hers.

"Can you tell me what happened to you?"

"No, it's not worth the time."

James takes his hand away and frowns. "So, why now? Why have you come here now?"

Sam's eyes soften, and she gives James a slight smile. "To help you."

James's frown deepens. "To help me? How? Why?"

Sam removes her hand from his arm and looks intently into his eyes. "To understand what your life's like now."

James tries to avoid her gaze by focusing on the floor. The carpet could do with a clean. "Now? What do you mean?"

Gently, Sam lifts James's chin and directs his eyes to gaze into hers. She speaks slowly so that James can absorb every word, "You were in an accident. You ran off the road, and I'm sorry to say your body didn't survive. You're now going with me on an eternal trip." She pauses to give James time to react.

James pulls away from her hand. "You're saying I'm dead. I can't believe that. Look at me. I'm just as alive as you."

Sam smiles. "That's right. You are."

The full weight of what Samantha is trying to tell him presses on his chest, making it hard to breathe. He forces a deep breath. "Um, Sam?"

"Yes?"

James expels the air from his lungs. "You're dead, too?" He reaches for her hand.

"Yes. A man took me from school and killed me. They never found my body."

"W-what?"

Sam squeezes his palm. "Don't think about that now. Focus on the future. Because you prayed so hard and missed me so much, they gave me the honor of escorting you to the other side."

"Other side? What's the other side?" James eases from her soft grip and wipes his face to get rid of the mess of tears.

"It's not called the other side, but it is a wonderful place for all time."

"And you and I will be together?"

"We have to see what transpires. For now, just hold my hand, and then let's be off."

Gingerly, James retakes her hand. He looks at her. "I have more questions."

Sam smiles. "All in good time, my man. All in good time."

Chapter Two

Though Sam's revelation has left James reeling, they continue down the road without saying anything. James looks over, and Samantha turns from staring out the window. She smiles and says, "You okay?"

"As long as I'm with you." He gives her one of those smiles that beg for reassurance.

"Don't you worry. No way would I leave you alone. Do you know how long I had to wait to come and get you?"

"No. How long?"

"I was seven when I died and then had to wait for another seventeen years."

"Do the years pass at the same time … ?" James pauses to pick the right word. "Uh, over there?"

"You mean over here. This is the new reality right here and now."

"But it looks like we're still in my Olds driving down the road."

"I know it seems that way. You see, there's a waiting period for you to get used to your new status."

"You've done this before?"

"I've never done this until now. I have to say, though, the instructions for handling such a thing have proven amazingly specific and useful so far."

"So, *does* time pass the same?"

"That's hard to answer. For instance, you prayed for … what? … Around ten years? Did it seem like ten years?"

"No."

"Then you can feel what it's like. Time is relative. I didn't think about how long it took for you to die. It just happened, and I'm here to take care of you."

"When you died, did it hurt?"

"No, I didn't feel anything. Like you, I wasn't aware of what happened. It just happened."

"Who came to take care of you?"

"Such a blessing. My grandma. She died when I was still a little baby. The first thing I remember is being in her arms. It was wonderful."

"Do you see her? I mean, over here?"

"I do. It's funny, though. Gran's real busy, and we don't get to see each other as often as I would want. She's one of the baby handlers."

"Baby handlers?"

"Hey, look up ahead. There's a general store. Let's stop. I have a hankering for a cold drink."

"I should be thirsty but just don't feel it."

"You don't get thirsty in the classic sense. You can feel a memory and then go ahead and revisit it. I loved ice-cold root beer, so that's what I'm going to have."

James slows the car. Some things he will never understand, so why not just follow her lead? He parks in front of the store.

Sam jumps out of the Oldsmobile and gives a little laugh. James heard that laugh around the playground when they were kids. He remembers, distinctly, the time she grabbed his baseball and burst out with that laugh while running away. Now, she hurries up onto the wooden porch. "Come on, silly."

He breaks his reverie and opens his door. The heat hits him as soon as he steps out of the car. Squinting against the bright sunlight, he sees Sam go through the double doors. James follows her and, momentarily, the darkness within stuns him. Through the gloom, he makes out a long bar on the other side of the room. When his eyes become accustomed to the low light level, he notices lamps hanging from the ceiling, which give

17

off a smell that he doesn't recognize. One or two near the bar are lit, and a thin layer of smoke hovers near the ceiling.

"Over here," Sam calls. She stands at the bar with one foot up on a brass rail. The bartender has a wrinkled forehead and doesn't look pleased, so James decides he better get over there and clear up any misunderstanding.

"Everything okay?" James looks first to the bartender and then to Sam.

"I was just telling the lady that women aren't allowed at the bar. Just not ladylike, and the boss doesn't want any trouble with the womenfolk in town."

Though taken aback, James manages to give Sam a look that broadcasts, 'behave yourself.' To the bartender, he says, "Well, sir, I guess we better move to a table, then. Will that be okay?"

The bartender smiles in relief. "Yes, it will. I'll serve you from there."

"It's not okay with me." Clearly, Sam has her hackles up.

James takes her by the arm and half drags her over to a table. He plops her down and pulls up a chair for himself. Other people in the bar stare open-mouthed at the two of them. "Sam, for heaven's sake. Quit grumping about the bartender and take a look around."

"What am I looking for?"

"These people appear as though they're from the 1800s. Look how they're dressed. There's not a zipper in the place. All buttons and suspenders."

Sam glances around the room. "I see what you mean. The women look like Miss Kitty from the show Gunsmoke." Sam pauses. "Oh, no."

"Oh, no, what?"

"I was warned while in training that there's a possibility that, while making our way back to the eternal home, we could encounter some turbulence."

James frowns. "So, is there some now?"

Sam sighs. "You bet. We've walked into a saloon and, I believe, into the nineteenth century."

James sits up straighter in his chair. "W-what? How can that happen?"

"It's a normal occurrence. See, life on Earth is made up of compartments. As we leave one plane, we move through these compartments at different times. Like right now, we're in the 1870s or so. Of course, I'm guessing."

The corners of James's mouth turn up slightly. "About the planes?"

"No, I'm certain about the planes. I'm guessing about what time frame we wandered into."

James leans forward. "Did you have to do this when you went to the eternal home?"

"No. I was just a child, so they took me in like they do with all children who die."

"Any reason for this turbulence?" James taps his fingers on the table.

Sam puts her hand over his to stop the nervous fidgeting. "My goodness, you're full of questions today."

"Good grief. I just died today, and here we are in eighteen hundred, and God knows what. I do have a lot of questions about this whole situation."

She squeezes his hand and whispers, "Shush. People are starting to stare."

"Okay, so I'll whisper." James moves closer. "Tell me. How do we find out where we are?"

Sam lets go of his hand "Let's do the scientific thing." She pauses to let James get sucked in. "We'll ask the

19

bartender." Sam laughs at James's expression. His eyebrows look like they'll cover his eyes if they get any lower.

"Uh, and raise all kinds of suspicions?"

Sam leans back. "About what?"

James places his palms flat on the table. "Who we are and where we come from."

Sam smiles. "He won't care."

"How do you know that?"

Sam waves her hand. "He sees strangers all the time. Oh, look, he's coming over now."

The bartender approaches the table, wearing another frown. Maybe he doesn't like the idea of having to fetch drinks. "Okay, folks. What can I get you?"

"Do you have root beer?"

Now a look of confusion replaces the frown. "Uh. I don't know what that is."

Samantha duplicates the bartender's perplexed expression. "What can we order to drink?"

The bartender's eyes look up to the ceiling. "I got rye whiskey and ale."

James gives Sam a look and then orders two ales. The bartender sniffs his acknowledgment and moves away.

Sam stares at James. "Why order two? I hate beer."

"It doesn't matter. We won't drink the ale anyway. We needed to order something. The guy was getting a little antsy."

"You're right. I think I better ask for information before we have to pay."

"Why's that?"

"You have any money?"

"Yeah, sure."

"2019 money?"

"Yeah, and I have cards too."

"Hahaha. Did you just hear yourself?"

James leans back in his chair. "We're in deep trouble." He leans forward quickly. "Oops, here he comes."

"Here we are, folks. Two ales. That will be four bits for the two." The bartender places the large mugs on the table.

James looks up at the man. "Can we run a tab?"

The bartender frowns some more. "A tab? I reckon I don't know that term."

"Oh, sorry. Uh, I mean, can we pay for the drinks just before we leave?"

"You going to have food?"

"That depends on what you have today."

"A real nice stew."

"Sure, we'll have food."

"Well, then, I'll just keep track of the bill and let you know what it is before you leave. Y'all passing through?"

Sam places her hand on James's, which he takes as a sign to let her do the talking. She smiles. "We're thinking of settling down somewhere and thought this town looked pretty nice."

The bartender folds his hands in front of his apron. "Well, ma'am, this here's a peaceful place good enough to raise your youngens."

"A couple of questions if you don't mind."

"Shoot. If'n I can answer, I would be happy to do so."

She gives him a smile. "Oh, thank you."

The bartender blushes.

"We didn't see a sign when we rode in. What's the name of this town?"

The bartender raises a hand to his face. "Dodge City, ma'am."

Sam lays her palms flat on the table. "Dodge City, Kansas?"

"The very same, ma'am. The Thirty-fourth state in this here union. Yes, ma'am."

"So, how long has Kansas been a state?"

"You *are* from out of town for sure. Kansas became a state in sixty-one. Just twenty-two years ago. I 'member it like it was yesterday. Big celebration. Was January 21st and like a second New Years. We were all having a tough time with the drought and all. The announcement that we were a state was like a breath of fresh air. A'course, the war came along in late spring, and we all joined the union. Them confederates would sometimes come over the line from Missouri. You heard of the Lawrence Massacre?"

Sam nods and scrunches up her face in concentration. "Yes, I read about it in school."

The bartender looks down at the floor. "Yeah, horrible. Over one-hundred-and-sixty boys and men killed." He stares up and straight at Sam and James. "Damn that Quantrill and his stinking raiders. We showed 'em, though. The union soldiers caught up with Quantrill in Kentuck, and he died there."

Sam entwines her fingers on the tabletop. "Where were you during the war?"

The bartender stands a little straighter. "I was a member of the eighth volunteer infantry regiment of Kansas. We walked all over the South, chasing rebs. Lots of action at Chickamauga, Missionary Ridge, Chattanooga, and Atlanta. We got into Alabama, Georgia, Louisiana, and even Texas. Never thought we would stop walking." He chuckles at the memory.

Sam hesitates but goes with her next question, "Were you wounded?"

The bartender shifts his feet. "Naw, not a scratch. We lost ninety-seven due to the battles. The rest to disease. About 210 all told."

Sam lifts her eyebrows. "Out of how many?"

22

"Our regiment had ten companies of one hundred men each, so … one thousand."

Sam lets out her breath. "That's near twenty-percent casualties."

"If'n you say so, ma'am. Never been much good at cyphers. Anyways, I need to get back to the bar. You want that stew?"

Sam points at James. "How about you? Stew?"

James nods. "Ah. Yeah, sure."

Sam looks up at the bartender. "Make that two."

"Yes, ma'am."

She holds up her finger. "One more thing. What's the name of this saloon?"

"This here's The Long Branch."

Sam sits back in her chair. "Okay, thank you."

The bartender backs away from the table. He seems to suspect something is different with Sam and James. With their different clothes, he would have to.

James brings his ale to his mouth. "This tastes warm."

"Pardon? I can't understand you with that swill in your mouth."

"Excuse me." James swallows. "The ale feels warm."

"Forget the beer. Do you know where we are?"

"Yeah, Dodge City, Kansas."

"In 1883, to be exact."

"My history isn't so good. What happened in 1883?"

"Wyatt Earp and Bat Masterson came to support Luke Short in what became known as the Dodge City War. Some folks wanted to close the saloon. In the end, Luke Short became part owner of the saloon. Then they forced him out of town. He went to Kansas City and got those guys to come back and help him."

"How do you know this stuff?"

Sam rolls her eyes. "I had a chance to study history."

All at once, a problem niggles at James. "I have a question."

Sam tastes her ale and wrinkles her nose. "Far cry from root beer. What's up?"

James leans closer to her so that no one can overhear. "When that guy gets back with the food, he'll want his money."

Sam nods her agreement. "I think it's time we bid this place adios."

James runs a hand through his hair. "How the heck we going to do that? The front door stands in plain view of the bar. He'll grab us before we get halfway across the room."

Sam holds up her hand. "We can will ourselves back into the car. Let me try, and then I'll come back to get you."

"Wait, Sam——"

"What?"

"You did it?"

Sam smiles. "Yes. I went back to the Oldsmobile. Didn't I disappear from here?"

"You did, but it was only a half-second."

Sam throws her head back and laughs. "Man, that is so cool."

James scratches his head. "How'd you do it?"

Sam waves her hand. "Easy. All you do is close your eyes and think of the place you want to be. In this case, the car."

"Let me try it?"

"Okay, go ahead."

James closes his eyes, and, in an instant, reaches the Oldsmobile. Just as quickly, he returns to the saloon. "Man, that was the best. It seemed like I was gone for five minutes. How long was it?"

"Maybe half a second."

"I visualized the Olds and popped into the front seat. I had a chance to look around, too."

"Anyone see you?"

James pauses. "I don't think so."

Sam nods. "Okay, then maybe it's time to leave."

James frowns. "You know one thing bothers me."

Sam takes a guess, "This doesn't look anything like the Long Branch Saloon on TV from the show Gunsmoke?" She smiles.

"How'd you know? It was way before both of our times."

The corners of her mouth turn down for an instant. "My dad got a DVD set with every episode. We would watch them religiously."

James taps the table lightly with his index finger. "Mine too."

Sam scowls. "Damn, how come we never talked about that as kids?"

"Don't know. Never came up." James sighs.

Sam touches his arm. "So, let's wait for the bartender to come back, and then we'll do our magic disappearing act."

James can't help smiling. "That is funny. So, when he asks for payment, we just disappear?"

"Yup. Might scare the bejesus out of him, but we really don't have a choice."

James holds up his hand. "The idea of disappearing gives me butterflies."

Just then, the bartender places the edge of the tray on the table for balance. He sets the bowls in front of them. The steaming stew smells out of this world. "My boss says this is on the house since you are new to town. He tossed in the drinks as well."

Sam leans back. "My goodness, that is so kind of him."

"Well, he's a good boss and a kind man. I hope you enjoy the meal. Here's some bread to help with that gravy. You're strange folks but nice. Y'all enjoy your supper."

"It's kind of you and your boss to feed us. Thank you ... uh, what do we call you?"

"Name's Short. Luke Short."

Chapter Three

The bartender walks away, and Sam shifts closer to James. "Do you know who he is?"

"I don't have a clue, and why are you whispering?"

"Luke Short is the guy who brought Bat Masterson and Wyatt Earp to Dodge City to reclaim the Long Branch Saloon. I told you that."

"I thought you said the owner of the Long Branch did that. He's just the barman."

"He and Harris formed a partnership. This is all going to come down very quickly. How's the stew?"

"Tastes pretty good. I'm surprised we dead folks have taste buds."

"Remember when I told you about memories. You're experiencing the memory of a stew."

James puts his spoon back in the bowl and sits back. "So, this could be crap, and I wouldn't know."

Sam cannot help but smile. "Not exactly, but close."

James wipes his sleeve across his mouth. "Makes you lose your appetite."

Sam shakes her head. "Well, you don't have to eat, so do what you want."

He eyes the stew again. "You going to try it?"

Sam pushes her bowl away. "I think we ought to go."

James sighs. "I'm ready. We going to walk out or just disappear?"

"I think the disappearing thing will be best." Sam closes her eyes.

"After you." Sam surprises James when she disappears so quickly. He looks over to the bar to see if anyone notices and feels shocked that no one has, or at least if they have, they don't seem interested in the vanishing girl. He takes a deep breath and visualizes the Oldsmobile.

In an instant, James finds himself standing outside the general store next to the vehicle. Sam sits in the passenger's seat already. James opens her door.

Sam smiles at him. "Wow, that was a blast."

James leans in slightly. "So, why's this a store out here and not the Long Branch?"

Sam looks up at him. "Hard to know. Maybe the coordinates are different once you get inside. In fact, this store looks like it belongs in the 1930s rather than the 1880s. I'm sure there's a reason, but for now, we need to satisfy ourselves with the experience we just had."

Sam's knowledge impresses James. "How do you remember all that history?"

Sam chuckles. "You may find this hard to believe."

James nods. "Go ahead. I trust you."

"While I was in training and waiting for you, I studied history."

His eyes widen. "No way."

"Yeah. I had access to all kinds of documents and books, which interested the hell out of me. The other cool thing is I can remember everything I learned. You don't get that skill in public school." As if she wants to drop the subject, she asks, "Should we continue driving?"

"For sure." James goes around to the driver's side, gets in, and starts the engine. "What about this Olds?"

Sam shakes her head. "What about it?"

"As we drive around, we'll need gas at some time or another."

Sam smiles. "I'm not sure, but I don't think this car runs on gas."

James gapes at her. "What *does* it run on?"

Sam rests her hands on her thighs. "Oh, who knows?" She raises one hand. "Maybe the eternal spirit." She drops it back on her leg and shakes her head. "I really didn't pay too much attention to any mention of fuel or vehicles. I figured things would just work. The sooner we get going, the sooner we'll get there."

James puts the gear shifter in drive. "Okay. I guess we can always walk if we run out."

Sam nods. "I don't think we'll run out. Hey, wait."

"What?"

"Look at those guys riding up the road." Sam points to the horizon where a dust cloud has risen. "It looks like five or six riders. I'll bet that's Bat Masterson and Wyatt Earp arriving in Dodge. Let's get back into the saloon. I reckon they're headed this way."

"Won't they think this Olds is something from outer space?"

"If we go back inside, the car will disappear."

James turns off the ignition. "You know this how?"

Sam lets out some air. "You know, you're kinda getting on my nerves." She sucks in another breath. "You know the drill by now. Just think of that table in the saloon, and I'll meet you there." Sam barely gets the last words out of her mouth when she disappears. James closes his eyes and thinks of the table in the Long Branch. He appears at Sam's side.

She looks up at James. "What took you so long?" Then she laughs at her joke.

James sits down, hard. "I'm new at this, and I think you should cut me some slack."

"That's pretty funny. Hey, the stew's still warm."

"Is there something wrong with your meal?" James and Sam startle and look up. Luke Short stands with his arms akimbo and a wet rag in his hand.

"Er, no," James says. "We just took a breather. We got to talking and pretty much ignored our food."

Luke purses his lips. "You want me to warm it up for you?"

James picks up the spoon and puts it to his lips. "N-no, that's okay. It seems warm enough."

"Okay, then. Excuse me. I see some friends coming in. If'n you need anything, just holler."

Luke goes over to the new arrivals and welcomes them. Evidently, he knows the five. The loud voices and laughter broadcast friendship.

"Is that Earp?" James nods in the direction of the group rather than pointing.

Sam squints. "It sure is. I had a picture of the Dodge City Peace Commission. Which is what they called themselves. It had Wyatt and Bat as well as the other guys who came to help Harris and Short get back the Long Branch."

James's eyes grow wider still. "Was there a huge gunfight?"

Sam smiles. "No. Everything got settled peacefully. The presence of Bat and Wyatt smoothed the way for a compromise. Don't forget, they were involved in the shootout at the O.K. Corral in Tombstone, Arizona, not more than a year before this. Wyatt's brothers Morgan and Virgil got wounded there."

"So why would they help Luke and Harris?"

"As far as the Long Branch was concerned, it was a matter of townsfolk against the cattlemen. The ladies of the town grew tired of the wild goings-on with drinking, gambling, and prostitution. They wanted the saloons to close, so the mayor came up with a resolution, and it was done."

"I still don't get it, but okay. You seem excited to see these guys, and I guess that's good enough for me."

Sam leans closer to James. "I think we ought to go to Tombstone and see the gunfight for ourselves."

James's eyes bulge. "Uh, hello? Aren't we supposed to be on some kind of quest to eternity?"

Sam smiles. "Yeah, but why not have a bit of fun on the way?"

"I remember Tombstone from their newspaper, the Tombstone Epitaph."

Sam sits back. "You do? I'm shocked."

"Yeah, I was a journalism student in high school and studied several newspapers."

James gets lost in his memories.

Sam suggests, "Why don't we visit the Epitaph office?"

James stares at her with pure delight. Then he takes her hand and closes his eyes. In a fraction of a second, they both find themselves seated in the Oldsmobile once again.

"Whoa, that was new."

"I took your hand, and we traveled together. You never tried that before?"

She glares at him, but her grin of delight belies her mock sternness. "I never came to get anyone before, remember?"

"Right. Yeah. I say we drive to Tombstone and check out the paper."

"Okay, but you'll have to trust me on this one. We'll take the Oldsmobile but won't actually drive."

James frowns. "How do we do that?"

"Close your eyes and think about the Epitaph as you remember it. Hold my hand, and let's see if we can all go, including the Oldsmobile." James takes Sam's hand and, for the first time, notices how warm she feels to the touch. Her delicate fingers wrap around James's in such a way that a pleasant heat spreads upward from her hand to his cheeks. He almost opens his eyes to take a look at the union but resists. A blackness passes through him, as if he just passed an intangible barrier.

"We're here."

James's eyes pop open, and until they clear, all he sees is a blurry building through the windshield of the car. "Where are we?"

"Tombstone, silly. Exactly where we wanted to go. We're outside the Tombstone Epitaph office."

James shakes his head to clear his vision and his mind. "My gosh. I can't believe we made it."

"We ought to go inside and, maybe, get a handle on what year we landed."

"Did you think of a year when you thought of the Epitaph?"

Sam furrows her brows. "No, I did all I could do to concentrate on the Epitaph."

James squeezes her hand. "Since the paper is still being published, we could have landed in 2020."

Sam looks at him, and her eyes narrow to slits. "You have got to be kidding me." She pulls her hand away from his. "I didn't realize the paper was still going. I assumed it died when Tombstone died in the late 1880s. I guess I should have concentrated on a date like 1881 when the gunfight at the O.K. Corral took place."

James shrugs. "Well, maybe next time we can take this as a lesson. So if it is 2020, we can just do it over."

"Okay, but my instructions are to guide you home, not take excursions all over the time continuum."

Sam's reprimand leaves James confused. "It was your idea to come here. You mean, we only have so many places we can go?"

Sam waves her hand in dismissal. "No, I don't think it's that. I just don't want to waste trips in case we do have a limit."

James heaves a sigh. "Since I'm the newly-departed mortal and you're the well-trained guide, you would think you would know all about this stuff."

Sam edges over to the passenger-side door. "I sort of remember you as a pushy kid. Don't make me give you a Dutch Rub."

James breaks out laughing, and Sam follows. The tension between them breaks, and they both get out of the Oldsmobile. James looks around and mentions quietly, "The area doesn't look like modern times."

Sam puts her finger to her lips and rolls her eyes. "Someone may be listening. The last thing we need is to have these other time dwellers thinking we're aliens or some other oddity." James nods and grabs the doorknob. He crosses his fingers and shows them to Sam. She smiles, and he pushes on the door.

A bell above the entrance announces their arrival.

A rather short man, wearing sleeve protectors and a green visor, greets them, "Hello, folks." He wears his glasses perched on his head, and he holds several sheets of paper. "Can I help you?"

"Uh." James pauses to gather his thoughts. "We're traveling and wanted to know where to stay in town. Um, we figured the newspaper office would be the best place to stop and ask. Oh, and can we buy a paper?"

"My goodness, young man. First off, yes, you most certainly can. You'll find a stack over on that table by the door. As for where to stay, I know of only one good place in town. The new Grand Hotel is taking in guests. Fire destroyed the old hotel back in May."

"Thank you ... uh ..."

"Clum. John Clum."

James puts his hands together. "Oh, Mr. Clum, I'm so pleased to meet you."

"Well, nice meeting you, Mr.?"

"Wainwright. James Wainwright and this is Samantha Tourneau. Sam, this is John Clum, the founder of the Tombstone Epitaph."

Sam opens her mouth to say something when John interrupts, "I see my reputation precedes me."

"Mr. Clum. I've been studying you since—"

"Come on, James. I'm sure Mr. Clum doesn't need to hear your history." Sam places her hand on James's shoulder. "He's a big fan, Mr. Clum."

"Well, I'm certainly flattered. Have you read some of my editorials, Mr. Wainwright?"

"I have, sir, and I must say, your stand on calling for law and order in Tombstone is one I can support."

Clum drops the papers on the desk. "Well, thank you, Mr. Wainwright. By the way, where are you and Miss Tourneau traveling from if I may ask?"

Sam answers before James can, "Mr. Wainwright and I come from Kansas City. We're headed for San Francisco."

Clum folds his arms. "My goodness, that is a long trip. Business or pleasure?"

Sam thinks quickly. "We intend to marry in San Francisco once we arrive."

Clum unfolds his arms and looks like he wants to hug Sam. "Oh, how wonderful. Allow me to extend my congratulations. How long will you stay in Tombstone?"

Sam takes one step back. "We just planned to stay the night, is all."

Clum mirrors Sam's step away. "Well, you must have dinner at Nellie Cashman's. They do all home-cooked food and make plenty of it. This little lady needs some fattening up, young man."

James blushes. "Thank you, sir. Er, how much for the paper?"

Clum smiles at James's shyness. "Please, take it as a gift. It's not much, but it's the least I can do for such a lovely couple. Mind you, now. Don't go on the south side of Allen Street. It isn't seemly for a proper woman to be seen there. Just stay on the north side, and you'll be fine."

"Thank you for your help, Mr. Clum." James takes a step toward the door.

Clum bows slightly. "My pleasure, Mr. Wainwright. Nice meeting you both."

Sam and James smile and turn to leave. James reaches for a paper, and the date at the top stuns him. He folds the paper and says nothing until the two have gone down the steps to the dirt street. "Sam."

"What?"

"The date on the paper is October 26th,1881."

Sam grabs the news sheet. "The date of the gunfight at the O. K. Corral? We have to find out what time it is now."

"Why does that matter?"

She gives the paper back to James. "The gunfight happened at 3:00 PM. We might have missed it."

James shakes his head. "Don't you think a newspaperman like John Clum would have dashed to the scene instead of sitting in his office if we'd missed it? The sun looks fairly high. What about my watch?"

"Go ahead and look at it."

James glances at the watch and then back at Sam. "Oh, man. It's smashed."

"Yup. The accident."

James puts his hands to his face. "Why didn't I notice that before?"

"It didn't matter before."

"So, let's say we are on time—where should we go to view the gunfight?"

35

Sam chews on her bottom lip. "Might be best to go to the photographic studio right next to the vacant lot where the fight took place. We could stand on the porch and look around the building. I'm curious as to why you actually want to see the battle?"

"This is history. I would love to see the most famous gunfight in the world. Who wouldn't?"

Sam puts her hand on James's shoulder. "People get killed."

He touches her hand. "So, we shouldn't see it?"

Sam draws her hand away. "I'm just saying that real life and legend are two different things. When people get killed, they bleed, and it isn't pretty."

James stands with his palms open. "But the historical part?"

Sam shrugs, "I just want to warn you."

Sam and James walk down the street and eventually come to the place where the shootout will take place. Sam points to the porch of the photography building. "We can see everything from there."

James points at the porch. "Of course, we'd have to look around the corner, which means we won't stay out of sight. What if a stray bullet hits us?"

Sam chuckles. "You're dead already. So what if a stray bullet hits you?"

James's eyes open wide. "So ... we can't get hurt?"

"Well, let's just say logic plays a role here. In my training, no one ever said spirits can't get hurt. Oh, wait. Yes, spirits can end up damaged if they can't complete their journey home."

James frowns. "How does that happen?"

"If the Devil tempts your spirit—"

James raises his hand. "Hold on. There *really* is a Devil?"

"You better believe it. If the Devil tempts you, and you fall for his crap, you could be denied your home."

"What do you mean?"

"For instance, if the Devil shows you what life would have been like without a war, and he gets you to do something that alters the future. You would have failed because of that temptation."

"Okay, so it's like an old paranormal movie?—Where you can't do anything to alter the time continuum."

"Correct. Did that help?"

James nods. "I'll say."

"Hey, you two. Could we talk for a moment?"

James and Sam turn around and come face-to-face with a tall, weathered-skinned man with a badge. On his hip hangs a cracked leather holster, which holds a gun. The weapon catches their attention. The man rests the base of his palm on the grip of the .44 caliber revolver Though a smile stretches his lips, it doesn't reach his eyes. "Name's Earp. Virgil Earp. I'm the marshal hereabouts, and I ask that you find a place off the street real quick."

Sam raises her hand to her mouth, and a gleeful expression lifts her features. She clears her throat and manages to croak, "Is there any trouble, Marshal?"

Virgil appears amused with this girl feeling impressed with his position. "Five men are coming into town, and they mean no good. I intend to stop them. There may be some gunplay. I ask you to leave for your own safety. Since you seem to be strangers in town, I could put you into a cell till the trouble is over if need be, but I'd rather you move under your own will."

Sam gets ahold of herself. "Yes, sir." She grabs James by the hand, and they walk a little further down the street. The marshal waves at them to keep moving.

James pulls his hand away. "We won't be able to see anything."

Sam nods in the direction of some riders. "Look, I'll bet those are the cowboys who stopped at the O.K. Corral."

James presses his palms against his temples. "This is all starting, and we got sent away."

Sam pulls one of his hands away from his head. "I have an idea. Let's take a left here and get off Allen Street. Then we go down to Fremont, the next street over, and work our way back to that photographer's place. Since his studio occupies Fremont, and the shootout takes place there, we should have a great view."

James smiles and lowers his hands. "Oh, I like that."

Sam continues to hold James's arm, and the two make their way to Freemont, which lays one block over. They hurry down Fremont and pass the rear entrance to the O.K. Corral. Sam pulls James up short. "The photographer's place sits six more doors down. We'd better ease up and take our time. We don't want to make any noise."

James turns and looks in the direction from which they came. "Okay by me. Also, would you look at those guys riding up."

Sam squeezes James's arm. "Holy shit. It's the cowboys. They came down Fremont street instead of Allen. We need to climb onto this porch and not look at them as they ride by."

Sam and James mount the porch and pretend to head for the store there. The cowboys ride past and leave a cloud of dust that gets in the eyes. The riders pull up in front of the photography studio. They dismount and strike up a conversation with someone on the vacant lot next to the studio. "Come on." She tugs his hand. "We gotta get there."

Sam pulls him off the porch. They walk at speed until they reach the studio, where they mount that porch. From there, they peer around the edge of the building. The two groups stand talking to each other. The loudest voice comes from Virgil Earp, who tells the cowboys to pack up and leave town. Someone among the riders replies, "You have no right to tell us what to do."

It looks like the two groups will remain satisfied with name-calling, but then one of the cowboys goes for his revolver. Virgil shoots first. After that, a thirty-second flurry of shots ensues. Once finished, the booms continue to echo off the buildings for another ten seconds. The cordite smell and smoke nearly overcome James. Once the air clears, he sees three men on the ground and three of the lawmen holding various limbs in an attempt to stem the flow of blood. The other two cowboys must've run off—at any rate, they're nowhere in sight.

While he stands staring at the scene, a shadow passes over the three men lying in the dirt. James whispers, "What's that?"

Sam whispers back, "If I were to guess, that shadow has come here to collect the dying men."

"My gosh. This is so gruesome."

"It is the way it is."

The shadow forms into the shape of a person.

James moves closer to Sam. "Who is it?"

"It looks very much like Adolf Hitler."

James's hand goes to his mouth. "What? You've got to be kidding me."

"No, that's who it is. Oh, God. He's taking one of the cowboys."

"Is he looking at us?"

Sam grabs James's hand. "That's what's so scary. He sees us now. Since we're on the same plane, he recognizes us as travelers. I don't think he's pleased."

"Why would Adolf Hitler come down to escort someone home?"

Sam squeezes James's hand even more tightly, "He's come as a representative of the Devil."

39

To underscore what Sam just said, the shadow person picks up the soul from the fallen cowboy and raises a fist.

"What the hell is that? Why is he shaking his fist at us?"

Sam lets go of James's hand. "The Devil does his work mostly unobserved. I think that guy who looks like Hitler is giving us a warning."

"What kind of warning?"

"I'm not sure. It could be to stay away from him or that he plans to come get us."

"Now?"

"No, not now. He's busy taking that soul to hell. I just think he meant something like 'I'll get you, my pretty.'"

"Like the witch in The Wizard of Oz?"

"Yeah, exactly."

James runs his hands through his mussed locks. "Makes my hair stand on end. Look, he's gone. Man, that was some vision."

"Here comes another. This time it looks more like one of us."

"Who is that?"

"I have no idea, but she sure looks like a mother."

The shadow woman takes two souls. The dead boys appear glad to see her, and the three hug for all their worth.

Sam says, "I'll bet that's Tom and Frank McLaury's mother. You could see her smile a mile away."

"She's waving."

Sam puts her finger to her eye. "Aw, I could cry. So beautiful."

"So, I guess the McLaurys deserved to go to their eternal home."

"It appears that way. I wish my mom could have met me when I came over."

"Uh, Sam? That would have meant that your mom died before you."

Sam shakes her head. "That didn't happen. She's still alive. She and my dad Live in Florida."

"Have you gone to see them?"

Sam looks down. "No. That would be awkward. I don't think a spirit should go visit family members."

"Why not?"

"Can you imagine if I showed up and then told my parents I had to go again. It would bring back the old hurt; only this time, it would feel much worse."

"Hey, you two. Over there on the porch." One of the shooters waves at them. "Come here."

Now isn't the time to refuse an order from a lawman. They step off the porch and walk to the man.

"You two were there the whole time?"

Sam takes the question, "Yes, sir, we were."

"My name's Wyatt Earp. My brother Virgil and Morgan, along with Doc Holliday, have been wounded. I wonder if you would give us a hand."

"We would be honored, sir."

"Honored?"

"Well, you put up one helluva fight. To me, you're heroes."

"Well, young lady, we shall see. I'm sure a stink will get raised since we just shot some of the meanest spawn of some of the meanest folks on this here Earth." Wyatt directs Sam to get under Morgan's arm and help him walk to the hotel. Doc Holliday tells James, "I can make it on my own, son."

Wyatt helps Virgil to his feet, who takes a look at Sam and tells the group, "These are the two kids I ran off earlier."

Wyatt throws back his head and guffaws. "Looks like they listen to you about as much as the rest of town."

Virgil joins the mirth, but a searing cough cuts it short.

The group hobbles to the hotel, where Wyatt calls for the manager. He demands a room and tells someone to run and

41

get the doctor. The hotel manager grabs a room key and holds it out to Wyatt with shaking hands. "What is the room number?" Wyatt's voice broadcasts his increasing impatience.

"It's two-oh-one."

"Don't you have anything on the first floor? These men are in no condition to climb stairs."

"Sir. The first floor is all bar space and gambling. We have no rooms down here."

"Okay, then. We need to use the bar until the doctor has a chance to look at these men."

Doc Holliday laughs and tells Wyatt, "Now you're talking sense."

Wyatt scowls at the joke but says nothing. The manager goes to the bar and asks everyone to take their drinks to the tables. Wyatt helps Virgil up onto the bar and lays him down gently. "Someone get me something for his head." Until several coats arrive, Wyatt keeps his hand under Virgil's skull. He murmurs to Virgil that everything will be okay. The way he says it, though, doesn't convince anyone present that he believes what he says.

While waiting for the coats, helpers lay Morgan on the bar top as well. He sighs and eases himself down onto the hard surface. Doc Holliday takes a chair and orders a double whiskey. The barkeep brings him a glass, and Doc asks him, "You have any cigars?"

Wyatt tells him off, "Doc, you ass. You may have a bullet in your lung, so don't get to smoking any cigars. Besides, these boys are in no condition to withstand getting suffocated from what you pass off as burning tobacco but smells more like refined horse dung."

Doc raises his glass. "A salute to the wisdom of my elder." He downs the whiskey and orders another.

Content that he's got Doc under control, Wyatt moves to Morgan. "How's it going, brother?"

"Ah, Wyatt. I've had more serious wounds falling off a horse. I have to tell you, though, the shot to the leg hurts a good one."

Wyatt puts his hand on Morgan's chest. "It's not supposed to tickle, you know."

Morgan rests his hand over Wyatt's, "Man, we got those guys good, didn't we?"

"Yup, we sure did. Looks like we killed the McLaury's and Billy Clanton. The other two ran off."

Morgan takes his hand away and lays it on his forehead. "Going to be hell to pay."

Wyatt pats Morgan's chest. "I know it, brother. I know it. Well, we'll just have to tell the truth and hope for the best."

"Yeah, and pray that old man McLaury ain't threatened half the county to testify against us."

Wyatt takes his hand off Morgan's chest. "Well, we got us two eye-witnesses." He waves at Sam and James. "You two come over here."

They walk like the guilty with slumped shoulders and a nervous shuffle. Still, they do what he tells them and join Wyatt and Morgan at the bar.

This time, James speaks up, "Yessir."

Wyatt points at the two. "I was just tellen' Morgan here that you two saw the whole thing. That's right, isn't it?"

Sam and James look at each other. James answers, "Yes, we did, Marshal."

Wyatt drops his arm. "Uh, boy. I'm a town policeman. Virgil over there's the marshal. Never mind; just tell Morgan what you saw."

Sam touches James on the arm. "Let me tell it. I had the better view."

"No, that's okay. I had just as good a view."

Wyatt looks from Sam to James. "What are your names again?"

43

The pair share another glance. Evidently, Wyatt thinks they're trying to alibi one another. "I'm Sam, and this is James."

"Okay, Sam and James. Let's get this straight. You didn't do anything wrong, and in fact, we're pleased you saw the gunfight. We just want to know what you saw."

In unison, James and Sam turn to look at each other and break into a big smile. Relief spreads across their faces, and they relax. "That's a relief, sir. James and I thought we were in trouble because your brother Virgil told us to leave."

Wyatt squints at the pair. "Why didn't you?"

James blurts out, "And miss the gunfight?" Sam squeezes his arm, and her nails dent his skin. James pales, and his blood drops to his feet, which twitch, ready for running away.

Wyatt places the heel of his fist on his .45 and leans back against the bar. Then he lifts his other hand to his chin and strokes the stubble. "So, how did you know there would be a gunfight?"

Sam squeezes James's arm a little tighter, hoping to keep him quiet. "When we met Virgil earlier." Sam clears her throat. "He, um, told us there might be gunplay."

"That sounds like Virgil. Hey, man, you awake?"

Virgil lifts his head off the coats. "Sure enough, Wyatt. Gettin' stronger every minute. Doc Holliday here's got some good medicine."

"You hear what these kids said?"

"About meeting them?"

"Naw. About you tellin' them about maybe there being some gunplay."

"Yeah, I said that. I wanted them to get offen the street."

"They did get off of Allen street and went up a block to Fremont. They's been on the porch of Flys photography studio. They saw the whole thing, they say."

"That could be good, depending on what they saw. Ask 'em."

Wyatt turns to Sam and stands away from the bar. "Okay, so what did you see?"

"When we got to the photography studio and stood on the porch, the men had ridden past us already. We saw them talking loudly to you all in the vacant lot."

"Did you hear what got said?"

"Just a little. It sounded like Marshal Earp told the men to leave town peacefully. Then one of the men yelled about not taking any more of the bullying. It was then that the man who did the shouting went for his gun."

Wyatt stands straighter. "You sure he went for his weapon?"

"Yes."

"Did any of the lawmen have their guns drawn?"

"I can answer that." James steps forward. "None of the lawmen had their guns drawn."

Wyatt spits off to the side and then sucks at his lips. "Would you say the cowboys started the shooting?"

James thinks about it for a second. "The outlaws drew first. Can't say who shot first. It all happened so quickly."

Wyatt leans back against the bar once more. He looks over at Morgan, and they share a smile. "If you could tell that story at an inquest, we would feel much obliged."

"It's the truth."

"That's why you need to tell it. There'll be a host of friends and family of those outlaws who will say we murdered them in cold blood. We need you to back us up. Can you do that?"

Sam moves closer to Wyatt. "Of course, we can. How long until the inquest?"

"Don't rightly know. But you both are welcome to stay in the Hotel at City expense until it happens."

Chapter Four

James and Sam get settled into the hotel. The manager had wanted to place them in two separate rooms, but Morgan complained about the expense and offered to put James up in the city jail. Sam convinced everyone that she and James were like brother and sister and would be fine sharing a room. The manager made some noise about this being a proper place, and Wyatt shut him down by mentioning the number of rooms they had available by the hour.

The doctor showed up at the bar and patched up the various wounds. While he stitched, he drank a few whiskeys, but all in all, the men hadn't gotten seriously hurt. Virgil, Doc, and Morgan walked out of the place on their own two feet. Before leaving, Wyatt made certain that James and Sam would stick around and offered to meet them for breakfast in the morning.

The night rose, and Sam and James had roamed around town as much as Sam thought wise, then returned to their room.

***

James takes a seat on the comfortable chair in the corner. "I'll sleep on this. It's quite comfortable."

"That's silly. You and I will share this bed. It's not like we're even human anymore."

"We're not?"

"Not anymore. We're spirits. Just the same, we can't go wandering around town at all hours of the night. Who knows how many townsfolk we would scare out of a year's growth?"

"So, we do sleep, then?"

"Not sleep as such. More like a period of contemplation. You lie down and take deep breaths and think wonderful thoughts. Before you know it, the morning will arrive."

"It would bring more fun to get some chains and go to the cemetery and wander around."

Sam gives James a playful slap. "I would expect that from someone who's still a kid." She goes over to the bed and lies down.

James grabs his arm as if her slap hurt. "Just kidding! So, we meditate?"

"Yeah. Here, come lie beside me." Sam pats the bed, and James goes to her. He furrows his brow, and Sam takes his hand. "I won't bite."

"It's not that. I have these feelings for you, and, to be honest, my thoughts aren't so saintly right now."

Sam sits up and pulls James into the bed. Then she wraps her arms around him and rolls into a spoon position. She continues to hold him tight. "Notice how the warmth of my body seeps into yours. We show affection for one another this way in the eternal place. Yes, you have memories of a different kind demonstration of affection, but tell me that the Earthly way is as satisfying as this."

Thoroughly enraptured by Sam's closeness, James can't speak. All his senses fly into a high state of awareness. The scents, sounds, and softness of her enter him and flow through his blood and nerves as if she's taken over his body. He undulates with pleasure and drifts into another plane, where all he can see or feel is a soft light and a vibration, which renders him helpless.

Held in that perfect state of bliss, an uncountable period passes, and then Sam calls to him to return. "It's morning, so we need to meet Wyatt."

James sits up, and for a moment, he doubts he's ever felt what he experienced through the night. He wants to ask

47

Sam about what went on, but she might take his question the wrong way.

Sam interrupts his reverie, "Did you enjoy the feeling?"

James pulls the sheet near his chin. "I, er, well, yes, I did."

Sam chortles. "You're acting like a kid who just copped his first feel."

He lets the sheet fall. "I suppose I feel a little confused."

"About what?"

"About that sensation."

"Call it pleasure."

"I've never felt like that before."

"Well, you've had sex."

James leaves the bed and pulls at his clothes, trying to cover up. "W-what do you know about my sex life?"

Sam throws her head back and laughs. "Do you suppose I never gave you a visit in all the years I waited around for you to cross over?"

James doesn't know where to look. "Damn. I never gave it a thought. Before I think the worst and die of embarrassment, tell me what you saw."

"You can relax. I didn't sit in the car while you fumbled with Darlene's bra, for heaven's sake."

James covers his face with his hands. "Oh, yeah? How did you know I fumbled with her bra?"

"Let's just say I was in the area. When things got a little gross, I left."

He lowers his hands. "What do you mean, gross?"

"Oh, you know all that fake moaning and stuff."

"Fake moaning?"

"Yeah, that Darlene sure made a load of noise. I guess it turned you on or something. Of course, she did that with all the boys."

"All the boys? All what boys?"

"Let's just say that Darlene kept busy and let it go at that. So, back to my original question—how was last night?"

James smiles. "What we did is the eternal version of sex, huh?"

Sam sits in the chair and shakes her head. She can't help smiling at James's question. "Is that what you want it to be?"

James hadn't expected such a question. He furrows his brow and sits on the bed. His answer will need careful weighing. As a kid, he never thought about having sex with Samantha. Hell, as a kid, he never even knew what sex was. When he first saw her at the edge of the road hitchhiking, her being a female pleased him. In fact, he'd even considered the possibility of the two of them getting together at some point.

Now he knows she's his boyhood friend, wanting to have sex with her sounds too creepy when he thinks about it. So how bad would it sound to her? "I, um ..." He pauses and clears his throat. "I enjoyed it."

"You need to be honest with me. Would you like that experience to take the place of sex?"

"When you ask that way, I have to say yes."

"Well, now, that wasn't so hard, was it? So, in answer to your question, yes, what we did was the eternal version of intimacy. It gives us a way to express affection in a more demonstrative fashion than just saying so."

"Will I be able to return the feelings?"

"You did."

"How come it felt like I was the only one on the receiving end?"

"We all interpret the feelings and experiences a different way. For instance, I felt that you were close, and I could hear your prayers to God for my deliverance. I could feel your passion and concern from way back when I disappeared. All of those expressions came to me as a welcome gift. I received so much more than I gave."

49

"How's that possible? I didn't feel as if I gave anything last night. From my perspective, I was the center of all that was good and had no awareness of you being close at all."

"I think that comes as a result of you getting separated from me for so long. On my side, I've always been with you, ever since the day I ceased my physical form. I think, over time, you will also have experiences that involve me."

"So, we'll have more of those?"

"I hope many more. Now, come on; we need to go down to the restaurant and meet with Wyatt."

James rises. A feeling of overwhelming love comes into his spirit. For the first time, he looks at Sam and sees her through different eyes. She has become part of him now, and he feels emotionally attached to her. No way can he even think about what life was like without her. "I love you."

Sam gazes into James's eyes and smiles. She rests her hand on his cheek. "I love you, too. I have my whole life." For a moment, neither one moves. James places his hand over hers.

They don't move for another minute until Sam breaks the spell. A union has formed between them. James opens the door and lets Sam pass through. He's never felt any better than he does right now and is sure Sam feels the same.

They take the stairway and go down to the bar. Wyatt has secured a table and waves them over. He stands when they get to him. "Here, Samantha, take a seat." He pulls a chair from under the table. James takes the one across from Sam. "I hope y'all are hungry this morning. They do a real nice breakfast here."

Sam and James make small talk with Wyatt, and the waiter comes and takes their orders. They continue a light discussion until the food arrives.

"I got word that the hearing will happen in three days." Wyatt talks between bites of egg, potato, and ham. "It seems that old man Clanton, the father of one of the boys who died,

50

wants to press charges for murder. Can you folks hang around Tombstone that long?"

Sam and James trade glances. Staying in town comes down to the matter of what the schedule will allow, and James has to defer to Sam, who asks, "How long will the hearing last?"

"Hard to tell. I would expect, with the calling of witnesses, it could last a month."

Sam slaps the table. "Oh, my goodness. That's impossible."

Wyatt pulls on his chin. "How about recording your testimony with the clerk of the court, and then you can get on your way?"

Sam sits back in her chair. "Well, that sounds just fine if that works for you."

Wyatt nods. "I reckon an affidavit would work just as well as a personal statement. Of course, you have to undergo cross-examination by the attorney representing the state."

Sam leans forward. "Is he available now?"

"Yeah. I spoke to him before I came over. He was the one who told me about the murder charge. He has space this afternoon."

They all agree that Sam and James will meet with Wyatt and the clerk later in the day to testify under oath and then sign the testimony.

Wyatt leans back in his chair and pulls a toothpick from his shirt pocket. "So, now that we have the arrangements settled, I'm wondering if I can ask a question."

James lets Sam answer, "Of course you may."

"Where y'all from?"

"What do you mean?"

"Where's home?" Wyatt shifts the pick to the other side of his mouth. He picks up his cup, puts it to his lips, and squints over it to look at Sam while he waits for an answer.

"Well, ah ..." Sam pauses. She looks Wyatt in the eyes. James can see that the man suspects something and won't accept anything but the truth. "James and I come from another time."

Wyatt sits still. The only indication that he heard Sam comes from the slight crinkle at the corner of his eyes. He sets his cup on the table and leans forward. "I figured as much."

James can't help himself, "So, what tipped you off? Does it bother you? Do you believe us?"

"Whoa, one question at a time. First of all, I do believe you 'cos it's the only explanation for the other things I've observed. Secondly, no, it doesn't bother me, but I care. I've studied time travel, and to know it's real excites me greatly. At least, I hope it's real, and you aren't pulling my leg."

Sam leans forward with her arms crossed on the table. "I can assure you, we're not pulling your leg, Mr. Earp."

"No need getting upset. I'm in your corner. Now, mostly, your clothes tipped me off. I've never seen denims with such a tight weave before. The cloth we wear is coarse and unrefined. Your shoes don't come from around here. In fact, I don't think anyone can make shoes like yours. That thing on your wrist—" He nods at James. "—gave me a final clue."

"My wristwatch?"

"Yup. Smashed as it might be, I never saw one like it. The band stands out the most. What's it made of?"

"Fabric. Velcro fastens it. Here, take a look." James unzips his watchband, and Wyatt pulls back from the ripping sound that the Velcro makes. James hands him the Apple watch.

Wyatt turns the device over in his hands. "My, my, my. Look at this thing. What material is it made out of?"

James scratches his ear. "Sort of metal but finished in black."

Wyatt zips and unzips the band a few times. "This thing is magic. How does it work?"

"You know when you get a burr stuck to your clothes?"

Wyatt nods. "Yeah."

James points to both sides of the band. "Velcro has one side like burr barbs and the other side plain. Put them together, and they stick."

Wyatt turns the watch over. "The back of your timepiece has this circle."

"It's where the power cord attaches to the battery."

Wyatt puts the watch on the table. "Battery?"

"Oh, my. I keep forgetting you don't have the technology of power storage yet. We can capture power and store it for later use. We call the storage place a battery."

Wyatt drums his fingers on the table. "Okay, then. This seems a little hard to understand. Just tell me what century you come from."

"The twenty-first."

He sits back. "Twenty-first? That's not so long from now. What year?"

"Twenty-twenty."

Wyatt strokes his chin. "That's ... let me think. One hundred-and-thirty-nine years from now."

"That sounds about right."

Wyatt sits forward again. "You have to tell me about all the advancements."

"We've seen a fair few."

"Would you tell me?"

James raises his hand. "You have to promise not to tell anyone. If you tell, we'll get into trouble."

Wyatt shakes his head. "There's no one I can tell. Hell, no one would believe me if I did say something."

James rubs at his temples. "I hardly know where to start." An idea strikes him. "Let's start with something you know. The telephone."

Wyatt's eyes widen. "Yeah, okay. The telephone is still around in 2020, right?"

"Well, yes, but almost everyone has their own phone, which they carry in their pocket. Here, let me show you." James glances around. Nobody else sits in sight, so he reaches into his pants pocket and takes out his smartphone. "This doesn't work in this time zone, but in my time, I can make calls all over the world."

"Let me see that." Wyatt takes the phone from James and turns it over and over. "It hardly weighs anything." He turns it to the side, and James imagines he is trying to figure out how something so thin can make calls all around the world. "Here, take it back. It certainly is a marvel."

"Let me show you something." James turns on the phone, and the many icons surprise Wyatt. He takes the phone back and looks mesmerized by the screen images. "Touch that right there." James directs Wyatt to the camera icon. Wyatt touches it, and a screen full of photos pops into view.

He almost drops the phone. "What the hell is this?"

"The device takes pictures. Those get stored, and I can look at them anytime."

"Can you take my picture?"

"I think so. Let me see." James tells Wyatt to smile and takes his picture. He turns the phone around and hands it to Wyatt.

"I'll be dammed. That is magic. You know what?"

"What?"

"I don't think I can take any more news from the future. This telephone is difficult to understand, and I think I would be just as well off not knowing what the future brings." Wyatt gets up.

James rises as well. "A wise decision, Mr. Earp."

Wyatt smiles, and this time his eyes light up too. "Call me Wyatt. Anyway, I got to get running along. I will see you two later, right? You won't up and run back to the future, will you?"

James shakes his head. "No, sir. We need to stay and bear witness to your innocence."

"Do you know how the hearing turns out?"

James looks at Sam, and she nods her concurrence. "We do."

Wyatt holds up his hand. "I don't want an answer. I know in my heart I'm innocent, so I just have to believe that the justice system will get there as well."

Sam puts her hand on Wyatt's sleeve. "I don't think you have much to worry about as far as the legal stuff is concerned."

Wyatt turns and looks Sam in the eyes. He doesn't hold her gaze for long, and his eyes soften a little before he turns away. "Much obliged." With that, and without another word, he leaves the Saloon.

James leans close to Sam. "Do you think he'll say anything?"

"No. I caught a look from him that makes me believe he feels grateful for our help. Knowing he and the others will be okay brought him great relief. No, he'll not say a word."

James remains perplexed. "Should we have told him about Morgan getting killed later this year, or Virgil getting badly wounded?"

"These are things people should not know. If they did, they might take some action that would alter history forever. If that happened, you and I would end up on the hook for spilling the beans."

"I'm beginning to understand. I thought it was weird Wyatt didn't want to know anything else about the future."

"Yes. Earp got scared knowing he wasn't going to be part of the future, which turned him off. It's a normal reaction."

Chapter Five

Sam and James go to the courthouse, and a staffer ushers them into a conference room on the main floor. They take seats, and the young man who greets them says, "If you could wait for the clerk and the lawyers."

When he leaves the room, Sam nudges James. "So, do you think we'll see Wyatt again?"

"I doubt it. It wouldn't seem right us sitting with him while the lawyers ask us questions."

Sam sits forward. "This hearing stuff is going to turn into a trial."

James folds his arms. "How do you know?"

"I studied history, remember."

"Oh, yeah. So, what happens?"

Sam sits back in her chair. "They find Doc Holliday and the Earps are innocent and that they acted appropriately."

James unfolds his arms. "So, why do we need to give our testimony?"

Sam shakes her head. "We don't really, but we gave Wyatt our word."

James frowns and glances at his hands. "Where does this sit with not disrupting the time continuum?"

Sam lets out a breath. "It's fine. As long as we tell the truth, we won't create any disruption."

Sam stops talking when she sees the knob on the door turn. A knock sounds, and a well-dressed man with a satchel comes into the room. "Excuse me. Are you here for the deposition?"

Sam speaks first, "You mean the testimony regarding the shootout?"

The man places his satchel on the long table. "Yes, that's it. My name is Thomas Fitch. I'm here to defend the Earps and Doc Holiday."

Sam smiles. "Hello. I'm Sam, and this is James."

Thomas nods to them both. "So, in a minute, a few more folks will join us. The governor appointed Lyttleton Price as the prosecutor."

Sam sucks in some air. "The governor? This case must be high-profile."

Thomas takes a seat next to James. "Yes, there are a lot of people who want to see the Earps go to jail."

James speaks up, "Jail? How come?"

Thomas leans back in his chair. "It is a long story but mostly about jealousy. Maybe someday I'll retire and get some slick writer to tell it for me. Another person attending is Ben Goodrich, lawyer for Ike Clanton."

James furrows his brow. "Why is he involved?"

Thomas puts his hand to his chin. "Old man Clinton is swearing out a murder warrant against the Earps and Doc Holliday. He wants his pound of flesh for the death of his son." Thomas pauses and then, almost as an afterthought, he says, "The final attendee is Will McLaury—the brother of Tom and Frank, who also died." Thomas looks down. "So, as you can see, it's going to turn into a circus."

Sam gets up from her chair. "I thought there would be a hearing and that we would just give our testimony and then leave."

Thomas motions for her to retake her seat. "Oh, it is a hearing, for sure. A preliminary hearing in front of Judge Spencer to determine if murder charges are warranted." Thomas consults his notes and clears his throat. "Now, all I need you two to do is tell the truth and don't answer any questions until you have thought out the answer. It's essential not to blab. Just answer the questions and add no more. I will be here to protect your rights. If anyone asks something that I don't think is proper, I will object. The clerk will record this session, so we have to make sure it reflects, accurately, what we say. If you don't understand any of the questions, please say, 'I don't understand the question.' This session isn't to see how witty or intelligent you are. It is to get to the truth. Do either of you have any queries?"

James and Sam shake their heads. Thomas smiles. "Miss Tourneau, would you come over and take a seat?"

She joins him at the table where he and James are sitting. No sooner has Sam settled than the door opens, and three men and an older woman enter. All wear stern expressions, so Sam and James know the other side has arrived. The woman takes a place at the head of the table and pulls papers and a notebook from her valise. She must be the clerk.

Thomas speaks first, "I want to thank you for attending this deposition. These two witnesses cannot stay in town, so we need to take their testimony for introduction into the preliminary hearing later. The court rules covering testimony will prevail. I will obtain a statement from each witness and then allow you to ask questions and cross-examine. Each side reserves the right to object anytime. Is all that agreed?"

Will McLaury raises his hand, Thomas recognizes him. "What if they're lying?"

"The law regarding perjury is unambiguous. They could go to jail. Anyone else?" No one else raises any objections. Thomas goes on to introduce the clerk, who blushes when he calls her competent. He then says Sam's name out loud. Sam perks up.

"Can you give your full name?"

"Samantha Evers Tourneau."

"Your state of residence?"

"New York."

"I understand you saw the gunfight that took place on Fremont Street in Tombstone, Arizona, on or about October 26th, 1881?"

Sam nods. "Yes, that's correct."

"Thank you. Now, Miss Tourneau, would you please tell us what you saw on October 26th, 1881, at about 3:00 PM?"

Sam fidgets in her chair and, finally, gets comfortable. She speaks but seems conscious of everyone looking at her. Her voice cracks but not enough for anyone to notice, "A lot of men gathered near the photography studio. The Earps and Doc Holliday walked down Fremont Street to intercept them. The men wore arms, and Virgil Earp told them to put up their hands. It was then that one of the men pulled a gun, and he and Wyatt shot at about the same time. After that, a whole bunch of shots rang out."

Thomas holds up his hand. "Excuse me, Miss Tourneau, but you said the men were armed."

Sam looks at Thomas. "Yes, that's correct."

"How do you know they were armed?"

"You could see their revolvers."

"Okay. Proceed."

"Well, when the shooting stopped, the only person not wounded was Wyatt Earp."

"So, in your mind, you believe the other men shot first, and Wyatt responded."

"Objection."

"Yes, Mr. Price?"

"Calls for conjecture by the witness."

"Okay, let me ask a different way. Do you know who fired their weapon first?"

Sam shakes her head. "I don't know who fired first, but I do know that one of the outlaws drew his gun first."

59

Thomas points to the clerk. "Let the record show the witness has indicated that Wyatt Earp did not draw his firearm first. One more question, Miss Tourneau."

"Yes, sir?"

"Did anyone else in the Wyatt Earp party draw first?"

"No, sir. No one else."

"I have no more questions. Gentlemen, your witness."

"Hello, Miss Tourneau. My name is Lyttleton Price. My job is to prosecute this case if there have been any laws broken. You understand?"

Sam puts her hands flat on the table. "I do, sir."

"Okay, then. Tell me how long you have known Wyatt Earp?"

"I met him yesterday."

"You never met him before yesterday?"

"No, sir."

"You and he aren't secret lovers, are you?"

Thomas half rises from his chair. "Objection. There is no evidence to that effect, Mr. Price. You are defaming this witnesses' character, and the slander laws are clear on remedies for that error."

"I withdraw the question. Thank you, Miss Tourneau. Let me ask you one more question. Are you and this young boy lovers?"

Thomas jumps to his feet. "Objection. Not relevant to the case."

Price holds out his hand. "I'm trying to establish if there are any credibility issues with this witness."

Thomas retakes his seat. "Who she loves holds no relevance here."

Price taps the table. "But committing adultery is against God's will, and if she were willing to commit that sin, perhaps the commandment regarding false witness would be the next to fall."

Thomas shakes his head. "You are barking up the wrong tree, sir."

"She did not answer the question."

Thomas points at Price. "She shouldn't have to answer such a question."

Sam raises her hand slightly. "I will answer, Mr. Fitch."

Thomas waves his hand. "I advise against it."

Sam speaks regardless, "James and I are good friends, not lovers."

Price stares directly into Sam's eyes. "Didn't you spend the night last night in the same room?"

"Yes."

"Where I come from, only man and wife do that."

Sam shrugs. "Or brother and sister."

"Is he your brother?"

"No, but that's how I see him."

Thomas raises his hand to cut off the dialogue. "Excuse me, Mr. Price, but this line of questioning has no relevance. You were not in that room, so there is no way you can attempt to describe what went on between these two."

Price leans back in his chair. "Fine. Thank you, Miss Tourneau. Anyone else want to question the witness?"

"I have one question."

Thomas nods. "Yes, Mr. Goodrich?"

"Miss Tourneau, I'm a lawyer hired by Ike Clanton, who lost his son. He's the one they say drew first."

"Yes, sir."

Goodrich frowns. "How do you know who drew first? Were you looking right at the two men?"

Sam gives Goodrich a steady look. "I was, sir. The first draw, I could see plainly. The gun came out of the man's holster. Then two shots followed."

"Have you ever met Mr. Clanton?"

"No, sir."

"Then, how are you sure it was him?"

"I'm not. I only know what I saw. The man was blond and young, and he drew first."

"And you saw that?"

Sam nods. "I did."

"I'm surprised you didn't look away, being a lady."

Sam shakes her head. "It happened too fast for me to turn away."

"Just one more question, Miss Tourneau. How far away were you when the shots were fired?"

"We were on the photographer's porch, which was maybe twenty feet from the shooting."

"Did you not feel afraid?"

"No. As I said, it happened too quickly."

"You sure you didn't duck or something?"

Thomas again holds up his hand. "I think, asked and answered, Mr. Goodrich. If there are no other questions, I would like to ask James Wainwright to take the floor."

"Yes, no more from me. Anyone else?" Goodrich looks around the room at the other participants.

Thomas retakes control, "Looks like no more." He turns and addresses James, "Could you give us your full name?"

"James Wainwright."

"Your residence. Just the state."

"New York."

"Now, please tell us what you saw."

"Well as Sam said—"

"We need you to tell us in your own words."

James flushes. "Okay. I was on the porch of the photography studio and saw the Earps and Doc Holliday coming up Fremont street. There was a group of men by the back gate of the O.K. Corral. When the lawmen got close, they asked the men to put up their hands. Instead, one went for his revolver, and then all hell broke loose."

"By 'all hell,' you mean shooting?"

James nods. "Yes, that's it."

"Any idea who fired first?"

"No, it was hard to tell."

"You sure?"

"Yes."

Thomas waves his hand. "No more questions. Anyone else? Yes, Mr. Price?"

Price wrinkles his nose. "Seems silly to ask this one a question. It's obvious they have cooked up the same story."

Thomas frowns. "Objection."

Price scoffs, "Yes, I know. These two have come to their story independently."

Thomas looks toward the clerk. "For the record, Mr. Price, both of these witnesses saw the same thing at the same time. Why would their stories differ?"

Price removes his glasses and rubs a spot between his eyes. "This does remind me of something, Mr. Fitch. I have a question for this witness."

"Very well, Mr. Price."

Price puts his glasses back on. He looks straight at James. "Tell me, young man, when was the last time you saw Wyatt Earp?"

James returns the stare. "This morning, sir."

Price glances down at his papers. "Where was that?"

"The Alhambra Saloon."

Price picks up a sheet of paper and looks at it while he speaks, "Where you met Mr. Earp for breakfast—is that right?"

James maintains eye contact with Price. "Yes, sir."

"What did you talk about?"

James frowns. "What do you mean?"

Price drops the paper. "Did you discuss your testimony?"

James shakes his head. "Only to the point of understanding the arrangements for today."

Price smiles as if he has a secret. "Did Mr. Earp tell you what to say?"

Thomas looks up from writing his notes. "Objection. A very broad question."

Price holds up his hand. "Okay, then let me narrow it down a bit. Did Mr. Earp tell you to say he drew second?"

James looks at the ceiling, "No. I saw what I saw."

Price turns to the clerk. "I would like the record to indicate that this young man and woman had breakfast with Wyatt Earp this morning, and they maintain that there was no discussion of how to testify this afternoon. I find that hard to believe."

Thomas drops his pencil on the table, "Objection. You are not being asked to believe anything, Mr. Price. The testimony is the testimony. These two are not here to convince the person responsible for prosecuting this case that Mr. Earp is innocent. They are here to tell the facts as they know them and let others decide. Your comment is totally out of order."

Price holds up both hands, with the palms facing Thomas. "Thank you for the education, Mr. Fitch. That will be all. You have the floor."

Thomas looks at each person. "Does anyone else have any questions? If not, these witnesses are excused."

The only sound comes from the scraping of chairs as the prosecuting team moves out of the room. Sam and James sit in silence while Thomas Fitch puts his papers into his valise.

He stuffs in the last and says, "That went pretty well."

Sam folds her arms and leans back in her chair. "You think so?"

Thomas looks at Sam and then James. "I do. Those guys wanted to place doubt on the veracity of your testimony."

Sam looks down. "I think they succeeded."

Thomas waves his hand. "I don't agree with you. They brought nothing to the table other than innuendo."

Sam looks at Thomas. "But, won't that influence someone reading the transcript?"

"No. What it will do is point out how thin the prosecution's case is. I was surprised someone like Lyttleton Price would stoop to such a tactic. Maybe he thought that was an easy road to travel."

"Well, I hope we didn't do the Earp-and-Holliday case any harm."

"Far from it. I think you helped."

Sam smiles and rises from her chair. "Well, then, Mr. Fitch, we need to move on. James and I have a long way to go to get back to New York."

"You know, I have some friends in New York. What part do you hail from?"

"We, ah, come from Long Island."

"Too bad. I don't know anyone from there. By the way, can I have your addresses in case I need to contact you?"

"Yes, just send it in care of the Long Island City Post Office. We pick up our mail frequently."

Fitch frowns and makes a note on a piece of paper. Then he pauses and looks first at Sam and then at James. A smile smooths his expression. "Very well, then. I've made a note of that. Thank you again for your help." Fitch gets up and offers his hand to each and then departs.

James says, "Do you think he bought the phony address?"

"Did you see his face? He knows I lied."

"Why didn't he call you out?"

"Why should he? He's got the testimony. He won't want to contact us. If anything comes up, he'll just say he tried, and the testimony will stand. So, now we need to close our eyes and think of the Oldsmobile outside the Tombstone Epitaph."

"Okay. Here we go."

Chapter Six

By the car, Sam leans down to check on James. She opens the door. "You okay?"

James looks up. "Oh, yes, I was just looking at my cell phone."

"Why?"

James shrugs. "It pinged, so I thought a text had come in."

Sam snickers. "You know that's impossible. We're not of this world, so how could you receive a text?"

James holds the phone out to her. "Okay, smart one, take a look."

Sam leans over and then takes the phone from James's hand. Sure enough, a text notification shows an unknown sender.

James urges, "Go ahead and open it."

Sam places the device back in James's hand. "It's your phone. You open it."

James rolls his eyes but studies the message. "Want me to read it aloud?"

"Sure, if that makes you feel better."

"It's time we met formally. I have much to discuss with you. Text 666 with a time and place."

Sam puts her hand to her mouth. "666? Is he crazy? That's the sign of the Devil. Lucifer just messaged you."

James drops the phone onto the seat. "Oh, man, this gives me the creeps."

"The creeps? I've never heard of the Devil sending texts to potential converts."

James's eyes open wide. "You think he sees us as converts?"

"I'm not sure about me, but since he has your number ...."

James scowls. "What should we do?"

Sam puts her hand on James's arm. "Ignore the text."

He turns toward Sam and touches her hand. "If we ignore it, do you think it will make him mad?"

"It doesn't matter if he gets mad or not. He wants to possess you."

James sits back in the seat. "Why me?"

"I don't know. Maybe it's 'cos you're a good guy. Good-guy fallen souls may fetch a premium price."

"Price? Where do they get sold?"

Sam takes back her hand. "Just a figure of speech. We need to get moving. Where would you like to go?"

James shrugs. "I'm not real sure." He turns on the ignition, and the engine comes to life. "How about we just use the road and see where it leads?"

Sam looks away and out of the window. "That's okay with me, but it can be a little risky."

James stares at her. "You mean we're at the mercy of accidental discovery?"

"Well, it is your eternal home, so I think you ought to pick."

James puts his hand on Sam's shoulder. "Wait a minute. Are you telling me we're shopping around for a place to spend eternity?"

"No. We're giving you experiences that last for an eternity, but if we find a place you like, it could become an eternal home. You have to admit being in Dodge City, and then Tombstone was pretty cool."

"Yeah, and those visits make me not want to be stuck in those times."

"Okay, then you need to pick something else."

James grips the steering wheel. "I still don't understand, but okay. I've always wanted to pan for gold. Do you think we could do that?"

Sam smiles. "Close your eyes and think of Sutter's Mill."

James turns off the ignition and closes his eyes. "I've never seen a picture of Sutter's Mill."

"Well, just visualize a river and some gold nuggets. Hold my hand, so we both end up at the same place." James reaches over and takes her palm in his. The feeling of motion hits them immediately.

When the sensation of movement stops, James opens his eyes and looks around. "Wow. What's this?"

Sam's eyes pop open. "OMG, you were supposed to think of gold and a river. It looks like you brought us up to the Alamo."

James shakes his head. "How could that happen? This place is nowhere even close to what I thought about."

"Somehow, this must have come into your mind. Anyway, you should take a look inside. Seems peaceful right now. I don't see any big holes in the building, so I'm guessing we've arrived before the battle."

James purses his lips. "I don't know about you, but I sure don't want to be around here when Santa Anna and his troops show up. You do recall they didn't take any prisoners? I also don't feel like explaining to a bunch of defenders that they're gonna lose."

Sam nods. "Maybe you're right. Let's drive on. There has to be another place that isn't so dangerous."

James touches her arm. "Before we go, I was thinking about both our visits: Dodge City and Tombstone."

"Thinking what?"

James removes his hand. "Maybe we are part of a bigger design and were sent to these places to make sure history remained intact."

"You better explain that one a little more. I'm not following."

James's eyebrows draw together. "We testified for Wyatt and Doc Holiday."

"Yeah. So?"

James waves his hand. "What if we hadn't? Maybe they would have gotten charged with murder."

"Okay. What about Dodge City? I don't think we did anything there."

James holds up a finger. "Remember when the owner gave us the free food and ale?"

"Sure."

James closes his fist. "Don't you think that was some kind of breakthrough in the owner's heart, which allowed for the settlement and reopening of the Long Branch Saloon?"

"You're stretching it."

James places his hand on the seat. "Well, okay. I just thought that leaving the Alamo might prevent some kind of event from happening, which would have occurred if we were there."

"Do you think something will occur as a result of us being there that won't happen without us?"

James sighs. "Yes."

"Okay, then we'll stay."

James nods. "I would like to leave, but we came here for some reason, and—hopefully—we can figure it out."

Sam holds up her finger. "Once we step out of the car, that will be it. We will be at the Alamo, and we will have no idea what year it is."

Playfully, James grabs her raised finger. "I'm willing to take the chance."

Sam pulls away. "Let's go, then."

James opens his door as if his next step would send him out onto the moon. He gets out of the car and shields his eyes

70

as he looks toward the mission. Already, Sam has climbed out of the passenger's side, and the slam of the door makes James jump. "Geez, take it easy on the Olds."

"You nervous?"

"Maybe a little. How about you?"

"Think about it: We're both dead. What do you think can hurt us?"

James shrugs. "I just have a funny feeling, is all."

Sam waves her hand. "Don't worry. We're okay."

The pair take a moment to look around. Away from the car, the scenery comes into full focus. They pause at the entrance to a compound. To their right and left, walls stand twelve feet high. Men on horses and with wagons pass through a large door.

Someone calls to them, "You down there. What business have ye here?"

The two look up to see a man at the top of the wall pointing a rifle at them. Sam answers, "We're travelers, seeking some rest at the mission."

The man waves his rifle. "Best be gone with you. There's a whole Mexican Army headed this way, and we don't think they'll be too kind when they ask us to leave."

Sam raises her hand. "I understand, but we have nowhere else to go."

The man shoulders his weapon and shakes his head. "Pass through the gates. I'll see ya on the other side."

Sam grabs James's arm and drags him through the entrance of the mission. Inside, they have to leap out of the way when horses and wagons dart through the gates after them. To the right of the big door, they find refuge. The activity inside the mission appears frantic. Men rush this way and that. Women carry buckets and rags. Suddenly, it dawns on James that the cloths are for bandages, and the women are busy preparing for battle causalities. He turns quickly to the voice behind him.

71

"Allow me to introduce myself. The name's Travis. William Travis, but my friends know me as Bill."

James follows Sam when she takes a small step forward. "Mr. Travis. Thank you so much for allowing us to enter. We won't be much trouble."

Travis pushes his hat back on his head. "Ha, ha, ha. Young lady, you could not even be compared to trouble like you are going to see if you stay."

"What do you mean?"

Travis leans against the wall. "In less than twelve hours, I expect the Mexican Army to attack this place. They have vowed not to take any prisoners, so if we can't hold 'em, it looks like we all could meet our maker."

Sam gestures at all the activity. "Is this why everyone is running back and forth?"

Travis stands up straight. "We're trying to get in supplies so that we might manage to hold out in case of siege. I guess what I'm saying is, y'all might be safer just heading North away from here."

Sam's voice lowers, "We're tired and could use a rest."

Travis shakes his head. "If that's what you need, I can't offer you a way to recuperate. I can give you some water and then, respectively, ask that you continue on your way."

James wants to help Sam convince Travis that they should stay, "I'm a good marksman, sir."

Travis smiles at their tenacity and rubs his chin. "I can see I'm not gonna talk ya'll out of staying. We could always use another gun. How about you, young lady? Can you load a musket?"

Sam straightens. "I could certainly learn."

"I've warned you two of the dangers of staying here. You seem hell-bent to die along with the rest of us. If that's your wish, I won't turn down your offer. I just hope to God that I'm wrong, and you two will live a long and happy life. Okay, why don't you report to Davy Crockett? You'll find him setting up the defenses at the palisades."

James smiles. "Yes, sir. Uh, where are the palisades?"

Travis points in the relevant direction. "To the right of here."

"Yes, sir. Thank you, sir."

James and Sam take off, running across the plaza. With the fortifications only about 50 feet away, they slow down and walk.

James glances around. "I didn't realize this mission was so large. Look at those walls—they gotta be two-feet thick."

Sam nods. "I read where the walls average about that in depth and nine-to-twelve feet high."

James makes a sweeping motion with his arm. "You wonder how the Mexicans could have breached these walls. See those cannons? I'll bet you know exactly what they are, too."

Sam blushes. "You flatter me. But, yes, I do. Those are eight-pounders."

James studies the cannons with interest. "Meaning?"

Sam takes his arm and points to the pyramid of balls beside the weapons. "They fire eight-pound balls."

James puts his hand on the wooden frame and looks up at the cannon. "Why are they up on these platforms?"

Sam gazes beyond the wall and gestures to imitate lobbing a ball over the perimeter. "I'm not sure, but I think it allows them to fire over the defenses at anyone on the outside."

"Makes sense." James takes his hand off the platform and sets off walking again. "How many people would you say are in here?"

Sam lets go of his arm. "I think over 200 when the attack started."

All of a sudden, James spins to his right. "Oh, smell that. We must have neared the kitchen."

Sam takes a deep sniff. "Yes." They have also reached the palisades, and a man stands at the top.

James puts his hand over his eyes to cut the sun's glare. "I think he must be Davy Crockett."

James and Sam approach the wall and shout up to the figure above. Davy looks down and frowns. "What do you want?"

Sam cups her hands around her mouth and yells, "Mr. Travis sent us to you. He said you could use a couple more hands."

Davy wipes beads of sweat from his forehead, points to the end of the structure, and yells back, "See that ladder over there? Climb up here where we can have a decent talk."

James and Sam wave to let him know they see the ladder. They go to it, and James turns to Sam. "He doesn't look remotely like Fess Parker."

Sam laughs despite herself. "Hush. Someone may hear you."

James laughs and puts his hand on the ladder. "Okay. You want to go first?"

Sam grabs James's shoulder. "Isn't it customary for ladies to go first?"

James bows to mock Sam's words and holds the ladder as she ascends. Though the rungs look like grass, they hold her weight. She takes her time. At the top, she throws a leg over the last rung and stands on the platform. "Come on up."

Quickly, James joins her on the top. They go over to Davy Crockett, who stands deep in discussion with a couple of the men. He waves the pair of them over. "You might as well hear this. We built this platform so we can fire our muskets over the wall. That covers the good news. The bad news is half your body gets exposed when you stand to fire. We should have built the platform a little lower to keep us fully protected, but it's too late to change it now. My suggestion is that you do all your firing from a kneeling position. Travis assigned you two to me?—Did I hear you right?"

James straightens to attention. "Yes, sir."

Davy takes note of his enthusiasm. "Okay, then. Do you have a weapon?"

"No, sir, but I'm a good shot, and Sam, here, can do the loading."

"Okay, we can use you both. Go to the magazine in the chapel and tell the man there that you need two muskets, powder, and balls. What you will do is ... I'm sorry, I didn't get your name."

"James, sir."

"Okay, James, while you fire, Sam will reload. You will pass each other the muskets. That clear?"

James nods. "Yes, sir, very."

"Okay, then go get your weapons. After that, stop by the kitchen and grab some food. You both look like you haven't had a meal for a while."

James and Sam thank Davy and go to the ladder. Davy shouts that they can take the stairs that lead to the cannon mount. "It's much easier."

They wave and do as he suggests. The steps seem like a grand staircase. James whispers to Sam, "Why didn't we think of this?"

Sam smiles. "It would have been presumptuous. Davy told us to take the ladder."

James agrees. "I think Davy is nice."

"He's a busy man, so we were lucky he took time with us."

James confesses, "You know, I can shoot straight but have never loaded a musket."

Sam laughs. "I figured that. How about we get someone to show us how?"

"That might be a tad better than standing at a wall while several-hundred Mexican soldiers try to kill us, and we have to figure out how to load a musket. We better find out what date we arrived at, as well. We don't want to stay around for the actual battle."

Sam nods. "I can't figure out why we came here yet, so I hope we can leave anytime we want."

James stops. "Wait. Once again, you're the guide, so why don't you know these things?"

Sam keeps walking, and James has to catch up. "Well, Mr. Up-in-my-business, I just don't. You'll have to get over it."

They reach the chapel.

James pauses. "This is strange."

"What is?"

"You ever visit the Alamo?"

Sam shakes her head. "No."

"I have. The chapel is all that survived from this huge mission after the battle. There's no stables, barracks, walls, and plaza. Just this chapel. It never occurred to me that, in reality, the Alamo was more than the structure I toured as a kid."

Sam stands quietly for a moment and then says, "Well, for what it's worth, maybe this is the place to come to during the attack."

James looks at the chapel with new appreciation. "Yeah, no doubt."

The entrance to the powder magazine stands before them.

Sam puts her hand on James's arm. "Do we knock?"

"Just go in, I think." James grabs the handle and swings the door open. Then he holds the door, and Sam enters the small, low-ceilinged room. James follows.

"What do you two want?" They come face-to-face with a scowling, bearded man in a buckskin jacket and coonskin cap.

James says, "Mr. Crockett sent us over for two muskets, some powder, and balls."

The big man rests his clenched fists on his waist and stands with arms akimbo, looking rather fierce. "Oh, he did, did he? I don't suppose he asked you to fill in for me while I take the time to fetch your needs?"

Sam gives him her biggest smile. "No. We would be happy to cover for you, though."

"Aw, never mind. It would take longer to explain what's needed than to simply get the muskets. I'll be right back." The guy disappears behind a roughly-sawn door.

James lets out his breath. "I guess he's not too happy."

Sam looks around the room. "I would think overworked is what. I'm sure he has a lot of things to do before a major battle."

James shakes his head. "You know, I get the feeling you're one of the nicest people on the planet."

Sam blushes. "Why, thank you. What brought that on?"

"The way you see the positive side of peoples' personalities."

Sam smiles. "I suppose, after so many years in the afterlife, I have a sense of what's important regarding others."

"Want to share?"

"Well, take this guy, for instance. Hard-pressed, he jumps ugly at us for no reason. I have a choice—get ugly back or try to understand his side of things."

James leans against the log wall. "So, you wouldn't consider responding to the attitude as important?"

Sam edges closer to him. "By getting ugly, all I will have accomplished is placing myself in a position of regret."

"Regret? But he started it."

Sam rests her hand over her heart. "And I would have said something that would have come out not at all as I planned, and then later, I would have regrets over my reaction."

James shrugs, still bewildered. "So what?"

"That's not how one behaves when wanting to become a better soul."

James stands up straighter. "You can grow in the afterlife? Grow as in develop?"

"We're always growing. That's the essence of life. It doesn't matter if you're a corporeal or a spiritual being. Growth is the key to life."

James snaps his fingers. "Damn. And here I thought I could loaf for eternity."

Sam grins. "There is an element of that, but I don't think you would be too happy."

James shakes his head. "Right now, it sounds good."

"I'm sure it does, but hear me out. It just came to me why we found ourselves at the Alamo."

"Oh, do tell."

"This bad-mood-guy inspired me. I believe we need to help someone here save their immortal soul."

James brightens, "That's a tall order. Who is it?"

"No idea. But it's bugged me as to why—if you were thinking of gold and a river—what caused us to end up at the Alamo? Now it's clear."

James holds up his hands. "I'll have to take your word for it."

The rough-hewn door swings outward, and the man returns. He lays two muskets on the counter along with a pouch. James and Sam move closer to pick up the supplies.

"This here pouch holds powder and your shot. Also, it holds extra flints."

James picks up the heavy musket and hands it to Sam. Not ready for its weight, she almost lets it slip through her fingers. The man's eyebrows just about hit his cap. "You two have never handled these before, have you?"

They can't explain away their greenness, so James admits, "No, sir, we haven't."

"Let's go outside, and I'll give you some pointers. God help us against the Mexicans with this kind of soldier. We'll be lucky we don't shoot ourselves."

Sam and James follow the big man outside. He shows them how to hold the weapon so that it's balanced. Then he gives them instructions on the powder, wadding, and ball. He pulls the ramrod and tells them the amount of pressure needed to make sure the load stays put. Next, he pulls back the lock and inserts a new flint and reminds them that the rifle is now ready for firing. Finally, he shows them how to ease the lock back to a resting position to make it safe if they're not prepared to shoot. "Okay, then, any questions?"

James shakes his head. "I think you were pretty thorough, thank you. Is there a place we can practice-fire this thing?"

"Yes. Go back out through the gate and take shots at a tree. Be sure to holler 'practice shot' before you do. Don't want you to become the first causalities."

James says, "Thanks for your help." Then he and Sam make their way to the gate. James explains to the sentry, "We're going out to try this musket. We need to sight-in."

The sentry reminds him, "Yell before you let a shot go."

James and Sam exit and head to the woods.

"Okay, I think I'm ready. Man, this thing weighs a ton. It's so long it's hard to keep the muzzle up high enough to hit anything." James cocks the rifle and does his best to keep the muzzle up. He yells as instructed and then pulls the trigger. The flash and smoke confuse him momentarily. His shoulder feels dislocated, so he lets the muzzle drop. The ball hit a tree about a hundred feet away. James rubs his shoulder to regain feeling.

Sam giggles and holds her hand to her mouth to hide her snicker. "Nice shooting, Wild Bill. How's that shoulder?"

James laughs at her jibes. "This will hurt tomorrow." Determined to reload, he follows the steps that the magazine guy laid out until he's ready to fire again. "How long did that take me?"

Sam rolls her eyes. "About ten minutes."

James frowns. "Oh, very funny. It was less than a minute."

"If several soldiers came after us, you would have one shot, and then you would be done."

James holds out the musket. "You want to try it?"

Sam lifts the spare weapon. "No, but I'd like to load this one."

James shrugs, "Okay, go for it."

Sam reaches into the pouch and retrieves what she needs. She has the rifle loaded and ready to fire in about half the time it took James.

He whistles. "I'm impressed." He lifts his musket and cradles it in his arm like he's seen the guys walking around the mission do. "Well, I've had enough practice."

Sam sighs. "Don't you think you ought to shoot these, so we don't have some kind of accident?"

James sees the wisdom in her words. He yells, "Practice shot," and fires his musket. Then he reaches for Sam's and repeats the process.

Sam says, 'Your accuracy is impressive."

They each cradle their musket. James winces when his weapon comes to rest. "Can you please grab the pouch? My shoulder's killing me."

Sam nods. "Sure enough. What will happen in a fight?"

James gives her a stern look. "I thought about that."

Sam locks eyes with him. "Tell me."

James glances away. "Don't you think it would be wrong for you and I to kill people? I mean, we're not supposed to alter history. What if someone we killed would have been spared in

80

the actual fight? On top of that, taking a human life is not something I would think appropriate for a dead person. Especially one looking for an eternal home."

Sam walks around until she once more has James fixed in her sight. "You bring up two good points." She pauses and takes his chin in her hand. "Maybe we should go on our way before the fighting begins."

James places his hand over hers. "That's what I think. I don't want to be responsible for anyone's death."

"I hear you. I just wish the reason we came here would become apparent. That we don't know bothers me."

James lowers his hand, and Sam does the same. He looks toward the mission. "We haven't found out what the date is either."

Sam rests her musket against a tree. "Oh, that's right. If we knew the date, we would know how much time we have until the actual shooting starts."

James places his musket next to hers. "When did the shooting start in reality?"

Sam doesn't have to think. "The first shots were fired on February 23rd at nighttime."

James wipes his brow. "Okay, then. We just have to ask someone the date."

Sam holds out her hand. "And broadcast to the whole group that we are so out of it we don't know?"

James looks at the mission again. "Don't you think it happens a lot in these troubled times? After all, they don't have radio broadcasts and such."

"Okay. You convinced me. Let's ask the sentry." They pick up their muskets and walk to the main gate. They both go up to the sentry on duty.

Sam breaks the ice, "Excuse me."

The sentry stood watching them from the moment they went to the woods. "Yeah, what is it?"

Sam looks down. "We wondered if you knew the date."

The sentry appears surprised. "The date? Well, it's a Tuesday, so maybe it might be the 23rd or the 24th. Hold on, let me ask someone."

Sam shakes her head. "Oh, that's okay. You're close enough."

The sentry smiles. "Okay, then. How'd the practice go?"

James answers, "Just fine, thanks."

"How's that shoulder?"

James laughs. "I think I'll live."

The sentry grins. "It takes a while to get used to. Get yourself something to fold up. It'll lessen the shock."

James nods. "Yeah, good idea, thanks. Well, we need to find a place to bunk. Nice talking to you."

"Try the jail. I don't think those bunks are spoken for."

James waves. "Thanks again."

The sentry gives them a little salute, and they both turn to leave. They head toward the jail. James asks, "You think it is the 23rd?"

Sam shrugs, "I'm pretty sure it's not the 24th. The first skirmish took place on the 23rd, and if it were the 24th, we would have heard something about it."

James frowns. "How bad was the skirmish?"

"The Texans didn't lose anyone, but five Mexicans died. The skirmishes went on until March 6th when an all-out assault from the Mexicans took place. All but five of the defenders got killed."

James's eyebrows raise. "So, we could—theoretically—stay until the 6th?"

Sam nods. "I suppose. If we find out why we came here earlier, we can leave sooner."

"What if we don't find out?"

"Then we'll leave anyway."

James sighs. "That sounds like a good idea."

They reach the jail.

A formidable giant of a man meets them. He stands in the reception area with his arms folded, and his expression carries a 'Don't mess with me,' glare. He doesn't say a word when Sam and James enter the low-ceilinged room.

Sam smiles. "A sentry told us that we might bunk here."

The giant continues to scowl. "No one told me."

"I'm sure the message got delayed. Anyway, would it be all right if we stayed here?"

"I'm not running a boarding house. This building is the jail, and it's supposed to be for those who break the law."

"Do you have room?"

"That's beside the point. I don't have time to babysit with a couple of green-horns when there might be some real need for the space."

James steps in, "How about just until some prisoners show up?"

The giant weighs the alternatives, and his conflict shows on his features. Eventually, he tells them, "How about you two clean up the jail in trade for your room?"

"You have a deal." Sam extends her hand. The giant looks at it and then waves them to the jail cells, through a door hidden by his massive frame.

Sam and James enter a hallway that holds four cells— two on each side. In each tiny space lies a bed made out of wooden slats and covered with straw. They contain no pillows or other bedding. A chamber pot sits under each bed. Sam wrinkles her nose at the sight. She asks, "Is there an outhouse close by?"

The giant smiles, shakes his head, and explains, "The sinks are in the animal corral, all the way around the long building and through a door opposite the main gate."

Sam says, "I'll have to get used to the pot rather than making a hike."

James hides a snort.

The jailer says, "It will be your job to clean and sweep the jailhouse every day. You take the chamber pots each morning to the sinks. Careful not to drop them on the way." He laughs at his last instruction. James can still hear him laughing after he goes into the front office.

"Man, that guy is weird."

"Shush, he might hear you."

James sits on one of the slatted beds. "This feels harder than my head. I can't imagine getting a good night's sleep on this thing."

Sam pats the boarding. "I don't suspect that a good night's sleep was a top priority for whoever built this place. Besides the chamber pots, I wonder how one stays warm in the night? I remember reading that the temperatures dropped to around 39 degrees this time of the year."

"I didn't see any blankets around."

Sam brightens. "I think we should check. I don't know about you, but the idea of meditating in this drafty place isn't high on my want-to-do list."

James holds out his hand. "Well, if we don't need to sleep, maybe we just wander around all night."

Sam shakes her head. "No, that would raise questions. Let's go see if we can find any blankets and try to make the best of it."

James reaches out and places his hand on Sam's shoulder. "Would the best of it include another intimate session?"

Sam squeezes his hand. "If you want it to."

James beams. "Yeah, I do."

Sam slides her palm free. "So, let's go find something to keep warm, and then we can come back to our jail."

James feels taken with the anticipation of becoming one with Sam. "Why do we need to get warm? Since we're dead, isn't it natural that we shouldn't need any of the Earthly comforts?"

Sam nods. "True enough—we wouldn't feel cold, but what would people say about sleeping in this hovel and not needing blankets? Right now, we have on the lightest of clothing, and someone will wonder how we do it. Especially if the temperature does drop."

James glances downward and then at Sam. "I suppose we need to act as normally as possible. And, now that you mention it, I feel as if I'm getting a chill."

Sam gives James a punch in the arm, and he winces in pain. She cringes. "I'm sorry. I forgot about your poor shoulder."

James rubs where it throbs. "Which begs the question— why the hell does my shoulder feel sore?"

Sam shakes her head. "I don't have all the answers. Maybe physical trauma is something we need to be careful about. The pain could be a warning not to become too confident in our deadness."

James laughs. "Deadness. You have a great way with words. Let's go and find some blankets. You think these long rifles will be okay here?"

"I would tote them. It seems like everyone carries their guns around. Doesn't seem like you're ready for a fight without one."

"Okay, but you need to tote one as well."

"Sure, fine. Let's go."

The two pick up their long rifles, and James grabs the pouch. They go through the door and tell the jailer, who sits at a table, that they will be right back. He looks up and grunts his understanding. Then he surprises them with a question, "You two get the text?"

James feels stunned. "T-text?" James's question hangs in the air like garlic fumes.

"Yeah, text. You think you can just ignore the man when he's trying to reach you?"

James stands with his mouth open. Finally, he speaks, "Who are you?"

"Not important. My boss wants to have a parlay with you, and you would do well to listen to what he has to say."

"B-but your boss. Uh … unless I'm mistaken, and if so, please excuse me, is the friggin' Devil."

The giant smiles. "You're not wrong, my young man. His Highness is proud to be labeled as such. Of course, he does prefer the name Lucifer."

Sam steps forward. "You know we're on a trip to the eternal place, don't you?"

The giant steeples his fingers. "Listen, sweetie; the whole underworld knows you two are on your precious trek. It's like we get an update-broadcast throughout the halls of hell on exactly what you're doing. I enjoyed that little eternal love session, by the way."

James clenches his fists. "Now, you watch what you say, hell-boy."

The giant lays his hands flat. "Or what, angel face? You gonna sock me in the jaw?"

"Hold on, James. I think we should find out what Lucifer wants. Do you know, uh, Mister …?"

The giant leans back in his chair. "Attila. Yes, *that* Attila, and I don't care to get any more shit from this pipsqueak."

"Who you calling a pipsqueak, Mr. Steroid rage?"

Sam holds up her hands. "All right, boys. We've had enough testosterone-speak for one day. Do I call you Mr. Hun, or what?"

"Attila will be just fine."

Sam folds her arms. "What does Lucifer want with us?"

"As I told you, he wants to talk. He has a proposition for you, and I think you ought to listen."

Sam rubs at her cheek. "So, we call, and then what?"

"His person will set up a conference, and you can hear him out."

"Is this the reason we found ourselves at the Alamo?"

"Naw. We would have found you wherever you went. So, you think there was a reason you ended up here? That's fascinating."

"Okay, well. Thanks for the heads-up, Attila."

"You won't answer, huh?"

Sam unfolds her arms and stiffens. "I don't see it as a subject up for discussion with a henchman of Lucifer."

"Aw, now you've hurt my feelings, and I thought we were going to be besties."

Sam turns to leave. "I would love to believe that. See you later."

"Count on it, sweet-cheeks. You should come with me to a pillage-and-burn party."

Sam ignores Attila's comment. "Come on, James. We need to leave."

"Yes, Jamesie. Do as Mommy says."

James clenches his fists. "Up yours."

"Like to see you try. I mean, I really would like to see you try."

Sam yanks James out the door. He almost falls over the threshold. "Okay, you can let go now."

"What are you trying to do? Have some sort of fistfight with Attila the Hun? You know how long you would last?"

James scoffs, "I'm dead, remember? He can't hurt me."

"Are you willing to take that chance? I'm not so sure of that."

James frowns. "What the hell was that whole scene, anyway?"

"Attila is a messenger."

James nods. "Yeah, I got that, but what could be so important that Lucifer himself would send a goon like Attila to deliver messages?"

"Remember when we saw Adolf Hitler at the O.K. Corral?"

James chews his lower lip. "Yeah, of course. How could I forget that?"

"What did he do?"

"He shook his fist at us and made a face."

"Exactly. Lucifer wants to discuss that incident."

James holds his hands out. "What's the big deal?"

"You and I are the only ones who know that the dark side has folks who help bad souls over to the other side."

James shrugs. "Yeah, so?"

"How would people receive it if they knew some monster like Adolf would escort them to hell?"

James sighs. "I wouldn't like it myself."

"Hell, no, you wouldn't. You would pray even harder to keep yourself righteous. What would happen to the soul supply for hell if a lot of folks followed your example?"

James purses his lips. "I guess there would be a shorter supply."

"Yeah, until maybe none."

"Then Lucifer would be king over nothing."

Sam nods. "I think you get it."

"So, he'll want some assurance that we will keep his little game to ourselves. Wait, why would we agree to that?"

"He's not that naïve. He wants to talk about some kind of reward-for-silence scheme."

James shakes his head. "Can we trust him?"

"No. Let's keep moving. That comment about us getting broadcast in the halls of hell made me nervous."

James smiles. "Not to mention that we starred in an intimacy-porn movie."

Sam smacks his arm. "Oh, stop. He just wanted to get you riled up."

James feigns injury. "Sure worked."

Sam laughs. Not knowing which way to go, they stroll to the infantry barracks, which sit on the same side as the jail but a couple of doors down.

Sam indicates the barracks, "If we can't find a spare blanket there, I don't know where we'll find one." They walk a little further and reach the first door of the building. James opens the door slowly and sticks his head inside. Because of the dim light, he can hardly make out what the room holds. It doesn't look like anyone occupies the space. He holds the door for Sam, and she goes through the entrance.

Sam whispers, "There's no one here."

"No."

A voice says, "You're both wrong." Sam and James swing around to their right to face the source of the words. A tall man faces them in a stance that can only say "fight."

Sam speaks quickly, "We're looking for a spare blanket. Do you have any here?"

"A few of us have night duty and are just waking up. If you've a mind to steal a blanket, you'll have to go through me first."

Sam shakes her head. "No, not stealing. We thought the barracks might have a couple of spares."

The tall man relaxes his arms. "Who are you two? I've never seen you before."

James says, "No, we're heading for New York, and we stopped at the mission for a rest."

The man smiles. "A couple of Yankees, huh? Well, I'm Private Tapley Holland. Who're you?"

Sam points to James and then herself. "This is James Wainwright, and I'm Samantha Tourneau."

The private smiles broadly. "Well, pleased to meet you. Fact is, I was born in Ohio."

Sam cocks her head. "Oh, you were?"

The private nods. "Yeah, but I moved to Tennessee when I was a kid."

"So, you're Yankee born and Southern raised?"

The private gestures with his thumb. "Yes, ma'am, that's me. I can get you a couple of blankets. Stay here."

Private Holland turns and disappears around a corner. After about three minutes, he returns with two blankets across his arm. "Here you go. I hope this will be enough. It looks like the quartermaster supplies have run low."

Sam says, "We're grateful. Thank you so much."

"Aw, think nothing of it."

Sam and James both thank the private again and head outside.

James takes a deep breath. "My goodness, it felt stuffy in there."

Sam waves her hand under her nose. "Yeah, and it smelled of sweat, and God knows what all too."

"I had hoped you wouldn't notice."

"How could I not? I'll bet all the men who sleep in there haven't had a bath for weeks."

"Good thing I'm dead, or I would probably want a shower right now."

Sam smiles. "Speak for yourself. A shower sounds pretty good to me."

Chapter Seven

With the light fading, James and Sam make their way back to the jail so that they can get inside and light a lantern or two. When they reach the jail door, James pauses. "You think Attila is still in there?"

Sam shakes her head. "I'm sure he accomplished his mission and went back to hell to report."

"I hope so. I didn't much like him."

"Oh, come on. I think he was sweet on you." Sam wears an evil smile.

"What are you talking about?" James frowns.

"When you said, 'up yours,' he lit up."

James scoffs, "That's just an expression. Let's go in."

Sam laughs. "You've gone red all over."

"I'm probably allergic to straw and hay."

"Oh, I'm sure that's it."

The two go through the door and find the jail-house empty. Because the building has only one small window in the front, James finds it difficult to pick out objects in the increasing darkness. Sam goes over to a small desk and lifts a lantern. "It's a coal-oil lamp. Let me bring it closer to the light." She moves to the window and smiles. "It has a nice wick. Do you have a match?"

James looks around and finds a box of wooden matchsticks. He takes the box to the window.

"The first matchstick went on sale in 1824. I'm surprised they have them here."

"Well. Here they are."

"Light the lamp for me."

James draws the match across his pants, as he has seen in the movies and on TV. It bursts into flame, and he lights the wick. Gradually, the orange flame becomes brighter until the room fills with a muted glow. Sam takes a few steps and beckons James to follow. She goes through the doorway and into the cell area. "No one's here. Let's go back and see if we can find a candle."

"I saw a couple on the desk over there. Hold the lamp high so I can see." Sure enough, he finds several candles on the desk. James takes one and lights it off the lamp. The room becomes brighter, and they can see better than before.

Sam touches James, and he jumps. "Let's move into the cell area and rest a while. I didn't mean to scare you."

"You just startled me is all. I wouldn't mind sitting down for a while. Also, I have many questions for you about what happened with Attila."

Sam frowns. "I hope I have answers, but I may come up short."

The pair go back to the cell area, and each chooses a bed. James takes one close to Sam's and looks for a spot to place his candle. He spies the rough bedpost—nothing more than a two-by-four timber. After he makes sure to drip some wax, James sets the stick in the hot gloop so that the candle won't tip over after the wax hardens. Once rid of the open flame, he props his long rifle on the wall, drops the pouch, and sits on the bed. He sighs with relief at getting off his feet.

Sam smiles. "That sigh comes from memory."

"What are you talking about?"

"That feeling of contentment comes from memory. You could stand for a hundred years and not feel it."

"Well, recollection or not, it feels good to sit down. What will we do about Attila?"

Sam sits up. "What do you mean by 'do?'"

"Should we take his advice and call up old Lucifer?"

Sam places her hands behind her torso and leans backward. "I can't see an upside to phoning the Devil. Can you?"

James shrugs. "Well, is there a downside to not calling?"

"I suppose he could get pissed off."

"And do what?"

"I don't know. Maybe poke us with a pitchfork."

James lays back on the bed. "You're kidding, right?"

"Of course. I've never run across this kind of thing before."

"Isn't there a helpline you could call?"

"Sorry, James. No helpline."

"It still worries me why we ended up here."

"Me too. It's odd to think of one place and go to another."

James rubs his chin and then stretches out on the hard bunk. He wishes he could come up with a quick answer. On the other bed, Sam sits cross-legged. James wants to know, "Doesn't that hard cot bother you?"

"I could ask you the same question."

"Right now, it feels good."

"Another memory."

"You didn't answer my question."

"Because I don't have an answer."

James raises his hand. "Let's call him, then. After all, he won't talk on the phone. According to Attila, it has to happen in person."

Sam rests her hand on her forehead. "Yeah, an in-person appointment with Lucifer. You know how nuts that sounds?"

James waves his hand in dismissal. "More nuts than a couple of spirits sitting in a jail cell in the middle of the Alamo in 1836?"

"Okay. I give. You're right. Make the call."

James holds his arms out, palms facing Sam. "Me? Why me? You're the ranking spirit here."

"You have the phone."

James pulls his arms back. "Oh. Okay. I see that. Hold on."

He digs through his pocket, comes up with the phone, then reads the message aloud to Sam. *It's time we met formally. I have much to discuss with you. Text 666 with a time and place.* Sam leaves her cot and comes to James's. He whines, "I thought Attila said to call."

"Just dial 666 and see what happens."

Hands shaking, James dials 666 and puts the phone to his ear.

Sam says, "Put it on speaker."

James hits the speaker button, and a hollow buzz echoes around the jail cell. At mid-ring, an echoey voice comes through, "Hello, Mr. Wainwright. So nice of you to call."

James stammers and says, "W-who is this?"

"I am the special assistant to His Majesty and Lord of the underworld, Miss Harpy. His Lordship instructed me to arrange a face-to-face meeting. You must feel so proud."

"I, uh, I'm not sure how I feel."

"Quite understandable, Mr. Wainwright. After all, it's not every day that royalty blesses us with a visit. Let me inquire about your availability."

"M-my availability? I don't have a schedule. I guess that puts me at your disposal."

"Interesting choice of words, sir. How about meeting at this time tomorrow?"

"What's the time right now? Could you tell me?"

"Eight o'clock at night in the central time zone. I do want you to know that His Highness is responsible for creating daylight savings time."

"Figures. Are we in daylight savings time now?"

"No. It is February 24th, where you are. Daylight savings time goes into effect the second Sunday in March."

James looks at Sam. "Where should we meet?"

"Unless you want to witness more skirmishes at the Alamo, I would go somewhere else."

"Any suggestions?"

"Well, His Highness is fond of Las Vegas, given the amount of pure sin that goes on there. Let's say the Picasso restaurant at the Bellagio Hotel."

"That sounds good to me."

"Oh, and bring that sweet guide of yours. I'm sure His Majesty would love to meet her as well. So, are we set? Eight o'clock, Bellagio, Picasso restaurant. I shall list the reservation under Mr. Sedit. You, of course, know that Sedit is the American-Indian name for His Highness?"

James rolls his eyes. "Yes, all set. And, no, I didn't know that."

"Very well, if I can do anything else, please call me. You have my number. Enjoy your dinner. Bye, now."

"Yes, goo—" The line goes dead.

Sam stands. "Holy shit. Can you believe that?"

James shakes his head. "Lucifer has an assistant every bit as scary as him. Was it my imagination, or did that voice sound like it came from the deepest part of hell?"

Sam folds her arms. "You can assume it did. I don't believe she works in a call center in the Philippines."

James smiles. "Did you enjoy the part where Lucifer wants you to attend as well?"

Sam unfolds her arms. "Gave me the creeps. You don't know what a nasty guy he is. If you think of everything that has gone wrong in the world, you can bet he was behind it."

"Why do you suppose he wants to talk to us?"

"As I said, he wants to make a deal for your soul."

James sighs. "What kind of deal would I make? I'm already on the right side of God, why would I give that up?"

"I have no idea."

James puts his hands to his face. "Are you sure we can't call someone to give us help?"

Sam sits on the bed. "I'm afraid we're on our own. No one can help us."

"What about God?"

"I'm sure he's busy. Besides, God would tell you to follow your heart no matter what Lucifer proposed. He wouldn't step in but would want you to make the best decision."

James sighs and stares at the floor. Sam takes his hand and places it over her lips. An irresistible impulse to kiss her moves him, and he acts on it. The sensation feels as if he touched an electrical wire to his mouth. The sparks blind him, and his head grows lighter.

James wraps his arms around Sam, and the two go into free-fall. Sam yells above the roar of the wind that pulls them down, "Hold me tight. We can't let go of one another, or one of us may get lost."

James tries to yell, but the noise proves too much. The wind blows his words away as soon as they come out of his mouth. Instead, he intertwines his fingers behind Sam's back and holds on for dear life. The fall continues until James can no longer remain conscious. He fights hard. The pressure of Sam's body, and the comfort of her arms wrapped around his waist, reassure him. As long as they have each other, they will come to no harm. He pulls Sam in tighter, and then the pull of unconsciousness wins, even though he fights. With no choice and little time, James vows to remember Sam forever and thinks of her while the blackness seeps into his soul.

Chapter Eight

The sun burns James's face, and his back hurts from spending too much time lying on it. He tries to move his arm, but a body weighs it down. The realization stuns him into wakefulness. Sam sleeps on his arm. James rolls toward her and touches her face, which radiates warmth. He thanks God that she is still Sam and then looks her over. She lies totally naked from head to foot, and the sight makes him blush. She stirs in a deep sleep. He lays back and, for the first time, notices that he's not wearing anything either. Something must have happened when they fell into whatever it was that brought them here. Perturbed, James looks around as much as he can without disturbing Sam. Desert surrounds them, with not much else but cacti and a couple of low hills.

"Uhhh, James."

"Yes, I'm here."

Sam covers her eyes with her arm. "Where are we?"

"In a desert."

Sam squints. "How did that happen?"

"I'm not sure, but I have a bit of bad news."

"Only a bit? That's not such a problem."

"We have no clothes."

Sam sits up quickly and covers her breasts with her arms. "No clothes? Did you look at me while I slept?"

"Only a little."

"How little?"

"Well, your breasts are beautiful."

"*James.*"

"Okay, so I stared."

"You just laid there leering at me while I was defenseless."

"No, I—wait a minute. I'm naked too. I didn't leer either. I wanted to make sure you were okay."

Sam stares at him. "Stand up."

James frowns. "Why?"

"So I can leer at you, and then we'll be equal."

James sighs and stands, in full view of his companion. "Will that do it?"

She takes her time looking him up and down. "Yes."

The corners of her mouth lift in the beginnings of a smile. She orders him to turn around, and he sighs again but complies. "You can sit down again."

"Satisfied?"

"Yes. You have a lovely body." Sam chuckles. "I can't help but think of Adam and Eve right now."

"I worried sick about you. Do you feel okay?"

"Yes. Come closer and hold me for a minute. That was quite a ride."

James sits beside her and wraps his arm around her shoulders. Gently, he pulls her toward him. Then he raises his hand to her hair and strokes. "What happened to us?"

"I would say old Lucifer summoned us. Probably, we're on the outskirts of Las Vegas."

"Can he do that without our permission?"

"I'm afraid so. As I said, Lucifer's powerful." Sam startles. "What's going on?"

James pulls back. "What?" Then he notices his growing arousal.

"Pay no attention to that. I have a beautiful woman in my arms with no clothes on, and I'm stroking her hair and soft skin. I'm getting turned on is all."

"Well, stop it. We have to figure out how to get to the Bellagio in time."

James lowers his arm. "Your tone did it. I've stopped it for sure. Can we find anything to wear around here?"

"The sun is hot enough to burn, so I'd sure like to cover up."

"Yeah, that is another consideration. Let's start walking."

James offers his hand to Sam, and she takes it. They both walk with care through the low scrub of the desert. Many small twigs and burrs make barefoot travel tedious. James talks to take Sam's mind off their circumstances, "It seems kind of funny that we've lost the power to determine our own destination."

"What do you mean? Ow, that's the second time I've stepped on a stick. Those things hurt."

"I could carry you. Maybe even piggyback."

"No, that's okay. I'm just complaining out loud. What did you mean about us losing our power?"

"Well, something or someone summoned us to the Alamo. We didn't control that move or ending up here."

Sam squints and glances at him. "Yeah."

"Also, look at the mess we've found ourselves in here. We didn't ask for this."

"Yup."

James slaps his thigh. "So, what's going on?"

"I did figure out we got 'summoned'—as you say—to the Alamo to meet with Attila and get the message from Lucifer."

James looks at Sam. "Okay. That Lucifer sucked us out of there after the conversation does give a good hint of that. The question is, do we have control over our destination or not?"

"You know I have no answers, right?"

James sighs. "Yeah, I know."

"Maybe we should just stop here and test whether or not we can transport ourselves."

James smiles. "Great idea. We do need to plan carefully, though. For one, we have no idea of where or when we've come to. For two, we need to think of a place that has clothes. Any ideas?"

Sam thinks for a moment and then brightens. "We should go to your place in New York. You have money or checks or something there, right?"

James grows animated. "That's a brilliant idea. We can pick up some stuff there, and I could go out and get you new clothes. If successful, it would be a no brainer to will ourselves to the Bellagio."

Sam grabs James's hand. "Okay, but you have to think about your place and hold my hand so that we can travel together."

James looks down at their clasped palms. "Yeah, I get it. You ready? Don't let go.

"It worked. We've reached my apartment."

Sam opens her eyes and looks around. "I suppose no one knows yet that you've died; otherwise, this place would have had visitors."

"Good point. I wonder when my folks will find out?"

"The accident only happened a day or two ago. You went off the road in a deserted place, so it may take a while to discover the crash."

James changes the subject, "Can I get you anything? A drink, maybe?"

Sam rests her hand on her hip. "How about a robe or something to cover up."

James smiles. "Yeah, I hoped you wouldn't say that."

"Though you enjoy my nakedness, we have work to do and should get to it."

"Okay, hold on. I have just the thing in my bedroom." James starts toward the rear of the apartment.

"And get something on yourself. Your buns look good enough to eat."

He stops and glances back. "Really?"

Sam laughs. "Just kidding. Get dressed."

James goes into his bedroom and finds his robe, which will be perfect for Sam. He pulls on a pair of slacks and a shirt then picks out loafers and dark socks. Next, James opens his chest of drawers and takes out his checkbook. He can't believe that he left it here when he headed out, but thanks his luck for the oversight anyway. All he has to do is go down to the local bank and cash a check. With over fifteen thousand in his account, he could get a grand without any trouble. James notices his wallet in the drawer with the checkbook. "How can this be?"

"How can what be?" Sam has come in the room unnoticed. "Give me the robe." She holds out her hands.

"My checkbook and wallet are here. That's impossible."

Sam finishes putting on the gown. "That does seem a little unusual. Wait, is your phone here as well?"

"Yes, over here on the side table."

"What's the date?"

"The eighteenth."

"When did you start driving to Kansas?"

"The nineteenth."

"Aha. So, what you did was remember every detail about your apartment from the last time you were here. You transported us to the time you recalled."

"Yeah, I get that. But if I did do that, then another me must exist here somewhere, seeing as I didn't leave."

"Good point. Which means we need to get out of here before the other you comes back. Where would you go without your wallet and phone?"

"I usually went for a run, and when I did, I didn't take my stuff. Just my key."

"What time did you run, normally?"

"From about 5:00 until 6:00 or 6:15."

"What time is it now?"

"Only 4:00 o'clock."

"Okay, then. You more than likely went early because you plan to leave tomorrow. We need to get out of here now."

"I hear you. Um, can we get you into a pair of pants and a shirt just to hold you? We need to visit the bank."

"Why not take the wallet?"

"But I wasn't missing the wallet when I left on the trip. If I took it, wouldn't that cause some kind of time warp or something?"

"Okay, let's get me into something decent and then go to the bank."

James nods and returns to his bedroom. He rummages in the closet until he comes up with a pair of slacks, a belt, and a white shirt, and then he goes back to Sam. "These slacks are an old pair, so they might work."

"Okay, let me try them."

James gives Sam the slacks and shirt, and she heads into the bathroom. James looks in the mirror to see if he has a reflection. He read somewhere that ghosts don't cast an image in the mirror. It disappoints him to see himself. Maybe he isn't a ghost, after all.

"How do I look?"

Jolted out of his rumination, James turns to look at Sam. Her get-up brings a smile. She reminds him of David Copperfield in the old movie after David's aunt dressed him in grownup clothes. James doesn't want to laugh, so he grins instead.

Sam has her arms down at her sides. "You might as well laugh. I look like I work for Ringling Brothers Circus."

"It will only take us a short while, and then we can get you a new outfit. If we've arrived here in the time before I got

102

killed, then the car should be in the garage where I left it. This will save a bunch of time."

Sam smiles. James looks through the bureau and sees the keys. "On second thought, if the live me comes back before we can return the keys that will cause a tear in the continuum. Man, this time-travel stuff makes you have to think."

Sam sighs. "Again, you're right. Dang it, I'd hoped I didn't have to walk down the street looking like this."

James takes Sam's arm. "We'd better get going." James tears one of the checks from the book and stuffs it in his shirt pocket.

They leave the apartment and return to the elevator. James punches the down button. For what seems like an eternity, they wait for the doors to open. They finally do. The other James stands in the car, concentrating on his heart-rate readout. Happily, he doesn't look up but exits and walks past them. Clearly, he fails to notice or recognize either of the pair, who stand frozen like deer in the headlights.

At last, they move and get onto the elevator. James hits the door-close and first-floor buttons simultaneously. When nothing happens, he whispers, "These close buttons are like pacifiers. They don't really do anything." Finally, the door slips shut.

Once on the street, James and Sam go to the bank on the corner. James heads into the teller's area while Sam waits in the foyer, and after what seems too much time, he finishes his business.

"Got the cash. Let's hit the store. Where should we go?"

"How much?"

"Two thousand."

"Lilly Pulitzer, then. I just love her summer look."

James consults his phone. "Let me see. The store is at 1020 Madison Avenue. That's 79th and Madison. We're on 82nd and Lexington. So, only a couple of blocks away."

The two of them walk down 82nd street until they reach Madison, where they turn left. When they reach the store, James sighs with relief, and Sam echoes the sentiment. They go to the first salesclerk they see, and Sam says, "I need a casual outfit and something a little dressy for dinner, please."

The clerk appears more than happy to help, and over seven-hundred dollars later, Sam has two outfits and two pairs of shoes. She goes to the dressing room and puts on the casual clothes immediately. When she comes out, James smiles. "You look great." Then he turns to the clerk. "Thank you, ma'am." He hands her eight-hundred dollars, and the clerk throws Sam an envious look. Sam takes James's hand and gives the sales woman a smug smile. Once they have their change, the two hit the street again.

James steers Sam to a café that has seating on the sidewalk. They order coffees, and James then leans closer to Sam so that nobody will overhear and whispers, "Have you ever been to the Bellagio?"

She whispers, "No."

No one pays them any attention, so James raises his voice to a normal level, "Neither have I. It will be hard to visualize a place that we've never visited."

"How about going to a travel agent and getting a brochure? Would that work?"

James smiles. "It's worth a try. I mean, how bad could it be?"

Sam shakes her head. "Don't say that. The desert seemed pretty bad."

James looks down. "Some parts were nice."

Sam half-smiles. "My butt, right?"

James winks. "You said it, not me. Here's our coffee."

The server places the drinks on the table. James gives her twenty dollars. "Keep the change."

Surprised but gratified, she leaves them to it.

James pulls out his phone while Sam enjoys her brew. He sips while he concentrates on searching for a travel agent. "Looks like a travel place operates across the street." Sam nods. "Oh, yes. I can see the office from here." "So, after we finish our coffee, we'll go over there." Sam nods at James's cup. "How does it taste?" "The coffee? Every bit as nice as when I was alive." "Good."

When they've finished their drinks, they cross 79th street. The travel agent offers several brochures, so he and Sam select two that contain photos of the front of the Bellagio. They thank the agent and promise to come back as soon as plans get finalized.

The pair leave the agent's office and head down 79th and toward Central Park. James says, "The park will give us the space we need from other people so that we can vanish from there." They laugh out loud, trying to imagine the faces of those who might see them one second and then not the next. Still chuckling, they locate a spot that seems remote enough.

James says, "Hold my hand." Sam takes his in a soft grip. "I'll look at this Bellagio photo until it burns into my subconscious."

"Just make sure you don't have any other thoughts when you start the process."

James stares at the brochure. "Don't worry. The only thing on my mind is the Bellagio."

Sam squeezes his hand. "You sure?"

"Yes. Well, confession time." James grins at her.

Sam looks into his eyes. "My breasts, right?"

"Just for a moment." James closes his eyes. "Okay, you ready?"

Chapter Nine

Sam opens her eyes. "Oh, my goodness."

"Can you believe it? Luckily, we didn't land in the pools."

"I'm glad you concentrated on the front of the place and not on the whole view."

James laughs. "I would have felt embarrassed if we'd shown up dripping wet."

"Not to mention my new dress. What should we do now?"

"Check-in. And you should change and freshen up. We have about three hours before our command appearance."

Sam nods her concurrence, and the two go inside the massive hotel. They find their way past hundreds of slot machines and to the front desk. The clerk asks, "May I help you?"

James says, "We would like a room, please."

The clerk raises an eyebrow. "Do you have a reservation?"

James looks down. "No. We just got into town and need a place."

"Could I have your name?"

"James Wainwright."

"Ah, yes, Mr. Wainwright. We do, in fact, have a reservation for you. Mr. Sedit's assistant booked a room for you."

"Mr. Sedit?"

"Oh, yes. The gentleman is a big friend of the hotel and almost lives here full time."

"That doesn't surprise me."

"I'll have someone take you to the Lakeview Suite."

"How much, per night, does that cost?"

"It is $1,100 per night, but Mr. Sedit has paid for the room already. He also wants you to enjoy yourself, so he has put a thousand-dollar credit on the suite, should you want to use the spa or, perhaps, take a chance at one of our many games."

"I'm stunned."

"You're one of Mr. Sedit's friends, and so we consider you a friend of the hotel as well."

The desk person rings a small bell, and another member of staff appears. "Please take Mr. and Mrs. Wainwright to their suite."

The young man smiles, takes Sam's dress from her, and guides them to the elevator. On the way to the twelfth floor, the guide explains all the activities of the hotel as well as the various events around town. They reach their level. Their escort says, "Please, step out of the elevator. This floor has its own staff, who you can reach by phone." He then takes them to a door marked in brass lettering, *Lakeview Suite*. The guide pushes the keycard into the slot, opens the door, and ushers Sam and James inside.

"This suite has two bedrooms and a kitchen. It offers over one thousand square-feet, so I'm sure you will feel most comfortable. If you need anything, just pick up the phone, and the concierge down the hall will answer. The lounge boasts a full courtesy bar and an assortment of snacks for your enjoyment. Let us know if we can do anything else to make your stay more enjoyable."

James takes the key and gives a twenty-dollar bill to the man. The escort smiles and thanks James but hands the twenty back. "Mr. Sedit has taken care of all the incidentals, including a healthy gratuity to me. Thank you so much. Have a pleasant stay."

The guide leaves, and James sits on the couch. "This is some place, huh?"

Sam performs a small twirl as she looks the place over. "It sure is. You have to wonder what old Lucifer is up to."

"What would you like to do?"

"A visit to the spa would be high on my list. We'll have to call and get a reservation."

"We?"

"Wouldn't you like a massage and some kind of special treatment?"

"I've never had a massage."

Sam raises her brows. "You're kidding me?"

"No. And if you died at seven-years-old, when did you find the opportunity for a massage?"

"I didn't. We have them at the eternal home."

"No way."

"Yes way. They come as part of the spiritual gift package."

"Spiritual gift package? The eternal home sounds more and more like a resort."

"You could say that. Obviously, I've never visited a resort, and so I wouldn't know. Call and get a reservation, please."

"What time?"

"How about five minutes from now?"

"Okay. It's ringing. ... Yes, this is room 1201. Oh, you know that. Can we have a reservation in the spa for now? Yes, please. Okay, that sounds good. Bye."

"What did they say?"

"Come straight on down."

"Man, I just love the power of money."

"Don't say that. You'll curse yourself."

"Whatever. Let's go."

James looks on the desk for the directory, which he uses to locate the spa. "It's on the bottom floor of this building." They smile at the convenience and head out.

The spa session is like heaven. James makes a vow that he will sign up early for a regular treatment once he gets to his eternal home. He and Sam relax in their robes and enjoy a glass of water infused with lemon. The time soon comes for them to go back to their suite so Sam can dress for dinner. They each go to their respective dressing rooms and change outfits. James feels as if he's donning old rags after the fresh feeling he got from the spa session.

Once in the room, James relaxes while Sam puts on her new dress. Vegas is relatively informal, but he's not sure whether or not he needs to wear his jacket.

Sam comes out of the bedroom, and now he feels sure he looks like a bum. She appears radiant in her new dress, and he can't help but join in her infectious smile. He asks, "Should I get a jacket?"

Sam shakes her head. "You look fine just the way you are. The slacks and shirt are decent enough, so I wouldn't worry. Besides, no one will notice you. They'll all stare at me."

James laughs and forgets his concerns.

"Can a girl get a drink around here?"

James looks at his phone—they have 45 minutes before they have to meet with Lucifer. "Sure, what would you like?" He rises and walks over to the bar.

"What do you have?"

"By the looks of it, anything and everything. I could whip up a nice Margarita if you would like."

Sam smiles. "Sounds delicious."

James goes about making the drink. He pours it into a glass from the frosted shaker, adds a lime slice, and takes it to Sam.

"Not joining me?"

James hotfoots it back to the bar and whips up another cocktail. In deference to temperance, he eliminates the lime slice and returns to the sofa, where he sits next to her.

Sam raises her glass. "Here's to a real adventure." She leans over, and James gives her tumbler a little clink.

He tastes his drink. "I didn't think we could imbibe in the afterlife."

"Who told you that?"

"Well, nobody, but it just seems that, like eating, it wouldn't play well."

"Unlike eating, drinking alcohol is not done because we need to do it to survive. We do it because it's fun. You like to have fun, don't you?"

"Yeah, I like to have fun."

"Well, come closer. It's time for a little pleasure."

"You feel okay?"

"Of course. It's just, here we are in this beautiful room, relaxing with a nice drink. I feel a kiss or two is appropriate for the situation."

James blushes. "A kiss or two? Kissing is okay?"

"Not only okay, but encouraged. It brings souls closer together and creates harmony."

Eagerly, he scoots closer to Sam, and she reaches out and takes his hand. She brings it to her lips and caresses his palm by moving it back and forth and blowing gently. With her tongue, she licks his palm while squeezing his hand. A tingling sensation runs down his spine as Sam continues to mimic oral sex with tongue and hand. He grows aroused.

She grins up at him. "I see you like my little simulation."

"Yes, and last time you scolded me when I grew hard."

"That was then, and now is now." Sam puts her drink on the coffee table, reaches over with both hands, and cups James's face. She draws close to him and thrusts her closest breast into him. Naked under her new dress, her hard nipple presses like a hard button, tantalizing his chest. The continued pressure in his pants prompts him to shift his position. Sam holds his head fast, and her hot breath arouses him further. Her pink tongue presses against her perfect teeth as she brings her mouth to his.

"What are you two doing?" James looks up to see another Sam towering over them.

The voice is hers, and James can't process. How come two Sams are here? One sits on the couch and holds his face while one stands with her hands on her hips and looks furious. The couch-Sam takes her hands off James's face and speaks, "Don't get your titty in a wringer, Miss high-and-mighty. I was just visiting to see if everything was all right."

"Who the hell are you?" Sam regains control and stalks around the couch.

"Mr. Sedit's assistant."

"Ms. Harpy?"

"The very same."

"Why do you look like me?"

Harpy smiles. "You don't like the way you look?"

Sam leans closer. "That is not germane. Why have you seduced James?"

"This big boy can take care of himself. I wouldn't call this seduction. By the way, it might be fun if you joined us for a threesome."

Sam stands up straight again. "Over my dead body."

"That train has already left, dearie."

"Very funny. Get yourself up off the sofa and get out."

"James makes a killer Margarita. Can I take it with me?"

"Sure. Take it a and go."

"Very well. It's been fun, James. You take care of that penis of yours. If you ever want a good time, just whistle, and I'll come. You bad boy, you."

Sam waves her hand. "Jesus. Just go."

"TTFN, gang."

Sam and James watch with their mouths open as Ms. Harpy sashays to the door and makes her exit. When the door closes, Sam turns on James.

"I can't believe you were making love to her … er … me."

"Sam, it was only a kiss."

"Yeah, sure. You and your libido, which refuses to die when you do."

"The woman has a real way about her. You can't fault me for wanting to love you."

"That wasn't me."

"And how would I know that?"

Sam pauses a moment and then sits. "Right. You had no way of knowing. So, if I came on to you, you would give in to temptation?"

"I don't think of it as temptation. I mean, like the Devil is tempting me? You're a beautiful person, and I've loved you since the second grade. Of course, I would make love to you if I had a chance. I don't think that's evil either. Just honest."

"Yeah, sorry. I suppose I don't have a leg to stand on. I have no idea what the rules say about eternal spirits having sex—I hadn't even thought about it until we awoke in the desert with no clothes on." Sam flushes and takes a breath. "When you got … when your body reacted to me, it shocked me … and then, um, I realized that I reacted to you the same way."

James pats the sofa beside him, and she lowers herself onto the cushion next to him. "This is a confusing situation, and awkward for us both, I'm sure."

Sam purses her lips. "Of course, we could sleep together and see what the consequences would be."

Her words produce a hot, tingly feeling inside James, and from her deep blush, he reckons she feels the same way. So, they're both longing to touch one another but haven't dared speak about it. His heart races.

Chapter Ten

James and Sam walk into Picasso, and the Maître D meets them. He welcomes them and says, "Mr. Sedit asks that you seat yourselves, and he will join you in a few minutes." He then leads them into the opulent dining room, past several diners and tables to a nook on the far side of the enormous room. The Maître D helps Sam into a chair, "A server will come over shortly." He clicks his fingers, and a waiter appears with an ice bucket and champagne bottle.

"Mr. Sedit apologizes for the delay and would like you to relax and enjoy a glass of wine. He has selected a 1995 Krug Clos d'Ambonnay and hopes you enjoy it. He will arrive shortly." The server opens the wine and pours two glasses. Another waiter places a plate of crackers with chopped egg and capers. A third server places a plate with a jar of Beluga Sturgeon caviar and two spoons. All leave without a sound or word.

James waves his hand over the caviar. "My goodness. Look at us."

"Yes, this is what you get when you hob-nob with the Devil."

"Mmm, try the champagne. It is the best I ever tasted."

"Oh, I'm sure it's the best in the world. Why don't you dig into the fish eggs while you're at it?"

"You know. Don't mind if I do." James shoves a heaped cracker into his mouth and chews. "Did you see all those Picasso paintings on the way in?"

"They were gorgeous. I bet they're genuine. Wow, you're right about the wine. By the way, the antics of that Ms. Harpy ought to tell you something."

A wicked smile lights up James's face. "What? Like the way she moved as she walked out of the room?" He pops another cracker into his mouth.

"You are such a pig. No, I'm talking about the fact that these people mean business, and I think they're after your soul."

James takes a sip of the champagne. "Why just mine? Why not go after yours as well?"

"They know I'm committed and have been since I was seven. You're new meat and, by the looks of you, wolfing down that caviar, a rather susceptible piece of new meat."

"Aw, come on. I'm just along for the ride. Nobody will convince me to give up my soul."

"You say that now but wait until the time comes and remember what you just said."

"Have a cracker and caviar. Put a little egg and caper on it. Delicious."

Sam sighs. "The old saying, 'if you can't beat 'em join 'em,' plays well here. Okay, give me one."

James builds the cracker and gives it to Sam. "Here you go."

"Mmm. This is so good."

"I'm glad you're enjoying the wine and caviar and am so sorry for arriving late. A few things came up that needed my immediate attention."

***

Sam almost chokes on her caviar and, quickly, dispatches her wad into her cheek. Sedit asks if he may sit, and both Sam and James make a feeble attempt to get up.

"Oh, please, keep your seats. Allow me to introduce myself. My name is Lucifer, and I don't believe I have to give you my portfolio."

"No, sir," James says. "We're all too familiar with your background. I'm James."

"Yes, James. I have followed your quest for your eternal home with interest. You must be the beautiful Samantha."

Despite herself, Sam blushes. "Not sure about the beautiful part, but you have the name correct."

Lucifer signals the server, who comes over with a champagne flute and pours him a glass.

Lucifer raises his drink. "To old and new friends." He touches their glasses in turn and takes a sip of the wine. A chill runs from the glass down Sam's arm. Goosebumps form where the chill passes. Her muscles react to the sudden cold. Involuntarily, her hand jerks, and she has to make a quick recovery to prevent spilling the wine.

Lucifer notices the movement. "Oh, my dear. Are you okay?"

Sam opens and closes her hand. "Yes, sir. Just a brief cramp is all."

"Maybe this room is too cold. Would you like it warmed?"

Sam flexes her wrist. "No, sir. It's fine."

"Well, I hope you two brought an appetite. This is one of the best restaurants in Las Vegas. I am aware, in the afterlife, food is not necessary, but believe me when I say that it can be enjoyed well after death. You would agree, huh, James?"

"I certainly do." James holds up his glass. "This champagne tastes delicious, and the caviar is to die for. Uh, so to speak."

"Well, tonight, I have a surprise for you. The chef will make a special dinner just for us. I do hope you enjoy it."

Sam grows annoyed, "Can I ask you a question?"

Lucifer smiles. "By all means, my dear."

Sam sets her glass down. "What do you want?"

Lucifer frowns. "I'm not sure I understand the question."

Sam leans forward. "Well, here you are, the Lord of the underworld having dinner with a couple of insignificant souls."

"You are too modest, Ms. Tourneau. After all, you and Mr. Wainwright here witnessed one of my team taking a soul. No other, as far as I know, has witnessed the same."

Sam sits back. "So, you want to make a deal to keep us quiet on the matter?"

"Not quite, Ms. Tourneau. I desire to make a deal to eliminate the need to worry about the information getting back to pre-death humans. After all, if people understood that, by their actions, Adolf Hitler would meet them on their deathbeds, don't you think requests for forgiveness would arrive en masse? Knowing that all-forgiving God of yours, they would all receive it. Then where would I be? My kingdom would stagnate. I would have no new souls to torment, and I would no longer be able to claim responsibility for every bad thing that happens to the pathetic human beings. In short, God will have won."

James says, "Excuse me, sir. Sam and I have no intention of telling anyone."

"I appreciate that, but you must see that I can't just take your word. In fact, I fully trust you mean well, but circumstances have a way of changing, and I simply can't take the chance."

James frowns. "What do you propose?"

"I would like you to work for me. I have an opening on my staff for an enterprising young soul persuasive in tempting his peers. These days, I find myself so busy. The world has become more crowded, and it is all I can do to handle those souls hell-bent on their destruction. You know the type. The killers, rapists, dictators, and congress representatives."

"Congress?"

"Just kidding. Merely a touch of 'Hell humor.' We always joke around about members of congress. You'd be surprised the number we have received over the centuries, but in general, most slip through our fingers."

James raises his hand. "So, what kind of work do you have in mind?"

Lucifer smiles. "Oh, really sweet assignments. Like trying to convert a young person to our cause."

James cocks his head to the side. "What kind of cause?"

"The cause of the anti-Christ. Man, have you not done any religious reading at all?"

James's cheeks flush. "Yes, but I'm still trying to get a handle on where you're going with this."

Sam touches James's hand. "He wants your soul."

"Ah, the silent beauty has a voice. I think it's obvious that if James comes to work for me, he will need to renounce his loyalty to his God and claim allegiance to me. That action, of course, will render his soul as a permanent part of my domain."

The corners of Sam's mouth turn down. "To do with what you will for all eternity."

"Oh, come on, young lady. Aren't we being a bit overdramatic? This is the twenty-first century for the Devil's sake. We don't do deals like in the old days. We have transparency in our dealings. If we agree on a job, that will be the job."

Sam scowls. "I don't understand why you can't simply send some nice-looking spirits to collect your souls. Then this wouldn't have become an issue."

"Ah, the goddess speaks of those things of which she has no knowledge."

Sam scoffs, "Well?"

"My dear. It's not that easy. When souls go to hell, they take on a personification of the spirit of hell. In short, they look evil. Adolf looks like himself because his visage is a symbol of evil. Others don't resemble their Earthly selves. They would scare the pants off anyone. The point is, I don't want soul collecting to become an issue. People are happy sinners, and I desire to keep it that way."

Sam turns to look at James. "I have to warn you, this ... eh ... spirit cannot be trusted. He is the Devil and not one to trifle with in a business deal."

Lucifer nods toward Sam. "She is correct, James. You should get everything we agree to in writing. That is the fair way to handle it."

Sam sits up straight. "And if you break this contract, unholy one? Who would arbitrate a solution?"

"Unholy one—I like it. Pretty dignified, I would say. My word is golden. I'll bet you can't find a single soul for all eternity who would say I took advantage of them. You want me to bring a few up here so you can interview them?"

Sam punches the tabletop with her finger. "No. What I would like is for James to renounce you and all your followers."

"I don't think he can do that right now. Just like you have those thoughts of possessing his flesh, he has thoughts that make him wish to follow me to see them come true. Ms. Harpy could have had him. You know that."

Sam sighs, "James, say something."

"I'm sorry, Ms. Tourneau, but James is in a small trance. You see, I wanted to have a discussion with you and not have to disturb our friend with the nature of it."

Sam's fingers drum the table. "I think you should bring him out of it so he can participate."

"In a moment, my dear. I just want to make this point first. James remains a long way from possessing a pure mind. He harbors feelings of lust that, at his state of eternal development, are not normal. He should have given up these feelings before now. Also, what is interesting, his feelings have begun to play on you as well."

Sam folds her arms. "That's not true."

"Oh, no? Let me play back a scene from earlier this evening. Look over there; you will see yourself and James."

Sam turns in the direction Lucifer points and drops her arms. A version of her stands in the room upstairs that looks like a hologram in the middle of the Picasso dining room. She sits on the sofa, not moving. All at once, her voice amplifies throughout the room. Her lips don't move, but the voice is hers just the same. The vision says, "I don't have a leg to stand on. I have no idea what the rules say about eternal spirits having sex—I hadn't even thought about it until we awoke in the desert with no clothes on. When you got ... when your body reacted to me, it shocked me ... and then, um, I realized that I reacted to you the same way."

A hologram-James pats the sofa beside him, and the holo-Sam lowers herself onto the cushion next to him. "This is a confusing situation, and awkward for us both, I'm sure."

The vision-Sam says, "Of course, we could sleep together and see what the consequences would be."

The voices stop, and Sam turns back to the Devil.

"Sound familiar?" Lucifer leans back in his chair.

Sam looks down at the table. "Yes."

"And do you know what your God might have to say when two of his angels get caught making love?"

Sam glares at Lucifer, wanting to hurt him with her eyes. "I have no idea. However, nobody has said that we plan to make love or commit any other sin together."

"Ha. I triple-dog-guarantee that you and James will not survive your little trip to eternity without doing the nasty. Simple chemistry, my dear. I must say if I were in James's shoes, I would jump your bones in a heartbeat."

Sam bristles. "Well, lucky for me, you're wearing your pointy-toed boots instead."

"So the deal I offer ... you could help yourself in the eternal struggle by getting rid of James before it's too late. If he came over to my side, you would free yourself from these urges."

119

Sam stares harder at Lucifer. "And James forever dammed."

"Yeah, but it's not like he will suffer. He can have all the wild sex he wants, and no one will judge him. He can do whatever he pleases, and—I'm sure—enjoy converting nice, clean souls to dirty, filthy ones like himself."

"You have no intention of seeing that James remains unharmed, do you?"

"Well, I can't supervise everyone on my team. By the way, I extend my invitation to you to join James if you wish. Then you can supervise how we treat him."

Sam puffs her cheeks and then blows out the air. "Yeah, that won't happen. I've invested time in my soul, and it's an investment I want to keep."

Lucifer smiles. "Very well. Now we've had this little chat, the time has come to let James join in. So, James, what does my proposition sound like to you?"

Suddenly, James sits up, wide awake. "Well, you make some good points, but I find myself with concerns. All in all, though I find your offer interesting, I'll stay with God."

Lucifer looks over James's shoulder and gestures for the waiter. "Well, then, we might as well order dinner."

Sam leans back. "That's it?"

"Yes, my dear. That's it. I see no need to go on and on. If you two can't recognize the benefit of joining my team, I can do nothing about it." Lucifer pauses and places his finger next to his head. "No, wait, I can do something. How about I show you some possibilities of what eternal life would look like on my side of the fence?"

Surprise grabs Sam's interest. "How will you do that?"

Lucifer puts his thumb and forefinger together. "With a snap of the finger."

James and Sam look around. The sight makes their eyes widen and mouths drop. The center court grass at Wimbledon surrounds them. They stand next to Roger Federer as the announcer introduces the Head of the All England Lawn Tennis and Croquet Club, who will present the winner's trophy to the 2019 men's champion. The pair blink in disbelief when the announcer gives James's name to the cheering crowd. The club steward shakes James's hand and offers him the Men's trophy. James doesn't seem to know what to do with it, but thanks the steward. Sam leans in close and says, "I think you're supposed to hold it over your head."

James lifts the trophy up, and the crowd loves it. The steward whispers that James should follow him. James looks at Sam, and she gives him a smile. "I'll see you later."

                        ***

James follows the steward's lead and finds himself presented to the Royal Box. To stand in front of Kate Middleton and Prince William strikes him dumb. Fortunately, he stands separated from the royals and won't have to talk to them. They acknowledge him, and he nods to them. The steward then takes him on a walk to the four sections of the viewing stands. The flashes from the cameras make James blink. After the fan tour, the steward takes him back to the center of the court, where the fans give him one last round of applause. The steward says, "You can pick up your gear and follow me to the clubhouse, where the reporters are waiting."

"Reporters?" Panic laces his voice.

"Yes, sir. The press has come from all over the globe and wants to interview you. Your story is a fabulous one, and the world wants to hear it."

"My story?" Now the panic fills his guts.

"Yes, you know, a former ball boy turned pro becomes the Wimbledon champ. Great story. Oh, and Miss Tourneau can join you as well."

James signals Sam to come with him, and he walks to the bench area. A large backpack with his name embroidered across the rear rests on a seat. He takes the bag, puts the two tennis rackets and towels inside, and hefts it onto his back.

"Do you believe this? That Lucifer has some strange sense of humor. He has forever altered history going forward and doesn't seem to give a damn."

Sam purses her lips. "I know, right. Novak Djokovic won the trophy, and now it appears you've taken it from him."

"I'm not sure we should go through with this sham, but I don't know how to get back to the Bellagio."

"Do you think the normal way will work?"

"It's worth a try, but we can't do it here in front of thousands, and who knows how many millions watching on TV."

"In that case, you have to meet with the press."

"Looks that way. Here comes the steward now."

Sam places her hand on James's back. "I'm with you every inch of the way."

James sighs. "Thank you."

"Are you ready, Mr. Wainwright?"

James turns to face the steward. "I am, sir. Lead the way."

The steward smiles and walks purposefully toward the clubhouse. As they pass under the stands into a walkway tunnel, the fans start chanting, "James, James, James."

Sam whispers, "Looks like quite a following."

"I don't know how he did that. History and all. I wish he'd given me some kind of memory of events so that at least I could talk intelligently to these reporters."

"Well, buckaroo, it looks like you'll have to fake it."

"Wish me luck."

The steward stops and tells Sam and James that they have reached the pressroom. He places his hand on the doorknob, wishes James well, and opens the door. The number of reporters crowded into the room shocks James.

He reaches back and takes Sam's hand. She gives his fingers a squeeze, and he takes a deep breath. He drops her grip and moves through the throng to a table set up on a riser at the far end of the room. He climbs the stairs and turns to look at the reporters. In an instant, hundreds of flashes from whirring cameras held above the photographers' heads blind him. The effect of the bright bursts of light makes his movements appear jerky, and he thinks he might get sick. Unsteadily, he walks to the table and sits in the chair, thankful he kept one towel out of the backpack. He uses the cloth to wipe the cold sweat from his brow. A microphone stand with about thirty microphones attached to it sits in front of him. He notices, in particular, the mics that have been duct-taped in place.

James takes a deep breath and then opens the press conference with a quiet, "Hello."

The questions burst forth from the gathered reporters, much like water from a fire hose. James holds up his hand and asks for some degree of quiet. As the room falls relatively silent, he begins.

"Ladies and gentlemen. I want to welcome you on behalf of the club. I would like you to know that winning here at Wimbledon seems nothing short of a miracle, and I feel grateful to my coaches and the many others who have helped me come this far. I have special gratitude to Samantha Tourneau for providing the support and encouragement that allowed me to win today. Beyond that, I have little to add. I hope you have a great rest of your day."

James gets up and steps off the riser. The reporters fire questions in a furious attempt to obtain a story for their papers and TV stations. James holds up his hands and continues to walk to the rear of the room with no further comment. He takes Sam's hand and keeps walking until he makes it out of the room. A closet lies straight ahead, and James opens the door. It appears nearly empty, so he shoves in Sam, follows her inside, and slams the door.

Sam pats him on the back. "Where to now, champ? By the way, nice speech."

"Close your eyes and think of the Bellagio. I'll do the same. We have about ten seconds until that door gets busted down and they drag us back to the conference."

Sam hangs onto James. "That was a bold move."

"Think now. Talk later."

Chapter Eleven

When Sam and James open their eyes, they find themselves in front of the Bellagio once more. "It worked, Sam. We're back at the hotel."

"Oh, thank God. I wasn't sure how you planned to handle the press."

"Does it matter? It was all a phony exercise anyway. Lucifer set it up, so I think it was an hallucination."

Sam opens her mouth to say something then pauses. James follows her gaze. A group of people stares at them. One points at James and says way too loudly, "Hey, aren't you James Wainwright, the tennis player?"

James and Sam cringe at the question. It means that they have returned to the Bellagio, but not back to the same era they left from. It looks like the nightmare will continue. Sam leans into James and whispers, "We didn't manage to control our destination this time."

James whispers back, "I think we controlled it very well. It's just we were off on timing is all."

"Off on timing? What if we get stuck where that stupid Devil put us? Forever."

"Shush, let me think."

Sam pats James a little too hard on the back. "Meanwhile, this crowd is growing and getting rowdier."

"Yeah, I understand. Here, take my hand and close your eyes."

James thinks hard about the Bellagio of before. He concentrates on the exact period he and Sam left. He opens his eyes slightly and sees the familiar outline of the Bellagio at nighttime, with lit fountains and windows. "Open your eyes. I think we made it back."

Reluctantly, Sam opens one eye then the other. "The lights look beautiful, but did we come back at the same time as we left?"

James rubs his head. "I think so, but we won't know until we go inside and return to the restaurant."

Sam pulls his arm. "Let's go, then."

James glances down—he wears the same slacks as when they departed. The pants give him further confidence that he and Sam have arrived where and when he wanted. He smiles at Sam, and the two walk to The Picasso. James looks around the room and recognizes some of the faces from the first time they visited. Of course, he could be kidding himself in his desire to believe they got back. Then he recalls the old guy with the younger women at his table. "We made the correct timeframe for sure."

Sam leans close. "How do you know?"

"I remember that old geezer with the young women the last time through."

"The guy in the white dinner jacket and the rose in his lapel?"

"That's the one."

"That makes me feel better. Look, there's our table, and Lucifer is still sitting there."

James goes ahead of Sam. "I want to give him a piece of my mind for that Wimbledon stunt."

"Ah, my children. You're back. How was the trip? Here, sit down, have some wine, and tell me all about it."

James and Sam take their old chairs. James hasn't taken his eyes off Lucifer since seeing him across the room. He cannot keep his eyes from flashing what he hopes looks like laser beams into the Devil's face.

Calmly, Lucifer holds James's gaze. "You seem upset. Anything wrong?"

James looks away briefly and then back again. "You're asking me if anything's wrong? Uh, let me guess. You had no control over what happened to us?"

Lucifer smiles. "Au contraire. I had full control. How did you like being the new Wimbledon men's singles champ?"

James looks down. "Maybe if I knew anything about tennis and worked my way up, it would have been the best moment of my life. As it was, it felt unnerving. I had to get out of there as fast as I could."

Lucifer pouts. "Aw, now you've hurt my feelings. You mean to say you're one of those do-gooders who think you have to earn power and prestige?"

James nods. "Yeah, I am. I don't suppose you would understand."

Lucifer shrugs. "I understand. I just don't accept the idea of having to earn what's rightfully mine. Or, in your case, what's rightfully due one of my own."

"Look, Mr. Sedit, I didn't like being on your team and think this little experiment of yours is over."

Lucifer steeples his fingers. "Do you remember the song by the Rolling Stones titled Sympathy for the Devil?"

James drums the table with his fingers. "Yeah, sure. Doesn't everyone?"

"You know the lyrics about World War Two?"

"I can't recall."

"They talked about Lucifer leading the blitz?"

"Ah, yes, I recall now."

Lucifer leans back and puts his hands on the table. "I love that song. It speaks to my overall personality."

James leans forward. "So, what do the lyrics have to do with anything?"

Lucifer puts a finger to his lips. "I might send you back to several unpleasant events in history until you decide to join

127

my team. If you join, the trips will end. If not? Well, you will have a lot of rather unpleasant moments."

James slaps the table. "Why don't you just kill me?"

Lucifer turns his hands over, palms up. "Already done. Can't happen twice."

James crosses his arms. "Well, I won't join your team."

Lucifer gives James a little wave. "Have a nice trip. I'll keep the girl with me until you get back."

James reaches out to grab Lucifer. "Now, wait a minute, Sedit."

"What's that, sir?"

"What's what?"

"You said, 'now, wait a minute, Sedit.'"

The guy who spoke wears an olive drab uniform and helmet, with an M1 Garand rifle slung over his shoulder. James recognizes it as World War II full battle dress. The scene becomes more apparent, and roughly fifty men surround James—all dressed the same. From somewhere off in front, explosions roll. All at once, he realizes that he's on a landing craft in a scene right out of Saving Private Ryan. "Shit, this is D-day, and we're heading for the shore."

The uniformed guy nods. "Yessir, that's exactly what we're doing."

The stripes on the man's sleeve signify the rank of a sergeant. James looks at his own sleeves, which have nothing on them. *Why did this guy call me, sir?* James holds a carbine in his right hand. His left hand moves to his collar, and he feels dual bars. That damn Lucifer has dropped him into a landing craft heading for the Normandy beachhead as a Captain. And, no doubt, all the men in this craft will depend on him to lead them up the beach.

James's mouth turns to sandpaper, and he gulps to get enough air to keep from passing out. His thoughts turn to what is expected of his men when they hit the beach. He missed whatever briefing took place. James comes to the realization he has no idea what to do. Sharp sounds of metal hitting metal reach his ears. It doesn't take an expert to know the noises come from German machine-gun bullets hitting the drawbridge of the landing craft. Once that thing lowers, those bullets will enter this vessel like water sprayed from a hose. "Get down, everyone," James yells. Then he calls to the coxswain to turn the landing craft ninety degrees before dropping the drawbridge so that they lay parallel to the beach. The boat responds to the coxswain's command, and the sounds of the rounds hitting the side seem deafening and relentless. The bridge drops, and James screams for everyone to get moving. The machine gunners didn't anticipate the move, so they still concentrate their fire on the broadside of the vessel.

James and the men closest to him make it to the beach. Behind him, others have fallen into the water. The landing craft, now empty, turns to make its way out to sea. James's heart throbs in his throat. With no way to go back, the only way is forward.

"Sergeant, give me a headcount."

"Yes, sir. We have about thirty survivors."

"All right, then. We can't stay here if we want to keep our asses. Pass the word that we need to get the hell up the beach. Where's the lieutenant?"

"Didn't make it, sir. He took one for a guy behind him."

"Okay, then. Let's fan out, and on my signal, move to the next hillock. You see it up there?"

"I do, sir. I'll meet you there."

"Don't let anyone get lost. I'll go ahead."

"Right behind you, sir."

James jumps up and screams, "Follow me." He stays low and runs as fast as he can to the next mound. The machine gunners sweep the hillock. James signals the men to drop to the ground and calls for the sergeant to join him.

"We have to get those machine gunners, Sergeant. Any ideas?"

"Well, sir. If we can get a few grenades over the nest rise, we might have a chance."

"We can't throw that far."

"I was thinking of launchers, sir."

"Oh, yeah. Good idea."

"You feel okay, sir?"

"Why do you ask, Sergeant?"

"You're bleeding, sir. Looks like one to the head."

James takes off his helmet and runs his hand through his hair. Blood covers his palm and fingers. Then he notices the hole in his helmet. If he were alive, this would have been a fatal wound. Why he bleeds, he can't fathom, but the fact remains he didn't sustain a serious injury. He puts his helmet back on.

"It's nothing, Sergeant. I guess I got grazed. I'm fine."

"Yes, sir. You just seem a bit different is all."

"Different? How?"

"You seem so sure of yourself, Captain."

"Maybe it's just I'm so pissed at these Germans."

"Glad you're not pissed at me."

"I'll take that as a compliment. Let's get these machine guns silenced."

A few men gather around James, and he gives instructions. "We'll launch fragmentary grenades simultaneously toward the nearest machine gun emplacement. If we can eliminate that weapon, we can lay down withering covering-fire directed at the other gun. We will then launch another barrage of grenades and more fire until we've silenced all the machine guns."

James further instructs, "Launch on my signal." They do, and the multiple explosions and flying shrapnel kill everyone manning the gun on the left. The men then take a chance, and all stand and empty their magazines into the second weapon in the middle. The gun crew never knows what hits them when seven grenades lay waste to the area.

James runs forward, and the gun on the right doesn't have a full field of fire. The Germans installed the weapon with the idea of raking the beach and never contemplated allowing the gun to swing ninety degrees to protect its flank. James runs toward the weapon emplacement and stays slightly above the crew's line of sight. He reaches the gun and drops to his back. From a supine position, James pulls two hand grenades from his pouch, yanks the pins, and releases the levers. Then he tosses them up and over a small hill created when the Germans dug a place for the gun. The explosion shakes the ground. James jumps to his feet and leaps over the top, firing his carbine. He could have saved a lot of ammunition since all the Germans lay sprawled around and silent. He waves to the men to join him.

"Damn, Captain, I've never seen anything like that."

"Like what, Sergeant?"

"A one-man army, you are."

"Aw, come on. It had to be done. Signal the rest of the men on the beach that we have a safe place to advance."

James sits down hard on the ground. A wave of exhaustion hits him like a fist to the gut. His adrenalin had pumped at the maximum level and now tapers off. In its place comes a weakness in his legs that begs for a time-out. He reaches for his canteen and pulls it from the holder on his belt. His hands shake when he brings the mouth of the flask to his lips. Most of the water runs down his chin, but he slakes his thirst. James continues to pour water into his mouth until the bile in his throat goes away.

"You okay, sir?" The sergeant stands in front of the sun, shading James's face. James has to shield his eyes to see the man since the sun's glare makes him all but invisible.

"I am, Sergeant. Just catching my breath."

"You deserve a sit-down, sir. That was some feat."

"Thank you, but nothing you wouldn't have done."

"Pardon me for saying so, sir, but I would never have exposed myself to getting killed like you did."

"I thought everything was under control. That gun couldn't swing to get me, and the other two were out of commission. Piece of cake."

"From where I was laying, sir, you saved our asses, and I'll not forget it."

"Okay, have it your way. After all, you are the sergeant, and I'm just a captain."

"Yes, sir." The sergeant breaks into a wide grin. "We're ready to keep moving, sir, if you feel up to it."

"Yeah, you bet. Let's go get those bastards."

Chapter Twelve

The company makes it through the day and comes to a stop at a small village about ten miles from the beach. The rest of the contingent show up. James's landing craft held fifty men, and another vessel also brought fifty. A corporal gives James a casualty report, and it looks like about thirty didn't make it. "Sergeant, please pass the word that all remaining platoon leaders attend a meeting in fifteen minutes, at the old farmhouse."

In the meantime, James uses a pump out in front of the building to fill his helmet. With both hands, he dips into the makeshift bowl and splashes his face. He takes a towel out of his kit to wipe himself dry. Then, feeling much better, he goes into the house and clears off a table in the kitchen, where he spreads out a map and tries to get a fix on where they have camped. James needs to contact his battalion commander to report in. Unfortunately, he doesn't know who's in charge or how to contact him. Perturbed, he calls in the corporal, who stands outside the front door.

"Yes, sir."

"At ease, Corporal. I need to get a hold of Battalion, and I'm not sure who's left up there."

The corporal takes off his helmet and fluffs his hair. "Last I heard, Colonel Simmons remains in command."

"Could you figure out a way to get in touch with him?"

The corporal puts his helmet on. "Let me get the radioman over here. He can do it."

"Thanks, Corporal."

"No problem, sir. I'll be right back."

Though he covered himself well just now, James doesn't have a clue how long he can keep up the charade of leading this group of men. He doesn't want to leave them in the lurch by just going back to the Bellagio, and at the same time, he hopes Sam is okay with Lucifer. The thought of his friend with the Devil makes him gag.

His thoughts turn to the current situation. It looks like he's established himself as a role model, and the men count on him to get them through this war. James needs to find someone else who has the leadership ability to take over. Until then, he's stuck. "Thanks, Lucifer," he mumbles.

"Excuse me, sir." The corporal's voice jolts James back.

"Yes, Corporal."

"This is Private Simpson, your radioman."

"Simpson, you get hoodwinked into this job?"

"Yessir. I've searched all over for you, sir. After Adams took a bullet, I became your radioman."

"I understand ... er, what's your first name?"

"Allen."

"Okay. From now on, Allen, you stay close to me, okay?"

"Yes, sir."

"Get me Colonel Simmons on the line. I need to brief him on our situation."

"Yessir. One minute, sir."

"How about you, Corporal? What's your name?"

"Jason Fellows, sir."

'Well, Jason, you're now part of my support staff. Go outside and ask the platoon leaders to stand down for a few minutes till I get hold of the Colonel."

"Yessir. My pleasure, sir."

Everyone needs a job to feel useful. What about the rest of the company? Do they all feel as disjointed from the main group as I do? Not sure how we got separated, but I would like to join up with the rest of the battalion.

"The Colonel's radioman is on the line, sir."

"Thanks, Allen. I got it. Hello, this is Captain Wainwright."

"Please hold for the colonel."

"Sure, I'll hang on. Hello, Colonel Simmons, sir. Captain Wainwright here."

"Captain, good to hear from you. Your location?"

"Sir, we've holed up in the village of Corenton."

"Are you secure?"

"Yes, sir."

"How did you get to Corenton?"

"We walked, sir."

"Captain, I'd watch the sarcasm if I were you."

"Sorry, sir. I wasn't trying to be smart." James clears his throat. "My company and I fought our way here, thinking we'd fallen behind."

"Well, you didn't. You're well ahead of the main force, Captain."

"Oh, I see. Well, I would come on up, because I don't think any Germans stand between here and your forces."

"Will do. Keep me advised, Captain."

"Yes, sir. Thank you, sir."

The corporal strides into the room. "What did the colonel say?"

"He wondered how we managed to get so far ahead of his troops. Let's get the platoon leaders in here."

"Right away, sir."

James continues to look at the map while the three sergeants file into the kitchen. The corporal says, "All accounted for, sir."

James invites them to take seats. Once the men settle, James leans against the table and looks from one man to the next. The faces of war stare back at him. In the last twelve hours, they have seen and experienced more life and death than for their entire lives. He wants to console them and let

135

them know everything will turn out okay but has no way to guarantee that outcome. After a deep breath, he says, "Smoke 'em if you got 'em."

The tension in the room lifts, and each man pulls out a pack of smokes and goes about their personal ritual of lighting up. One asks, "Would you like a smoke, sir?"

"Never got the habit. Thank you, though."

The three sergeants, to a man, tell him he's a lucky guy.

James clears his throat. "Well, fellas. We've done good today. I just got off the line with Colonel Simmons, and he chewed me a new one for getting ahead of the Brigade." He waits for the laughter to die down. "So, despite the Germans, and in spite of losing over thirty of our comrades, we made it this far. The colonel ordered us to remain here until he and his country-club members can get here." James laughs with the rest. "I won't kid you about what lies ahead. We have a long road to Berlin, and France gives us a sizeable area to clean out all the Germans. I tell you this, though, if y'all continue to do the kind of job you did today, we'll get this thing wrapped up in no time.

"Until the colonel gets here, we need to make sure this town stays secure. I told the colonel that no Germans stood between him and us. Let's make sure my word stays good. I want you guys to set up regular patrols and ensure we maintain robust security throughout the night. I imagine the colonel will want to stay here, and we should do everything we can to help with that.

"We don't want some stray sniper to take out our leader, after all." James detects a quiet pride in these men that will carry them forward. "So, if you all don't mind, let's get to work and secure this area. Oh, and gentlemen. Please stay safe. Thank you. Any questions?"

A hand goes up. James gives the sergeant the floor.

"What about getting resupplied? My team's running low on ammo. The BAR and .50 guys have complained about being down to their last bandolier."

"Yeah, I would assume the colonel will bring supplies with him. Corporal Fellows will radio to make sure. If not, we'll see what we can garner from the rear. Anyone else?"

Another hand. "Yes, Sergeant?"

"Should we transport the wounded, sir?"

"I would keep the men comfortable until the medical team arrives. They will take them back to the beachhead quickly enough and with more support than our small group can. We just can't afford the manpower right now. Anyone else?" No other hands go up. "Okay, then, I'll stay in the vicinity, so if anything comes up, just ask me when I make my rounds. Right, you three decide the sentry rotations and anything else needed to make us secure. You may go."

James stands and watches the men leave. All in all, he believes these professional soldiers will do a great job. In all probability, they won't need him much longer.

The corporal breaks James's train of thought, "I contacted Battalion, sir. They confirm they have ammo."

"Excellent news, Allen. Would you please let the team know that resupply is coming? Also, did you get an idea of how long it will take the colonel to arrive?"

"They're moving slowly, sir. Colonel Simmons remains cautious in case they come across any enemy troops. Most likely, it will take them a few hours."

"So, they won't get here until dark?"

"Looks like it, sir."

"Call them back and let 'em know that we have picket lines out. Let's hope the teams don't shoot each other. We should give them a recognition sign."

"How about we yell, 'Carrots.' And they reply with 'Bugs Bunny.'"

"Damn, Allen, I like that. Yes, let the colonel's team know the recognition sequence. Pass the word to our team as well."

"Yes, sir. And thank you, sir."

"For what?"

"For taking my suggestion. That's a first for me."

"It was a great idea. Now, go along and make it happen."

Excited about his new-found respect, Allen leaves the room, and James watches him scamper from one sergeant to the next.

James turns to consider how he might leave this time-segment and get back to the Bellagio. He needs to wait for the arrival of the colonel, and then an opportunity to slip away may present itself. Many men go missing in combat, and James thinks this offers the easiest way to make the transition.

The corporal returns to the house. "I've notified everyone, sir."

"Good job. We've taken care of everything. It's time to go see the wounded."

"Yes, sir. They will be pleased to see you, sir."

"Well, that's not the reason I want to see them. I need to make sure that no emergencies arise that might require special handling. Though I told the sergeants we wouldn't take the casualties to the rear yet, I want to make sure none wouldn't survive under that order."

"Good idea, sir."

James and the corporal go out to the yard, where the soldiers have settled the wounded. At least twenty men lie on ponchos on the ground. Stone walls keep most of the men safe, should any action start up again. A lone medic moves from one man to the next, checking the status of each. Concern lines the man's features. The subtle downturn of the medic's mouth tells

James that the most critical are not doing well. He approaches the medic. "How are we doing, Corporal?"

"Fine, sir. I'm keeping these guys alive for now. A few will need surgery before too long. I can't stop the internal bleeding, and I'm running out of plasma."

"Understood. The battalion medics should arrive shortly."

"How soon, sir?"

"Maybe three hours."

"Some of these guys don't have three hours, sir."

"Damn, Corporal. We have no way to transport them. How many we talking about?"

"At least six, sir."

"That would take twelve men plus yourself to get them to meet up with Battalion now."

"Well, the way I see it, sir, if we leave and double-time it, we could meet Battalion in an hour or two. That would give them a chance, sir."

"Okay, Corporal. Let's figure out how to carry the injured and still make double-time."

"We can make stretchers out of blankets and tree limbs."

James cups his hands around his mouth. "Hey, Sergeant. Come here for a minute, will you?"

The sergeant waves and trots over to where James and the medic stand. James gives him a briefing and orders the selection of twelve men. "Make stretchers to carry the more seriously wounded to the rear. Our medic will select the six most in need."

"Yes, sir."

"And, Sergeant?"

"Yes, sir?"

"Make sure none of you gets hurt."

"I'm going, too, sir?"

139

Eternal Road

"Yes. I need someone with experience of nighttime navigation to find the battalion. Take the radio and Corporal Fellows with you. Stay in contact with Colonel Simmons's team, so you don't get shot approaching them. Private Simpson tells me they're jumpy."

"I understand, sir. You can count on me."

"I hate to reduce our numbers here, but we have to try and save these men."

"Understood, sir."

"Allen, get me Colonel Simmons."

"Yes, sir. One minute, sir."

Private Simpson radios the battalion and reaches the Colonel's radioman. He hands the receiver to James. After a brief wait, the colonel comes on the line. "What's the status of your company, Captain?"

"My men have dug-in at the village, sir, and we've secured the perimeter."

"Good, good."

James gives the colonel a situation analysis and an update about the state of the wounded.

"Mission approved, Captain."

"I'm sending our radioman so that he can update you on where the detail is at all times."

The colonel expresses his satisfaction with the plan and disconnects.

"Okay, Allen, you're free to go with the detail. Make certain you have plenty of batteries."

"Yes, sir, I will. This receiver has a generator as well, so a couple of guys at the winder can keep me on the air if we run out of power."

Chapter Thirteen

James's team reaches the battalion in time to save all six of the wounded men. They then return to James's company and inform him that the forward element of the brigade is about forty minutes behind. "Well done, men. Did you encounter any enemy soldiers along the way?"

"No engagements or sightings, sir."

For the first time in over two hours, James no longer feels he might have made a mistake. He breathes deeply and lets out a sigh of relief.

The first of the troops arrive in the village. They all laugh at the Carrots and Bugs Bunny recognition. Finally, Colonel Simmons arrives in his jeep. James gives him a smart salute as the colonel gets out of the vehicle. Simmons extends his hand, and James takes it.

"I want to congratulate you and your men for your bravery. You secured more terrain faster than any other unit landing at Utah Beach. There may be a Silver Star in it for you."

James looks down at his feet. "Sir, if anyone deserves an award, it's the men of my company. They did their duty and behaved with honor."

"Yeah, I get that, Captain. None of them personally took out three German machine gun nests and exposed themselves to enemy fire like you did."

"How did you know about that, sir?"

"A reporter and photographer witnessed the action. Unfortunately, with so many bullets flying around, they couldn't get a photo. They said they felt certain you would get yourself killed. It astonished them that you made it through all that."

"I guess I got fortunate, sir."

"I would say incredibly fortunate. I see you sustained a head wound."

"It's nothing, sir. German bullet wasn't as hard as my head."

"I like you, Captain." Simmons glances around. "Is there a place we can sit a minute with the rest of my staff?"

"Yes, sir. The farmhouse offers several chairs and tables. You can make yourselves comfortable in there."

The colonel issues orders for his group to set up camp for the night. James watches as men and material flow into the village. Guards get stationed, and the food trucks form a makeshift dining space. The colonel orders his staff inside the house.

Once everyone has settled into the small building, the colonel asks for quiet.

"Gentlemen, we have received our orders. We shall proceed to St. Lo, which lies about twenty miles south of here. We won't, however, make a direct march. Miles and miles of hedgerows run between here and the target. Our orders request that we proceed from here to St Lo with all due dispatch. Right now, our forces are bombing St. Lo to eliminate as many of the enemy as possible. Why St Lo?—You may ask. In the briefing that General Hobbs gave, he indicated that St Lo occupies a major crossroads. If we don't take the city, then the Germans will gain unlimited access to move men and material at will. This mission will not prove easy. I want each company to stand at a state of readiness. We will kick-off tomorrow at zero-six-hundred hours. I would suggest everyone get a good night's sleep. The major here will hand each of you the battle maps. Our positions are marked in blue. You will notice that the lines are tight. We want to keep them that way. I don't want one of you to get out ahead of the main group. Not this time. To do so could mean annihilation. Any questions? If not, you are excused. Captain Wainwright, could I have a word?"

James had blushed some when the colonel mentioned not getting ahead. He now flushes a full shade darker. The rest of the officers file out and leave him standing in front of Colonel Simmons.

"Have a seat, Captain."

"Thank you, sir."

"Any idea why I wanted to talk to you?"

"I would guess because my team and I got ahead of the battalion."

"Damn right, Captain. You jeopardized the lives of your company as well as leaving a flank of the troops exposed. A German patrol could have slipped between you and the battalion and wreaked havoc on us. Did you think of this when you went off half-cocked to prove God knows what about soldering?"

"No, sir. We took the objectives one at a time and then found ourselves out in front."

"Not out in front, Captain. Exposed. Totally vulnerable to an ambush or getting cut off or taken prisoner."

"Yes, sir."

"Some think you a hero. In fact, I'm certain stories are getting sent back to the states talking about your cowboy antics. I want it clear from now on that you will not repeat that reckless behavior again."

"Yes, sir. I will not repeat it."

"And, Wainwright."

"Yes, sir."

"My little act out there was for your men. I wouldn't want them to think that the Lone Ranger is leading them. You got damn lucky, and you and your company survived. Do I make myself clear?"

"Crystal, sir."

"You may go."

James stands at attention and gives the colonel a smart salute. Simmons returns the courtesy, and James leaves. Once through the door, he sighs with relief. Private Simpson, standing by the door, surprises him.

"You hear all that?"

"Yes, sir, I did. Let me just say the men have a great deal of respect for you, and that old war bird has it wrong."

"Thank you for the support, Allen. That old war bird called it true. I should have paid more attention to where we were in relation to the rest of the battalion."

"Hogwash, sir. We took the country with relatively few causalities, and we were right to keep moving. It's not your fault that old war bird's team is out of shape and can't keep up."

"Let's not keep referring to Colonel Simmons as an old war bird, shall we?"

"Yeah—sorry, sir. It chafes my chaps that the old guard can't see how good some of the youngsters are."

"I appreciate that, but he is right. This is a significant campaign, and the job needs teamwork. We have no room for, as the colonel said, 'Cowboy Antics.' Let's keep the colonel's discussion with me between us, okay?"

"Yes, sir. Not a word from me."

Even as Private Simpson says those words, James feels convinced the man will blab the whole incident around the company. James sighs. If Simpson does blab, then James can do nothing about it. He just hopes no one will allow the information to get back to the colonel.

James and Private Simpson walk back to the company's gathering place. James holds an informal meeting and informs everyone, "In the morning, we will move out to St Lo." He lets them know the reason and that it will prove a tough assignment. Then James shows the map around and explains where they need to deploy during the operation. "We will take this slow and make certain we don't leave the company to our right exposed to any sneak attacks. Now, if you guys will excuse me, I need to eat something. I haven't had anything all day."

"Sir?"

"Yes, Sergeant?"

"We all think you're a hero and feel proud to follow you, sir."

"Thank you, Sergeant. You are all heroes as well, and I'm proud to serve with you."

"We just felt you needed to hear that, sir."

"I'm humbled, Sergeant. Thanks."

The sergeant smiles and then sits back on the ground. James goes to his pack and pulls out a k-ration packet, which he opens and takes out the four-pack of cigarettes. "Hey, Sergeant. Catch." He throws the cigarettes, which the sergeant catches with one hand. The soldier lifts them in a gesture of thanks. James nods and smiles.

Today has been a good day, no matter what the colonel says. James dumps out his carton of food and realizes that his hunger is such that it will override any consideration of how the food tastes or its quality. He opens the can of pork loaf and uses a cracker to scrape out the meat. His pack contains a mess kit with cutlery, but right now, he feels too tired to get up and get it. The cracker works fine, and since he has four of them, he continues. Though the food pack has a beef bouillon packet, he has no fire to heat the water, so James puts it back for another time. He finishes the pork and then opens the chocolate bar.

The sweet, creamy delight tastes like heaven. James savors its rich flavor and then takes a few swallows of water from his canteen. A nicely sized piece of Dentine chewing gum finishes the meal. James tells himself that this is dessert even though some kind of tart-like thing lies in the box. The snappy gum feels good in his mouth and reminds him of being a small boy. Frequently, he would go to the corner store and buy a pack of gum. His parents wouldn't allow him to chew it in case he choked on it, but he still did—behind everyone's backs—and getting away with such a move made the gum all the better.

145

James leans back and thinks of a time when he and Sam were kids, chewing gum and playing a game with the clouds. The idea was to guess which cloud the other was describing. Sam had such a way with her imagination. She almost always saw an animal in her clouds. He would say he saw trains or cars. Sam could never get the name of the vehicle but would eventually identify the cloud that looked to James like a car.

The camp has grown quiet, and James realizes almost all of his men have fallen asleep. Maybe he should get some rest as well. He moves his pack to where he can lie down with it under his head. The June night feels humid, and he considers getting a blanket out of the rucksack but then decides he can manage without it. The dew will only get the bedding wet, and who knows when the sun will shine again? James stretches out, and his body presses into the ground. Even though the hard dirt offers little comfort, it feels like a good place to rest in his bone-weary state. James closes his eyes and his mind soon takes its leave, and he thinks of nothing.

***

The camp stirs as if it is one being. The sounds of men waking builds to the point that those still asleep soon awaken too. The smell of coffee wafts in the air, and men work to set up the tables for a hot buffet breakfast.

James rubs his hair, which reminds him of the head wound. He sits in a momentary state of stunned shock. The morning brings a new day and the realization that he and his men will have to fight for survival presently. The stiffness in his body makes rising and moving a chore. James hasn't lain on the ground too many times before, and not since childhood, and now he remembers why he's avoided that dubious pleasure.

The sergeant next to him asks, "Are you okay, sir?"

"I confess, sleeping on the ground, coupled with yesterday's activities, has me a bit lame."

The sergeant laughs and proceeds to the chow line.

James grabs his mess kit and follows the sergeant. What the battalion cooks have managed to assemble for breakfast amazes him. The tables hold toast, SPAM, scrambled eggs, and some kind of orange drink. James's interest fastens onto the coffee. He fills his canteen cup, pleased to see milk and sugar. Though canned, the milk tastes mighty good in the coffee. While slurping at his brew, Sam's words about memories of food and drink come back to James. He's convinced that the taste of this coffee is more than a mere memory. His dinner last night was something he's never eaten before, so he has the same feelings about that food too. It could be that Lucifer has, in some way, made him more mortal. Now that he thinks about it, why did he bleed from his head wound? Could it be that the Devil has the power to bring him back to life, and is using that ability to try and entice James to join him?

James takes another sip of coffee and now feels he needs to return to the Bellagio sooner rather than later. He has a strong intuition that Sam will need him before too long. Though unsure where this feeling comes from, he feels confident that she is attempting to let him know to go back. The best way to return would be to wait until the group has moved out. Once they've headed out, it would prove a simple matter to go into the farmhouse and imagine the Bellagio and when he left there.

Almost as if the battalion read his mind, orders get passed to saddle up. The colonel calls for one more meeting and gives each of the company commanders their instructions. They will move across the country, and it is vital that the countryside remains free of enemy troops. Each company commander acknowledges his assignment. The colonel dismisses the leaders and wishes them well.

James calls his company together and provides a similar briefing. Purposely, he gives them explicit instructions on which area they will occupy. He cautions them to stay in sight of each other and that no one should get lost or out in front of the main body. All his men seem to understand what's needed. He thanks them all and tells them to move out.

The sergeant falls back to be with James.

"Sir?"

"Yes, Sergeant."

"You feeling okay?"

"You keep asking me that, Sergeant—why?"

"That speech back there. It sounded like a farewell address to me."

"How so?"

"Hard to explain, but I got the feeling you won't accompany us to St Lo."

"Nonsense, Sergeant. Why wouldn't I go to St Lo?"

"Well, call me ridiculous, sir, but I've known guys who predicted that they weren't going to make it home. They get a sense that they will die without seeing their home again."

"You think I'm about to die?"

"No, sir, it's just that a briefing to the entire company is unheard of. Usually, the company commander briefs his staff, and then they brief their men. The whole thing felt like you wanted every man to know what to do because you won't be there to take care of them."

"I have no premonitions whatsoever, so you can relax, Sergeant."

"Okay, sir. Thanks. That's good to know."

"Thank you for your concern."

"See, there you go again, sir. No company commander thanks his sergeant for raising a concern like I just did."

"Okay, Sergeant, let's leave it at this. Maybe I'll die today. Maybe not. We have no way of knowing."

"Okay, sir."

"One last thing before you go. I need to pick up maps and stuff from the farmhouse. I'll just be a minute, so you take the men and make sure you stay up with Charlie Company on your right. I'll catch you after that curve over there."

"Okay, sir."

Chapter Fourteen

James watches as the sergeant walks away. He can't help but feel gratitude for the concern the man expressed. Someone cares about him, and his chest swells. But he can't allow the sergeant's demonstration of comradeship to stop him from going back to the Bellagio. James plans on making his getaway as the troops leave the area.

Most of his company have pulled out, and the sergeant marches in the lead. James waits until nobody remains in sight before going into the farmhouse. Once inside the building, James concentrates on the Bellagio and the nighttime restaurant.

"Bewegen Sie den Kapitän nicht und machen Sie kein Geräusch."

James spins around, startled. A German soldier points a sub-machine gun at his gut. The insignia on the man's helmet announces that he is SS. James holds up his hand and smiles. The German uses his weapon to indicate that James had better put up both hands. James places his hands on his head. " Where did you come from?"

"Schweigen."

James doesn't understand German except for a few words. The scowl on this fellow's face keeps James quiet. It appears this guy has gotten cut-off from his unit and has remained out of sight since yesterday. He looks quite dirty and, in all probability, hasn't slept or eaten since the American troops settled in the village. His red-rimmed eyes broadcast his weariness. James feels sure the soldier hadn't anticipated anyone returning to the farmhouse once the troops had moved out, and so had taken refuge here. James takes a chance, "Sprichst du Englisch?"

"Ja, ein bisschen. A little."

"Good. Can we talk? Sprichst?"

The German takes a moment to determine the meaning of James's question. Then the man smiles and straightens up. "You Americans talk. Wie wäre es mit? What talk?"

James knows he must proceed with care. He gestures with his eyes to indicate his hands on his head. The German nods, and James eases his hands down to his sides. The German points to James's sidearm and mimics unhooking the web belt. James moves with caution and releases his belt, at which point, he allows one end to reach the floor. Then he lets go, and his sidearm thumps to the ground. The German gestures for James to have a seat. James drops onto a chair opposite. Satisfied that James will not try any funny business, the German sits too but keeps his automatic trained on James's midsection.

Again, James goes for a bold move, "Do you want to surrender?"

The soldier smiles and shakes his head. "I sit with gun. You ask Kapitulation. Is very funny, no?"

"You are surrounded. There is no way out. You could surrender with honor."

The German sits without saying anything for a few minutes. James cannot tell from his eyes what he thinks. He must know that to expose himself among all these troops would amount to suicide. An average person would realize that the end of the road has come. James admires the spirit of wanting to continue the fight, but with these kinds of odds, the better part of valor is to give up. The man opens his mouth to speak but then sits deep in thought once more. Finally, he says, "Woher weiß ich, dass ich nicht erschossen werde?"

"Ich verstehe nicht. I don't understand."

"Ya." The German appears perplexed on how to communicate. He resorts to hand gestures and forms a pistol shape, which he puts to his head. "How not?"

"Oh, I get it. How do you not get shot?" James puts his hands on his head, gets up, and mimes walking out of the doorway with his hands still in place. A glance at the soldier shows that the man doesn't feel comfortable with that move. James can do nothing other than take the German into custody himself and turn him over to the soldiers responsible for prisoners. The only problem with that plan is it will delay James further in his desire to return to the Bellagio. He sighs and makes more hand gestures to the effect that the German could surrender to him. "I will keep you safe."

The guy smiles and nods. Then he stands and offers James his weapon. James takes it and offers a small bow of respect. The German then takes off his belt and hands over his sidearm. Next, the man reaches inside his battle jacket and produces a dangerous-looking knife, which James takes as well. The German holds out his hands and rotates them in the universal gesture to indicate he has no more weapons. James nods and smiles. The soldier has done the right thing to ensure he will live.

James retrieves his own weapons belt and lays the German's kit on the table. He indicates for the soldier to follow him outside. The man smiles and seems to understand. James waits in the yard, but the German seems reluctant to follow. James waves his hand, and cautiously, the guy puts one foot over the threshold. The rest of his body follows, and he seems ill at ease with the exposure. Together, they follow the direction of the departed troops. While they walk along, James wishes he could talk more with the German. He would like to know how old he is and what he plans for the rest of his life. Unfortunately, the language barrier means the men must walk in silence.

James catches up to his men. The sergeant comes over. "Hey, Captain, what do you have there?"

"This German soldier got separated from his unit. I need to get to Private Simpson and radio the brigade that we have a prisoner."

The sergeant gives the German the once-over. "You search him?"

"No. I'll leave that to the MPs."

"How do you know he doesn't have a weapon?"

"He got the drop on me. We left his automatic and sidearm in the farmhouse. He surrendered voluntarily. You got a cigarette?"

The sergeant digs in his fatigue pocket and comes up with a four-pack, which he hands to James. "Don't blame you for starting smoking, Captain."

"Not for me, Sergeant. They're for my prisoner." James extends the cigarette pack to the German, who takes one and smiles. "Got a light, Sergeant?"

"Jesus H Christ. These guys have shot at us and killed us, and you're giving him cigarettes."

"A cigarette, Sergeant. Here's the rest back. Now about that light?"

The sergeant gets out his Zippo lighter and flips it on. He holds it for the prisoner, who takes a deep draw. When he snaps the lighter shut, the German thanks the sergeant. The sergeant reaches around, pulls his canteen from its cover and hands it to the prisoner, who takes it and, with shaking hands, untwists the cap. After several long gulps, the German returns the canteen and takes another drag of his cigarette. James smiles at the sergeant's charity and gestures for the prisoner to follow the moving troops. "Keep an eye on him, Sergeant. I need to find Simpson. Give the guy a K-ration. I doubt he's eaten today."

"The corporal should be upfront somewhere. He wanted to wait for you, but I told him to go ahead to the lead where he might be needed to call in an airstrike or something."

The sergeant hooks a thumb in the direction of the German. "Should I bake him a cake?"

James can't help but laugh out loud at the sarcasm. "The k-ration will do, thanks, Sergeant. I'll go find Simpson."

James moves through the men trudging across the field. The corporal marches up ahead. Maybe James could just disappear while he walks among the troops. But leaving without letting the battalion know about the prisoner might be a mistake. After all, he spent some time saving that guy and wouldn't want him to get shot now. James thinks of how he forced the sergeant to do a good deed and smiles to himself. *What would the prisoner have done had I not returned to the farmhouse? I suppose he would have gotten captured and ended up the same.* Even as he thinks it would have unfolded that way, he can't feel sure. Maybe Lucifer set this up so it would appear that James saved the German's life. If so, that would give a powerful example of what could be done working on the Devil's team. James can almost hear Sam's rebuttal. She would tell him not to fall for such an obvious trick.

James reaches Simpson and gives him the information on the prisoner. Simpson radios the news to his contact in the brigade. James thanks him and lets him know he'll be right back. He turns around with the intention to meet the sergeant to tell him to keep the prisoner with him until someone from Battalion shows up. After a couple of steps, though, a shot rings out. The entire company hits the dirt. James stays standing. The shot came from the sergeant's rifle. It was too good to be true that Lucifer would allow a piece of goodness to happen on this go-around. James goes to the sergeant. "What happened?"

"He pulled a knife and came at me."

James goes over to the dead prisoner and looks at the knife in his hand. He's forced to take the sergeant's word since it appears that, for whatever reason, the German decided to commit suicide. James feels certain the good thoughts he just had about saving the prisoner got interpreted by the Devil as a negative event. Too bad he couldn't understand that, for a brief moment, James had thought how much satisfaction it would bring to do good in the world no matter the boss. James wipes that thought from his mind.

"Okay, Sergeant. We'll let graves registration handle this. I should have searched him."

"As it turned out, sir, no harm done."

James looks at the sergeant without saying anything. He turns and walks back toward Simpson. The men have all resumed their advance after word got passed that a prisoner tried to make a getaway. James posits it that way to Battalion as well. He talks to a lieutenant to explain what's happened. The lieutenant expresses disappointment that he will have to relay the information to Colonel Simmons, seeing as the colonel had shown pleasure in having a prisoner to interrogate about troop placements on the German side. James tells him, "Well, you'll have to wait for the next one."

Now James must figure a way to disappear without getting noticed. An inner debate rages about the consequences of just vanishing. Sure, some folks might get a big shock, but so what? He would have left them in good stead, and besides, he doesn't owe these men anything. He came here, did a good job, and now he can leave.

James decides to simply disappear. To do so with the fewest witnesses possible, he figures he can ease on back to the end of the column, and while everyone concentrates on marching forward, he can vanish. With this in mind, he stays in place and allows the rest of the column to pass him. The sergeant approaches. "I'm sorry about the prisoner, Captain."

"Think no more about it, Sergeant. You did what needed doing and should have no regrets."

"Thank you, sir. Want to walk with me?"

"I'm going to cover the rear for a few minutes, Sergeant. I'll catch up."

"There're some fine bushes over there, Captain, if you need a latrine."

"Thank you, Sergeant. I'll visit them. You keep going. I'll catch up."

The sergeant smiles and turns to go. James thinks the bush idea is a great one. Perhaps, when James fails to show up, the sergeant will think he got grabbed by another German. Of course, the man will suffer a guilty conscience for not staying behind, but that will be a fleeting emotion. James ambles over to the bushes and to a point where he can no longer see the men. He closes his eyes and concentrates on the Bellagio and the time of his departure. He can almost hear the sounds of the Vegas strip when a voice interrupts his concentration.

"How did you get here?"

Chapter fifteen

James opens his eyes and blinks. A man stands in front of him and doesn't look too pleased. "Excuse me, sir. Did you say something?"

"Yeah. I said, how did you get here?"

"Not sure what you mean."

"I was walking on the sidewalk and minding my own business, and you appeared out of nowhere. You weren't here a second ago."

"Sir. Have you been drinking?"

"I had a couple of shots in the bar. Wait a minute. I'm not drunk if that's what you're trying to say."

"Our eyes can do funny things, sir."

The guy sighs, "Sorry to disturb you." Then he goes on his way. James looks around but doesn't see the Bellagio anywhere. He wishes he'd asked the guy where "here" was. James feels quite confused about where he's landed. This looks like a big city, and he believes it's in the US, given the guy's accent. To see if he can determine his location, James walks around a little. A newsstand operates up the street. Surely, he can figure out something by buying a paper. He reaches into his pocket, and change jingles beneath his questing fingers. He has three quarters, which should be enough for a paper. Inspiration hits, and he checks the quarters for the dates. He doesn't want to pass money from the future if he has arrived somewhere in the past. All the quarters show various dates. The oldest reads, 1991. The newest shows, 2005. The middle one comes from 2000.

James reaches the newsstand and takes a look at the papers. His eyes widen when he reads the date at the top of the New York Daily News. The date shows September 11th, 2001. He was only five-years-old when the terrorist attack on the Twin

Towers took place. Like every student in school, the date got well etched into his mind. In James's case, the date also marked the beginning of the end for his family. His father worked as an employee of Cantor Fitzgerald and died in the attack. At least, folks told him as much. His father's body never got recovered, and so the Twin Tower memorial remains sacred ground for James.

His heart beats so furiously that he thinks it may jump out of his throat. James looks up, and the towers loom into the deep-blue sky. His mouth goes dry with the realization that he has come here before the planes have hit the towers. Will he have time to go to his father's office and warn him and everyone else about the tragedy about to take place? Frantically, James searches for a clock. Finally, he sees one on the corner outside a jewelry store. It shows eight-forty. James recalls from his studies of 911 that Flight 11 hit the North Tower, where his dad worked, at 8:46. James screams a curse at Lucifer for putting him in this position, and then he sprints toward the towers. He must make a try at giving some of the folks on the upper floors a chance to get down before the plane hits. The way the terrorists directed the aircraft into the building, and the fact it crashed between the 92nd and 99th floors, meant no one above the 99th level could make it out. His dad works on the 99th story.

James reaches the lobby of the North Tower. He goes to the elevator banks and spots the lift that serves the 99th floor. Repeatedly, he punches the button. The indicator shows the car stopped on the 92nd floor, and it seems to stay there forever. James leaves the bank and rushes to the reception desk. A uniformed security guard sits behind the barrier. "You have to warn everyone. An airplane will hit the North Tower in minutes." James stops and looks at the huge clock behind the surprised guard. It reads 8:43. "The plane will hit in three minutes." The guard gets up and starts around the desk. He wears a microphone on his shirt and uses the device to talk urgently to someone. James prays that the man is warning the building.

"Sir, I need you to calm down." The guard puts his hands on James's shoulders. James tries to shrug them off to make another break for the elevators. The guard proves too fast, and before James knows it, he is wrestled to the floor. The guard continues to call for assistance. The people in the lobby all try to get out of the way, and the effect puts James and the guard in an isolated circle, surrounded by gaping bystanders. Two more guards arrive, and James struggles with them as well. He screams, "You need to help people."

The guards continue to order him to be quiet. James refuses and, finding the strength of two men, almost breaks free. A rumble and shaking of the building render the guards, James, and the bystanders into a stunned silence. "Too late." James ceases to resist and covers his face with his hands. He no longer needs to struggle. His sobs follow the deep sense of failure. Lucifer has punished him for not joining his side. James admits to himself that the Devil is an expert in this kind of mental game. James squeezes his eyes shut and concentrates on the Bellagio.

The release of pressure from the guards tells James he has reached another place. Slowly, he opens his eyes and finds himself in front of the longed-for hotel. The fountains and lights indicate he has arrived in the evening. He goes through the massive front doors and enters the Picasso restaurant. Immediately, he sees the old guy with the young girls and breathes a sigh of relief that he has made it back. He continues to the table where Sam and Lucifer sit.

The Devil smiles and waves his hand toward James's old chair. "Welcome back. Please, join us. We're almost ready for the main course. Did you enjoy your little trips?"

James looks at Sam to make sure she's okay. She doesn't broadcast any signs of alarm, so apparently, his trip to Normandy and New York took only seconds. It pleases him to know Sam didn't have to spend a lot of her time entertaining Lucifer.

James takes his chair, intertwines his fingers, and leans forward. "That was some excursion. I have to admit that you had me going for a while. I had thought how nice it would be to go back in history and help others. You took care of that, though."

Lucifer places his palms together in a sign of supplication. "My dear James, you know that German died at the hands of the allies. If you had saved him, who knows what historical catastrophe would have happened."

James opens his hands. "You lost the opportunity to have me join you. Killing that German was the final straw."

"How'd you like visiting your father's tomb?"

James's lips stretch across his teeth. "That was a cute stunt too. Makes me love you even more."

"I could have given you a word of advice had you asked."

"Yeah, what?"

"Instead of running around like a chicken with its head cut off, you could have simply pulled the fire alarm. You might have been able to save a few on the upper floors."

"And to use your tired excuse, who knows what historical catastrophe that would have produced."

"Maybe your father would have lived."

James waves Lucifer off. "It doesn't work. The guilt thing has the opposite effect. I get to see your true evil when you play those games."

Lucifer sighs and drops his shoulders. "Well, I've reached the point of admitting defeat. You and the lovely Samantha would have made delightful coworkers, but now you leave me no choice. I have to put you on notice that I will watch your every move, and at the right time, I will capture your souls. You see, no one messes with the Devil."

About to say something in return, James pauses when Lucifer disappears.

Sam leans over to James and places her hand on his. "Are you okay?"

James smiles at her concern and gazes into her eyes. "I'm fine. I must say, playing games with the Devil is no fun."

"That was a low blow sending you to the Twin Towers."

"Well, I would expect something like that. I can't figure out what Lucifer hoped to accomplish by such cruelty."

Sam squeezes his hand and takes a moment to answer. "I think he wanted to demonstrate his power. The first experience at Wimbledon seemed exciting, and from what I could see, it would have been pretty cool."

"Speak for yourself. I didn't look forward to answering questions from the press. I don't know anything about tennis, and it would have been a laugh-fest for sure."

"Oh, you don't know that. Anyway, since I wasn't along, how did that other experience go?"

"You mean landing in France with bullets flying everywhere? I even took one in the head."

"You're kidding. Did it hurt?"

"No. I didn't even know it happened. As I explained to Lucifer, it seemed cool to save a life. I didn't know much about being a soldier but got satisfaction leading a bunch of guys past all kinds of danger. And then someone shot a prisoner that I'd saved."

"Who killed the German?"

"He pulled a knife, and an American sergeant shot him. I'm sure he should have died anyway, and would have had I not been there. At that point, I knew I wouldn't follow the Devil. I reckon he sent me to the Twin Towers out of spite. He knew my dad died there, and he wanted me to feel guilty because I couldn't save him."

Sam moves closer to James. "How awful for you."

"I felt a bit of a mess for sure. I never even thought about pulling the fire alarm. As it happens, a security guard wrestled me to the floor. I was there when the plane hit. I could feel the building shake from the impact. It felt brutal."

Tears swell in Sam's eyes. James's heart pounds with the recognition that she cares for him, and her tears flow for the pain he went through. He realizes that living through eternity without her is impossible. James needs to find out the prospect for the two of them sharing eternal space. "Um, Sam?"

Sam uses her finger to wipe the tears away before they reach her cheeks. She looks down at the table to compose herself and then turns to James, "I don't know the answer to your question."

"How do you know my question?"

"It would be the same as I would ask."

"How can we spend eternity together?"

"That's the one."

James turns his hand over and entwines Sam's fingers in his. He gives them a slight squeeze and looks onto her eyes. "I don't think I can live without you."

Sam pulls her hand away. "You can't say that. My job is to ensure that I escort you to your eternal home. Nobody said anything about you and I spending the time together. I have no information that says it's possible."

"And you have no information saying it would be impossible."

Sam pauses for a moment to think. "You're right, but the fact remains, we haven't received permission. For all I know, when we get to your eternal home, we won't even remember what has gone on. We might not even know each other."

James sighs. "I can't believe that would happen. Tell me."

"Tell you what?"

"Tell me that you don't love me."

Sam stares James in the eyes. "I do love you, but that's beside the point. I must complete my mission, and if that means getting separated from you, that's the way it will be."

"We can't fight it or ask someone for a special dispensation?"

Sam looks away. "For all I know, the Devil put these feelings in us. Maybe it's one of his little schemes to win."

James closes his eyes. "The Devil could never come up with such beautiful feelings."

Sam claps her hands. "Let's leave this subject as something we need to investigate. In the meantime, we should get out of this place and continue our journey."

Before James can answer, a waitperson comes over and asks if they would like anything else. When they both shake their heads, he places a leather folder on the table.

James stares in surprise. "What's that?"

"Your check, sir."

"I thought Mr. Sedit would take care of the bill."

"Not to my knowledge, sir. Is there a problem?"

"No. Just give me a moment. Can you come back in a few minutes?"

"Certainly, sir." The server frowns but backs away from the table. Out of the corner of his eye, James can see the server go to the Maître D. He can just imagine what the server is telling him. James picks up the leather folder and looks at the check. The total bill makes him pale. He slaps the folder closed and whispers to Sam, "The bill is twelve-hundred dollars. Do you have a credit card?"

Sam almost breaks into a laugh but controls herself. "No, of course not. The Devil is having the last laugh. Why don't we just hold hands, close our eyes, and wish our way out of here?"

James frowns. "Easier said than done. Do you know where the car is right now?"

"No, but just envision it in your mind."

James does as Sam suggests. He thinks of the Oldsmobile and its position outside the Bellagio. In what seems like seconds, he and Sam are transported to the location. Sam laughs when she opens her eyes. James feels afraid of what she finds so funny, so he keeps his lids squeezed tight.

Sam slaps him on the back. "Open your eyes, silly. We've reached the car."

Slowly, James opens his eyes. The Olds looks precisely as it did when they left it. Sam lets go of James's hand and goes around the front to the passenger side. She opens the door and gets in. James goes to the driver's side.

In the seat, he turns to Sam. "So, what made you laugh?"

"I was delighted we made it back to the car. I'm not sure what I would have done if we hadn't."

James digs in his pocket for the keys. "Let's just drive, and then we can figure out where we should go next."

"I'm good with that." She leans back in the seat. James starts the engine and pulls out of the Bellagio parking lot. At the junction, he turns south on the main highway and heads for the hills on the horizon.

Chapter Sixteen

Sam and James have driven along US highway 95, heading South from Las Vegas for about a half-hour when they spot something up ahead. James squints but can't make it out. "You see that up there?"

"Yeah, but I can't make it out."

James shields his eyes with his hand. "Hold on, I can see it. For heaven's sake. It looks like a wagon train."

"What would a wagon train be doing heading south on this road?"

"Whoa. The paved highway just vanished. We're on dirt now."

Sam puts her hands on the dash. "Don't you think we better stop or turn around? It's not a great idea to come running up the rear of a 19th-century wagon train in a 20th-century car."

James slows the Olds, "How about we stop here? Maybe they'll make camp soon. What time is it?"

Sam waves her naked wrist under James's nose. "Now, how would I know?"

James blushes. "I forgot. Okay, let's stop, and I'll get out and look at the sun."

Sam smiles. "Sounds good, Mr. Astrometry."

James breaks to a stop. The dust cloud behind them washes over the vehicle like waves over a rock. He puts his hand up to signal Sam to wait until the dust settles. The heat of the day penetrates the poorly insulated machine. Once the air-conditioner stops, the car will turn into a hot-box in no time. James turns the engine off. Immediately, the warmth seeps into the cabin. James opens the door, and the full effect of the temperature—somewhere in the hundreds—hits him. For the first time in his life, he has a difficult time catching his breath.

Sam gets out of the car and shields her eyes from the sun's reflection off the hard-packed desert floor.

"Holy moly. This is hot."

"Yes. By the looks of the sun, we're in the hottest part of the day. I reckon it's about five o'clock. That train won't go much further. We can walk and catch up to them."

"You crazy? We may be dead, but I sure don't relish walking in this kind of heat. The calefaction could kill us."

"Very funny. These temperatures won't kill us. It's just hot is all. I'll bet when the sun drops behind those hills, you'll want a sweater. And, speaking of that, we don't have anything to wear out here in the desert."

"Maybe those kind people will loan us something."

"I wouldn't count on it. After all, we're strangers, and they've probably had it up to their necks in outsiders." James rubs his forehead. "Do you remember the Native American tribes that habituated this area? Like between here and Needles?"

Sam rubs her forehead too. "Let me think. There were several, but primarily Paiute and Shoshone."

"Okay. We may need to know more once we figure out what year this is. You okay with trailing the wagon train?"

"We don't have much else to do. Lucifer worries me, though. We didn't choose this location, and I'm afraid it might be another one of his set-ups."

"Well, if it is, we'll just come back to the car. See that tree over there? Keep it in mind, so we can get back to the Olds in this time and space."

"I got it. Smart thinking."

"I'm getting wiser as I get older."

"I can see that."

"Let's go."

Sam and James move around the vehicle and walk in the direction of the wagon train. James says, "We should come up with a story to explain why we're way out here."

They discuss several scenarios and then settle on the fact that they've followed the wagon train with their own. They left Kansas City late and have been on the road since. Unfortunately, their wagon broke down, so they had to leave it. They took their horses and as much as they could carry. Then, during a thunderstorm, the horses broke away and ran off with most of their supplies. They didn't know what to do, so they kept on following the wagon train. They are so glad they caught up finally since they ran out of food and water yesterday.

When they catch up with the train, just as they make camp, they tell their story. Sam even manages a tear or two to cement the vision of the two unfortunate folks caught in the wilderness without a thing to their name.

The wagon master buys the tale and makes arrangements for Sam and James to ride in the company wagon. He also finds them each a blanket and a raggedy hat to keep the sun away. Next, he assigns them a work detail, which includes feeding and watering the horses and helping out around the camp. He makes it clear that when they strike-out tomorrow, the two will ride up with the driver. James and Sam express their gratitude for the assistance.

They arrive in camp in time to help the cook make the night meal of Jonnycake, beans, and molasses. James has never eaten camp food like this and feels surprised at how good it tastes. The cook explains, "Usually, I put in a piece of bacon, but we're running low."

James says, "I don't miss the bacon at all. This is delicious."

After supper, the cook directs them to a creek, where they wash out the tin plates and cups. They also fetch fresh water and fill the water barrel lashed to the side of the cart.

167

When they finish the chores, the cook stretches out near the fire and lights his pipe. Then he gazes at the stars and marvels at the bigness of the sky. Sam and James sit on the ground near the fire. As they relax, the boss comes out of the dark and sits by the flames.

"How do you two like wagon life?"

Sam and James look at each other and wait for the other to start. Finally, James says, "We want to thank you for your hospitality. We're both happy to travel with you. We did have one question, though."

The boss leans on one arm. "Go ahead and ask."

"Why does the train head south? Shouldn't you go west?"

"We want to avoid a situation we heard about going on up in the Utah territory."

"Trouble?"

"Well, a bunch of folks settled in Utah under their leader Brigham Young. We hear tell of a massacre of some travelers from Arkansas with the Baker–Fancher wagon train. They called it the Mountain Meadow Massacre, and about a-hundred-and-twenty men, women, and children got murdered. No one can prove it, but it's thought it were them Mormons. I didn't desire to take any chances. If we head south, we can connect to an east-west passage to California."

"How long before you connect?"

"My scout is out now, and it shouldn't be too far. Another hundred or so miles."

Sam sits quietly, thinking, and then asks, "How long ago did the Mountain Meadow Massacre take place?"

"Last September ... so, almost ten months ago."

James recalls, *The Mountain Meadow Massacre took place in September of 1857, so this makes the date July, 1858. No wonder it feels so hot.*

The boss prompts, "That answer your question, young lady?"

"Yessir. I just wondered how long ago it all happened. Have any more massacres occurred up there?"

The boss spits into the fire. "Not that we've heard of. Still, I didn't want to take any chances."

James speaks up, "I can't blame you at all. How about Indian attacks?"

"So far, luck has stayed on our side. The natives have left us alone, mostly. We keep on the alert at all times. That's one reason I don't want you walking around and insist that you stay in the wagon. It would be a sorry thing to have you kidnapped. My understanding is the Indians don't return the women they take without a fight."

Sam folds her arms. "Don't worry about me, boss. You won't catch me wandering around."

The boss smiles and gets up from the fire. He declares, "Time for me to turn in." Then he walks into the darkness and disappears.

James thinks it's a good idea to turn in as well.

Sam tells him, "Stay close in case I need you."

"I'll stay right next to you." Then he teases her, "You scared?"

"Of course not. I don't like sleeping out of doors, given the kinds of animals that could wander around."

James pats the ground beside him, and Sam lies down next to him. They both face the fire with James positioned on the outside as they fall asleep.

***

The morning sun breaks the horizon and shines directly into James's face. He gives Sam a pat. "Time to get up, sleepyhead."

169

Sam moans and makes a move to roll over. James pulls her blanket off, and she grabs it back to keep from getting too chilled.

James stretches. "Looks like a nice day. We better get to feeding the horses."

Sam groans and sits up. "I can't believe I slept so well. How did you sleep?"

"Man, like a rock. I thought this hard ground would keep me awake, but it didn't. How come we fell asleep all of a sudden?"

Sam yawns. "I can't figure that out. It may have something to do with occupying a certain period. I think we become more human and alive when we've made a transition away from the present." Sam pulls the blanket to her chin.

"Get up, and let's get to work. We have to earn our keep."

"I know. I know. Does the year 1858 mean anything to you?"

"Sure, that's when the Mountain Meadow massacre happened. You know about that?"

'I do know some history, thanks. … So, does the date mean anything for us?"

Sam shrugs. "I'm not sure. It will take me a few minutes to think back on history and see if anything else of significance occurred."

"Can you process while feeding and watering horses?"

"Of course." Sam gets up and wipes her face with her hands.

James and Sam go to where the horses stand tethered. They pick up the water buckets and carry them to the little stream, which babbles in the sparse woods behind the wagon train. Upon returning to the horses, they find the boss there. He smiles, pleased to see them going about the chores he gave them yesterday.

"Morning, boss."

"Morning, James. Sam. Everything all right?"

"Yes, sir. We're about to get hay for the horses."

"They would enjoy some of that fresh grass under those trees. Why not hobble them over there and let them have some of it? This oasis is rare in these parts. Mostly cacti and scrub. When we leave this Garden of Eden, we'll need the hay."

James and Sam each take a horse and lead them to the grass. They put their buckets within reach of the horses and then go back to the camp. The cook has started the porridge already—a huge pot of it. He calls Sam and James, "Come get a bowl."

While they sit eating, the cook says, "While on the trail, we'll have to eat cold rations." That explains the ginormous pot.

Chapter Seventeen

When they finish and wash up the plates and bowls, the cook tells them, "Go get the horses and hitch them to the wagon."

Sam asks James, "Do you know how to hitch a wagon?"

James shrugs. "I don't have the first clue."

"We'd better tell the cook, then."

"And let these folks know we didn't tell the truth about having a cart of our own?"

"Yeah, I see what you mean. Well, let's hope the process is intuitive."

They gather up the horses and lead them back to the wagon. James notices a bunch of stuff that looks like it might be for the horses. He gets it and brings it over to where Sam holds the animals. James looks at the straight bar attached to the wagon and thinks about the set-up. From old westerns, he knows one horse goes on one side of the bar and a second animal on the other. He takes the first horse and puts it on the left of the bar. The horse dances around and becomes agitated. James switches that horse to the right-hand side, and it calms. Then he takes the other horse and puts it on the left side of the bar. The horse seems content, so James knows they are now in the right position as far as the horses are concerned.

Looking at the leather straps and such, he spots a couple of bits attached to bridles. He understands that the bits go in the horses' mouths, and the harnesses attach to the horses' heads. He asks Sam to steady the one horse and, gently, puts the bit in its mouth. Quickly, James buckles the bridle at the nose and behind the head. He does the same with the other horse. Next, James runs long reins to the wagon and attaches them to the handbrake. Now he has to figure out how the long bar attaches to the horses. Shortly, he sees that the leather straps need to go over the horses' bodies and under their bellies, and that they attach to the long pole and then to the yoke down by the front wheels. James continues to work while Sam steadies the two animals. Pleased with his work, James stands back and wipes the sweat from his eyes.

He pulls off his hat and wipes his brow with his shirtsleeve. "What do you think?"

"Nice job. Let me lead these two a little forward, and we can see if it works."

"Yeah, great idea. I think I figured it out. Thank heavens whoever took that stuff off the horses last night didn't undo every buckle."

Sam encourages the horses to take a couple of steps. When they do, the wagon follows. She and James break into big smiles. James wants to give Sam a high five but looks around and sees the boss coming over. James says, "The horses are hitched and ready."

The boss takes a look and seems satisfied that they've completed the job correctly. He tells James, "Give the cook a hand with loading the wagon. Sam, gather your blankets and put them in the wagon."

Sam asks, "Are the horses and wagon okay without being tethered?"

The boss laughs. "Those beasts aren't too eager to go anywhere and are quite content to stand here for as long as it takes."

Sam nears the cold, dead fire and picks up both of their blankets. She looks around to see if she and James have left anything else. It seems like they have everything, and Sam returns to the wagon and places the blankets under the seat. Then she holds onto the side of the cart and climbs up onto the bench.

James comes up to her side of the wagon. "I see you've made yourself comfortable."

"You won't believe how hard this seat is. It feels like sitting on concrete."

James looks under the bench. "Yeah, I can imagine. It has a spring attached to the underside, but I'll bet it doesn't help much. Maybe if you get tired, you can lay down in the back."

"What about you?"

"I'll be fine. I got an ole butt big enough to cushion. I could change up with the cook and take turns driving. That would at least take my mind from the discomfort."

The cook shows up at the driver's side of the wagon. He indicates that it is time to get in and then pulls himself up with a grunt and sits on the seat. His weight causes a little ripple in the bench. He looks over to James and watches him struggle into the cart. Sam now sits squished between the two. James turns slightly sideways, which gives Sam a few more inches. She smiles and whispers, "Thank you."

James blushes, unsure whether it's because she thanked him or the way she said it. In any case, it was a nice thing for her to do. James wonders about this whole wagon-train experience. After all, as he pointed out, finding this train happened quite by accident. That fact gives him an uneasy feeling in his stomach. James wishes he could talk to Sam, but that's all but impossible with the cook sitting so close. Maybe he could use some code to communicate his doubts about the train to his companion. "So, Sam."

Sam has to lean back a little to see his face. "What?"

"Do you reckon Sedit will give us any trouble?"

The cook speaks up before Sam can answer, "What kind of injuns are the Sedit?"

James leans forward to look at the cook. "Oh, no, sir. They're not Indians. Sedit is an old friend of ours, who we left back in Nevada."

"Nevada? Where's that?"

Sam puts her hand on James's leg as a sign to stop talking. "What James means is the Utah territory. Our friend lives near the Sierra Nevada mountains."

The cook wipes his nose on his sleeve. "Oh, I get it. So why would he cause you trouble?"

James stops Sam and lies through his teeth, "Well, we owe him a little money, and we figure he might come after us for it."

"A lot of money?"

"Under a hundred."

"Naw, nobody would chase you for a lousy hunnert."

James smiles at Sam. "That's what we figured. Say, cook. Do you think the Indians are friendly around here?"

"There's no sech thing as a friendly Indian, son. They's all savages and would just as soon lift your hair as look at you."

"I suppose we will go through the cliché of Indians attacking us, Sam."

"What the hell's a cleeshey?"

Sam tries to end the banter before the cook gets too pissed off, "A cliché is an over-used manner of speech."

"Over-used. What do you mean?"

"For example, if one were trying to describe a guy who never has time to rest, we could say he's 'busy as a bee.' That phrase could be considered a cliché because it gets used so often to describe busy people. You understand?"

"I never heard 'busy as a bee' afore."

"Oh. Well, okay. Then to you, it wouldn't be a cliché."

"I guess I won't never understand."

"Let's just leave it at that. You don't need to understand the word, and James here used it differently. Okay?"

"You sure are nice, ma'am. I'm good with that."

James rolls his eyes, and Sam gives him a stern look. James takes the hint and forgets about using code with Sam. He will wait until they find themselves alone, and then he can have a decent conversation with her. He gives her a 'zipped-lips' sign and then mouths the word "later." Sam nods.

The day unfolds into hour after hour of sitting on the sometimes-unbearably hard seat of the wagon. The scenery crawls by at such a pace that Sam and James have to catch themselves from dozing and falling off. At times, they take turns walking beside the wagon and spelling the cook, who takes to lying down on the floor in the back. The cook can fall asleep in seconds, or so it seems. He will stay out for maybe a half-hour and then return to driving. James has grown used to the reins and guiding the horses around various bends and curves. Although he reckons the horses would have navigated any of the turns without his guidance. Still, he takes pride in learning.

At noontime or thereabouts, the cook goes to the rear of the wagon and makes supper while the train continues plodding along. "No cause to stop," he says. Pots rattle during the preparation for the noon meal. The cook stays in the back and rings a triangle that suspends from the very rear of the cart.

One by one, the drovers and the boss ride up to the rear and pick up a tin plate of whatever the cook has prepared. He hands out cold porridge with molasses drizzled on top, along with an apple. The men back away and eat their meals while seated on their walking horses.

After the crew have eaten and returned their plates, the cook comes to the front and hands Sam and James a similar plate. James has never tried cold porridge before, and he feels doubtful he can eat it now. James dips the edge of his spoon into the porridge, making sure he catches some of the molasses in the process. He puts it in his mouth, and the okay taste surprises him.

Though the porridge tastes bland, the molasses adds a sweet note to the concoction. Of course, hunger makes good sauce, and before he knows it, James has eaten his entire portion. He bites into his apple and feels like this will be a good day. Sam picks at her meal. She asks the cook, "Where do you keep the apples?"

He helps her off the moving wagon and shows her the barrel lashed to the side. The man explains, "The workers need the fruit to stay healthy."

Sam tells him the story of the British navy stocking limes on ships for the same reason. The cook doesn't ask where Sam got her information, which James thinks is a good thing.

The rest of the day passes much like the morning. Sam and James keep trading-off places with the cook. He mentions more than a few times that he likes having the two around. "It gives me time to think about the night's meal and to stretch my legs."

It pleases James to hear that. At least nobody sees them as a burden. When the shadows grow longer, the boss rides up ahead to scout a campsite. He comes riding back and passes the word from wagon to wagon that a good campsite lies about two miles up the trail. James has become wagon weary and looks forward to having the leisure to walk around.

They reach the campsite after all the other wagons. The cook pulls up the horses. "James, you and the lady can get these animals settled for the night."

James goes about his duties, and Sam helps. They get the horses tethered in a shady spot and feed them hay. The grass around these parts appears dry and doesn't look like it will provide any moisture at all. The boss tells them about a stream not too far off. Sam and James grab a couple of buckets and head off toward the water. The walk proves a little further than the boss indicated. When they get there, Sam takes off her shoes and puts her feet in the stream. "Oh, this feels so good."

"I'm sure, but the horses are dying for a drink, and we better get back."

"Just a couple of minutes won't hurt. In fact, I would love to take off my clothes and lie in this water. I feel so dirty."

"On second thoughts …" James wouldn't mind getting clean himself. He takes off his shoes and shirt.

Sam's eyes widen. "So, go on. Take off your clothes and join me."

Chapter Eighteen

To James's surprise, Sam giggles and then stands up to pull off her jeans. She follows with her blouse and undershirt. Then she turns her back on James and slides her panties down her thighs until they drop to her ankles. She steps out of them and then into the stream. Because of the shallow water, she has to lie back and let the stream flow over her body. She moves her hands all over her torso and does her best to get rid of the grit and dirt. "I would have liked some soap, but this is the next best thing."

James enters the water, and like Sam, lies on his back. He positions himself so that he and Sam lie foot to foot. Sam rests upstream from him, so she has the advantage of getting the water first. James lies back and lets the stream course over his face. He holds his nose but still comes up sputtering. Once he clears his eyes, he takes a long, appreciative look at Sam's naked form. The water works its way around her firm breasts, and the chill raises her nipples. James wonders what those buds would feel like between his lips. Her legs spread apart slightly in the current, which exposes her inner thighs and private parts. James grows aroused, so he averts his eyes and looks up into the sky. The last thing he wants is to let Sam see that he's having lustful thoughts about her. While he gazes at the clouds, the water cools the heat rising in his loins.

Just about to glance back at Sam, James pauses when her eyes meet his, and she places her hands on him. "You are Sam, right?"

"Of course, I am." She shushes him and begins to caress him lovingly. Her hand drives him wild as he tries to maneuver himself to a position where he can reciprocate. Finally, he settles where he can place his hand over her soft folds. Sam undulates with his strokes, and James lifts her out of the water onto a dry part of the bank

He continues to bring Sam pleasure until she asks him to enter her. When he slides into the tight warmth of her, Sam's wetness takes him by surprise. Together, they reach for climax. The crescendo of reaching an orgasm together echoes through the woods, and they both chuckle at the noise. When they've finished, they hold each other close and enjoy the afterglow of their lovemaking. As all good things must come to an end, James suggests that they get up and finish their chores.

They dress and then fill the buckets. Walking into camp, they imagine that others are wondering what they have been up to for so long. Sam and James ignore any looks and go about watering the horses. The cook comes up and tells them, "I would appreciate you helping out with dinner."

They follow him back to the outdoor kitchen. He explains, "I need you to help me hand out the food to the trail hands. Tonight's meal will be bacon, beans, and cornbread. Since we're running low on supplies, I can't let the hands help themselves like we normally do. I need you to take their plates to them after I fill them. Tomorrow, we need to shoot some game. It's the only way we can keep everybody fed."

Sam asks, "Are you running short because you have two extra mouths to feed?"

The cook shakes his head. "Two more means nothing."

That makes James feel better, even if he doesn't totally believe what the cook said. James asks, "What can we do to help during the hunting excursion?"

The cook says, "We will take a couple of horses out early. Hopefully, we'll find a deer, and failing that, even squirrels or possums will work."

The group finishes up with the bacon-and-bean dinner. After all the dishes are done, James and Sam pick up the horses' water buckets and set out for the stream. This offers the perfect chance for a chat. "Do you think we will get into trouble?"

"What kind of trouble?"

James looks down at his bucket. "You know. Our lovemaking. Do you think we made a mistake?"

"I don't think so. We're almost in a live state right now, so I think what we did was perfectly natural."

James sighs. "That's a relief. It felt so good, and I would hate to have it come to a bad ending."

"You should quit worrying. I've prayed on it and feel at peace."

"I'm glad. Another thing that bothers me is why we ran into this wagon train?"

Sam shakes her head. "I've thought a lot about that and haven't come up with a plausible reason."

"So, thinking back in history, is there any major thing about to happen that we might witness?"

"I can't think of a thing. The civil war's three years away. There're no native American uprisings that I can remember, and the Gold rush has happened already."

"There's got to be something." James takes the bucket from Sam and drops it into the spring. The pail fills quickly, and he changes it with the spare.

"I don't think so. It has to be something Lucifer plans to do that will threaten our souls."

"We've demonstrated that he'll not be successful. What else can he do? Maybe we should return to the Olds and just keep moving."

Sam chews her bottom lip. "It could be that this isn't the Devil's work at all."

James frowns. "What do you mean?"

"Maybe God decided to send us here for some reason."

"Any way to find out?" James picks up both buckets.

181

Sam reaches for one of the pails. "Here, let me have one. I don't know how to get more information other than just riding this out to see where it goes."

"Do you think there would be any harm in leaving?" James lets Sam take the lead back to camp.

"If Lucifer lies behind this visit, I would say no. If God orchestrated it, then we could well find ourselves in a heap of 'What part of my wishes didn't you get?' sort of trouble."

"Yeah, I can see that. So, I guess we stay until we see who's running things."

Sam nods. "That would be my suggestion."

James and Sam reach the horses and place the buckets on the ground in front of them. Eager for the water, the animals suck up a good portion. James decides he'd better go back for some more. Sam agrees, and they head back to the stream. James says, "I feel a little nervous about waiting to see what happens, but it does seem the only logical course of action."

With the pails filled, they go back to the horses once more. This time, the animals show little interest. The cook comes up and reminds James, "We'll need to get an early start." Then he tells Sam what to do to get the morning meal ready. "I expect me and James here will come back from hunting a little after you have the breakfast ready."

Sam nods. "You can count on me."

Satisfied, he wishes them a good night. "It might be a good idea to turn in early."

James and Sam both wish him a good night. Sam goes over to the wagon and fetches the two blankets. "I don't think we'll need a fire tonight. It still seems rather warm."

James agrees and takes his blanket. "You want to bed here together?"

"I would love to. Just don't get any ideas. I don't need half the cowpokes on this train watching us."

James laughs, wraps his blanket around himself, and lays on the ground. He pats the spot beside him and bids Sam to snuggle in. She wraps up and lays beside him. "Look at the beautiful stars."

James sighs. "They are so dense. I haven't seen stars like this since visiting the planetarium at the college."

"I know, right. See, there's a shooting star. Make a wish."

"Do wishes come true where we're going?"

Sam nods. "Yes, if they come from an innocent heart."

"Did you make a wish?"

"I did."

"Can you tell me?"

Sam sighs, "If I do, then it won't come true."

James chuckles. "So, the rules in eternity are the same?"

"Yes. They work the same for wishes in life. Now, you'd better get some sleep. I figure you'll be rising at about three in the morning."

"You make it sound way early. Okay, then. Night."

James and Sam soon fall into a satisfied and deep sleep. When the cook taps James's shoulder, he finds it hard to believe that he didn't fall asleep mere moments ago. The cook whispers, "Time to get moving."

James looks over and sees that Sam remains asleep. He decides not to wake her and figures someone will make some noise in the morning to rouse her. He gets to his feet, and Sam says, "Be careful."

"I will. Go back to sleep."

James tries to keep as quiet as possible while he gets the horse ready to ride. He puts in the bit and buckles the halter. The cook waits by his side, all ready to go. Since they have no saddles, they will have to ride bareback. James feels a little shaky as he gets on the horse's back. He grips the animal

183

with his legs. The cook leads the way out of camp, and before long, the wagons have disappeared in the darkness.

After about a ten-minute ride, the cook holds up his hand. James reins his horse to a stop. They both dismount. The cook ties his horse to a shrub, and James looks around for one as well. A small scrub sits about ten yards away. He takes a step, but the cook whisper-shouts for him to freeze. James stands as still as possible, but his heart pounds against his ribs. The cook swings his long rifle from his back and rests it on the horse's back. He stares down the sight of the weapon, and although James cannot see what he's aiming at, he jumps along with the horses when an explosion and fire erupt from the gun.

The cook yells at James, "Hold the horses," and runs off into the night. James can hear the cook somewhere out there, but he can't see him. What he shot at remains a mystery. James looks down for a second, and the cook appears, making him jump. "Got us a nice buck."

James cannot get his tongue to work, given the incredible feat that the cook just pulled off. Finally, he manages to say, "So, how did you see him, let alone shoot him?"

"Well, boy." The cook pauses. "You see that there deer had a glint in his eye, and I seen it when he turned his head."

"But how?"

"Not sure it was the stars or what, but it was as clear to me as day. All I had to do was aim for the glint, and I bagged him. Now, come with me and let's get him dressed and back to the wagon."

James and the cook lead the horses to the dead deer. The cook takes his knife from its sheath and runs the blade along the belly of the carcass. Then he strips out the innards. "I would love to make use of the organ meats, but we just don't have the time to prepare them, and they would spoil before we get to camp tonight." He speaks lovingly of the deer liver, and

James wrinkles his nose. The cook spots the grimace, "I wonder about you sometimes, son."

When he's cleared the buck of all the organs, he says, "See if there's a creek nearby. I could smell water close."

After stumbling around in the dark, James finds a streamlet. He hollers to the cook, who tells him to come back to the deer. When James returns, the cook says, "Grab the hindquarters." James does so, and he and the cook carry the carcass to the creek. The cook then puts the deer in the water and washes it thoroughly. He had removed the head while James went in search of the stream. The cook tells him to go get the horses, which he does. When he gets back to the creek, he and the cook heft the deer onto the back of the cook's horse. "We'll have to take 'er slow. I don't want this here deer falling on the ground."

Chapter Nineteen

The cook and James walk their horses back toward the wagon train at a leisurely pace. When they reach roughly a mile away, the cook holds up his hand. James stops his horse and wonders why the cook has halted. "They should have fires going by now," he whispers. "It's almost daybreak, and the other wagons should be up."

"What do you think the problem is?"

"I'm not certain, but it sure don't seem normal. Let's leave the horses here and go on foot. We need to keep real quiet in case injuns have attacked the train."

Bile rises up James's throat. Fear for Sam paralyses him for a moment, and then he whispers. "What if it is Indians?"

"Then we're in for a bad time. The two of us can't hope to take on a whole hunting party. The best we could do is to try and parley an agreement. That's if everyone's still alive. If not, then we will be forced to hide out until they leave. Otherwise, we're dead as well."

James's knees weaken. Although Sam is dead already, it seems to him that these lives they slip in and out of have some precarious elements. Just like eating, James wonders if he and Sam could get killed in their spirit world. They can get hurt—he got a scratch or two stumbling around looking for the creek. For the first time, he worries about mortality, even though he took a bullet to the head during his sojourn to war-torn France. It could well be that while they live in a specific period, they could become mortals. His D-Day head wound certainly bled enough. Of course, the bullet should have killed him, most probably, but it didn't. That thought helps his breathing return to normal.

To keep a low profile, the cook hunches over as he walks. The tops of the wagons make silhouettes against the slight sliver of light from the dawn sky. The cook flops onto his stomach, and James follows suit. Then the man wriggles close to James and places his mouth at his ear. "It looks like some men have gotten the drop on the boss and crew. I can see them sitting on the ground with the settlers. They have about ten guys standing guard over them. They all have rifles."

"What can we do?" James whispers.

"I gotta think about this for a moment. It looks like there are a bunch of marauding thieves. They will load up a couple of wagons with whatever seems valuable and then kill those they rob. Real nasty types."

"The two of us need to do something."

"Yeah, but what? We have one rifle between us, and it's a single shot at that."

"I might have an idea, but it could sound wild."

"Right now, we can't get too picky. What are you thinking?"

"If I can go to a place where I know they have plenty of men and guns and get us some weapons that will turn the tide, we might stand a chance. It will mean that you'll have to stay here for a few minutes while I make a trip."

"What the hell are you talking about?"

"Yeah, I didn't think you would understand. You'll just have to trust me on this. I'm going to go a few yards back the way we came. I'll be right back. Don't move."

James runs back toward the stream. He stops, closes his eyes, and thinks hard about the last look he had at his company in Normandy. When he opens his eyes again, he sees the backs of the men as they move away from him.

"Hey, Captain. I've been looking for you."

"Yes, Simpson? What is it?"

"Battalion called. They're sending someone to get the German."

"Thanks, Allen. Where's the sergeant?"

"Up ahead, sir. You want me to fetch him?"

"No, that's okay. I'll go myself. You have enough to do carrying around that radio."

James leaves Simpson and double-times it to catch up with the sergeant. He hollers for the soldier to hold up. The sergeant turns around and smiles. "Everything come out okay, Captain?"

James laughs at the crude joke. "How can I lay my hands on an automatic weapon and antipersonnel grenades?"

The sergeant furrows his brow. "You starting your own war, Captain?"

"No, Sergeant. I saw a few of the enemy in the next wood, and I don't think this little carbine will be enough."

"Well, sir, we've all got you covered. You're not a one-man army."

"I can appreciate that, but could someone loan me a BAR and some grenades?"

"Okay, sir. Not that I understand what you plan to do, but I can get you the BAR. Would you like a Thompson as well?"

"Sure, Sergeant. If one runs out, I can use the other. I'll shoulder the carbine."

The sergeant asks James to follow him, and he goes over to a group of men. "The captain needs to borrow your BAR, soldier."

"What will I use, sir?"

The sergeant gives the man his M1. "Hand over a pouch of ammo as well. Each of you put a grenade in the pouch."

James now has a fully-automatic, 30-caliber rifle capable of firing twenty rounds from one magazine. The pouch contains ten to twelve magazines, as well as six grenades. More than enough to finish off those ten thieves.

The sergeant leads him to another guy, who carries a Thompson sub-machine gun. "The captain needs your weapon and magazines."

The soldier protests but, finally—after James offers him his carbine in trade—gives James the gun. James assures him, "I will return your Thompson within the hour."

The guy seems satisfied.

James puts the Thompson magazines in his pouch and slings it onto his shoulder. He shoulders the Thompson as well and grips the BAR with both hands. James thanks the sergeant and walks back along the lines toward the bushes where he came from. Once he is out of sight, he closes his eyes and thinks of the field where he left the cook.

"Show me your hands." Cook has his gun leveled at James's belly.

James comes up short and shows the cook his palms. "It's me. James."

"Damn, you made the hair on my neck stand up. What the hell is all that stuff?"

James sits on the ground and beckons the cook to do the same. "This is our armament. These weapons will add a few more men to our posse."

The cook sits there, wide-eyed, and then he edges away.

"Here, let me show you these guns. This one is called a Browning Automatic Rifle or B-A-R for short. This puppy … er, this weapon has a magazine of twenty rounds, and you can either pull the trigger once per round or just pull the trigger, and the twenty shots come out faster than you can say, 'I need to reload.' This contraption on the front is a bipod. It folds out like this so you can rest the rifle on the ground. See, like this." James flops onto his stomach with the BAR out in front of him. "You would make a tough target, lying down like this."

"What's this other thing?"

"A Thompson sub-machine gun. It, too, is fully automatic, and all you have to do is pull the trigger. The

189

magazine holds 30 rounds and empties fast. These rounds are .45 caliber and will knock a guy off his feet when you hit him."

"I see that, but how do we get the drop on those guys without our folks getting in the way?"

"You and I walk into camp and tell these thieves to put up their hands."

"You think they will do that?"

"They will once they see how these weapons perform. Also, I have several antipersonnel hand grenades. The only problem with them is if our folks are anywhere near these guys, then they could get hurt as well."

The cook pulls on his chin. "So, let me get this straight. You and I walk into camp. We tell these guys to put up their hands. What if they don't?"

"Believe me, when they see the destruction that these weapons can do, they will gladly surrender."

"How do we demonstrate that destruction as you called it?"

"Just point the gun in the air and give a short burst. They'll get the idea."

The cook looks over the two weapons and seems puzzled. James shows him how to load each and what it takes to eject the magazine and insert a new one. After a few minutes, the cook handles the BAR. "I'm used to a heavy gun, and this one feels more substantial than the Thompson."

James gives him four magazines and shows him how to tuck them in the waist of his pants. "I'll watch after the grenades and, if necessary, use them."

The cook seems happy with that decision. Finally, the two stand armed and ready. James says, "Follow my lead."

While they walk toward the wagon train, James looks back to see if the horses are secure. The two of them stand tethered and seem at peace, nibbling on the sagebrush.

The sun shows over the wagons. James takes an indirect route so that the sun doesn't shine in his eyes. His eyes dart left and right to make sure no one comes between them and the group of thieves gathered near the wagons. Nobody has spotted James or the cook yet, and so they continue to edge toward the group. When they reach about a hundred yards out, James holds up his hand. The cook stops. "They still don't see us. I guess guarding our folks has kept them distracted. I see a couple have begun to load a wagon. It looks like they're taking everything of value. Let's keep walking. When we get to fifty yards, I'll shout at them."

"What's to stop them from taking hostages?"

James pauses for a few seconds. Then he grabs the cook and pulls him into a squatting position. "Is there a way to get word to our people?"

"Word about what?"

"To tell them we're here and to run away when we make a showing."

"I don't see how that's possible."

James thinks for a few more seconds. "The only thing we can do then is to drop the thieves as quickly as possible. That won't give them an opportunity to take prisoners. That means we can't offer them the chance to give up. You okay with killing these guys?"

"Hell, yes. They have our folks, and there's no tellin' what they'll do once they have the wagons filled."

"Okay, then. We'll have to sneak up on 'em and then open fire. Just as we do, we need to yell for our folks to get down. These two guns have enough firepower to kill these guys, but we have to be careful and aim high. As far as I can tell from here, all our people are on the ground, and these guys are strutting around like gods."

James and the cook agree to take it slowly and stay as low as possible while moving closer. Once they reach about twenty yards away, James whispers, "You should deploy your bipod and stay on the ground." The cook's aim will be better as a result. The cook moves into a prone position. James checks, "Can you see the thieves?"

The cook confirms, "I have a good view."

"We fire on a count of three." James plans to go down on one knee to empty his magazine.

"I'm ready."

"Okay then," James whispers. "On three. One, two, three. Get down."

At the sound of three, the cook opens up with the BAR. James gets to one knee and sprays the campground with the .45-caliber rounds. Almost in a heartbeat, the magazine empties, and James ejects it and slams in a new one. James yells, "Follow me," and runs toward the fallen thieves. The cook had the wherewithal to take out the men loading the wagons, so when he and James make their way to the camp, they meet with no resistance.

The prisoners sit in stunned silence. They blink as they realize what's just happened. Splatters of blood and brains stick to their clothes and, in some cases, their faces. James yells for Sam, and she answers. He runs to her, and—thank heavens—she's unhurt. "Get some rags and water, and let's try to clean these folks up."

Sam gets up and nods. James goes from person to person, checking to see if they are okay. Most don't understand what just happened and look at James as if he was the one who held them hostage. The cook finds the boss and unties the ropes holding him. "What the hell happened?"

The cook tells him about James's weapons. He casts a glare of distrust over at James. The rest of the people walk around and take stock of their surroundings.

Some of them look at their wagons, now riddled with bullet holes, and then stare at James with questions in their eyes. One of the men murmurs, "Did you have to kill all those men to save us?"

James feels as though the blood of the thieves is now on his hands. His and the cook's. The man who spoke reaches into his cart and pulls a bible from under the seat. He and his wife walk over to where the thieves lay, get down on their knees, and then pray.

The boss comes over to James. "That's some firepower you have there, son. Mind telling me where you got it?"

"That's not important right now. Those guys were going to rob and kill you all. I just couldn't let that happen."

"You sure scared the bejesus out of us."

"Couldn't be helped. Cook and I didn't want these guys to have a chance to grab hostages and create a worse problem."

"It might take some doing, but I think I'll come around to thanking you after a bit. It's just I have never seen men taken down so completely before."

"I can understand that, for sure."

"I wouldn't ask these folks to thank you right now, either. They're too stunned to say anything. I'm sure they will realize you did what had to be done, but right now, they all feel guilty. After all, to save them, you had to kill others. If they had a choice about that, they might have wanted something different."

"Why is that, sir?"

"These people are Christians. They believe in the sanctity of human life and aren't comfortable trading one life for another."

"Even if it's their own or their families'?"

"I think especially if it's their own."

The boss walks away, and Sam approaches. James tells her of the conversation. Sam says, "Their attitudes don't surprise me. You did a brave thing in saving their lives but at a high price."

James wonders what she means.

Sam elaborates, "I think I know why we came to this train."

"To save these people?"

"Well, that may be part of it, but I think it goes deeper than that."

"All right. Why did we come?"

"Well, I mentioned the price of saving these folks. We arrived so that you could release them from the bonds of self-hatred."

James puts the back of his hand on his forehead. "Self-hatred? What do you mean?"

"Notice they're all looking at you like you did something bad?"

"Well, yeah, who could miss that?"

"In actuality, they believe that you valued their lives more than they did. Mistakenly, they think they're upset because you took someone's life to save theirs. That's not it at all. They're unhappy because you demonstrated that their lives are more valuable than the band of thieves."

"So, what does that mean?"

"You set a higher value to their lives than they have."

James slaps his thigh. "I still don't get it. So what?"

"They have to live up to that higher value. In other words, they have to become worth what you spent for them. Now, whoever sent us here can thank you for setting these folks on a higher plane of expectation."

"We ought to get out of here and continue the quest for an eternal home. All this mumbo-jumbo about higher planes makes my head hurt. So, who the hell sent us here?"

"My guess is that God wanted you to get these folks to value their lives so that they wouldn't throw them away too easily. You accomplished that, but now they don't like you."

"Did I disrupt the time continuum by killing all those guys?"

"I reckon they would have died soon anyway. No way could such crimes would go unpunished."

James wipes his face with the palm of his hand. "Yeah, I agree. At least, I hope we're right."

"I wouldn't worry about it for now."

James squints. "So, is it time to move on?"

Sam gives him a smile. "I'd say so."

James takes Sam's hand, and the two of them walk further out on the prairie. James closes his eyes. Then they pop open again. "We can't leave these World-War-Two weapons here in 1859." They agree that they will have to get the BAR from the cook and then go to Normandy and return the arms to the sergeant.

James tells Sam, "Stay here with the Thompson sub-machine gun and grenades, and I will go and retrieve the BAR."

"Okay."

James sets out to find the cook. He catches up to him as he arrives in camp with the horses and dead deer. "I need your gun back."

"I had hoped to keep this. It would make the best hunting rifle."

"I'm sorry, but I have to return the BAR to its owner."

The cook gives in and hands James the weapon.

James returns to Sam and takes her hand. "I will need to carry everything back. Do you want to come with me or stay here?"

"I'm not comfortable staying here. These people are upset, and there's no telling what's in their minds. I would rather come with you."

"Okay, then. Hand me the pouch and the Thompson, and we'll go to Normandy and then back to the car."

When they're ready, James thinks of the sergeant and the scenery around the marching troops.

Chapter Twenty

"Hey, Captain. Where did you get to?"

The question startles James. It seems that every time he does this time-travel thing, he isn't sure it will work out. Every time it does work, it surprises him. "Hi, Sergeant. Had to run an errand is all."

"I see you have a beautiful prisoner."

James still holds Sam's hand, and he drops it unceremoniously, at a loss for words. They didn't do an adequate job of returning undercover. James figures his alternatives are, one, grab Sam, close his eyes, and get to the Oldsmobile right in front of the sergeant. This will cause some kind of commotion. Or, two, try to say something that will make sense. Before he has a chance to do anything, Sam speaks up with a French accent.

"Zis capitan rescued me from ze Bosch. I'm so grateful." Sam gives the sergeant a big smile and thrusts out her breasts, meant to broadcast that she feels grateful to all the soldiers. The sergeant blushes at the obvious intent of her body language.

"Uh, well, sir. I guess you won't be needing these weapons."

"Thank you, Sergeant. They came in quite handy."

"For the rescue, sir."

"Yes, Sergeant, for the rescue. Now if you will excuse me, I need to walk this young thing back to her village. It's a couple of kilometers away, so I might be gone for a few minutes."

"Take all the time you need, sir. Do you want someone to go with you?"

"I can handle the escort duties. No one else needs to get involved."

The sergeant smiles, and James returns the gesture. He figures to let the sergeant think what he wants. Sam did an excellent job of covering for the two of them. Now it will be an easy matter of just going back toward the beachhead until they get out of sight.

James and Sam bid the sergeant a goodbye and head off.

James turns to Sam. "That was fast thinking."

"Thank you. I thought it was pretty quick myself."

"Your French accent sounded superb."

"Thank you, kind sir."

They both laugh out loud at having gotten away with the theatrics. After a while, they look back. James can no longer see the company of men. He takes Sam's hand and tells her to remember the Oldsmobile parked on the prairie in 1859. She nods and closes her eyes.

High overhead, the sun makes the car appear as if it's on fire. James and Sam approach their respective doors. Once inside, James starts the engine to get the air conditioning running. He smiles at Sam, who sits fanning her face with her hands. "The air will cool us down in a minute."

"I hope it hurries. I'm burning up."

James nods. "That was some adventure. I don't think I want my eternal home to be on a wagon train. And I still don't understand why those people got so weird."

"Just mark it down to experience, James. That's all you can do."

"I guess. Well, I see the road has reappeared, so we might as well get going."

Sam nods her agreement and leans back. The air conditioning kicks in, and the cool air hits their faces. She glances at James and appears troubled. "It's too bad that those people didn't appreciate your effort to save them. It will be interesting to see how history treats that episode. I'll have to look up any historical mention of the killing of those highway men. Those automatic weapons sure made a mess of those guys. It isn't any wonder the people felt so stunned. They'd had no exposure to that kind of weaponry." Sam shrugs. "I hope I got it right about God being the one to direct us to the wagon train."

"You said he would be fine with what I did."

"Yes, but I'm not totally convinced I'm right."

James says, "Great. Okay, so where do you think we should head?"

"Is there a place you would like to see?"

"I've always had an interest in Mars. Maybe we should go there."

"Very funny. We have no good reason to go to Mars. I thought, maybe, you would say into the future."

"We don't know anything about the future, so it's hard to focus on where we should end up."

"Yeah, I know. Well, you should make up your mind before Lucifer makes it up for you. Wait. Is the car picking up speed?"

"It is. The speedometer shows a hundred, and the brakes aren't working, either."

Sam puts her hands on the dashboard. The acceleration increases and pushes them both back in their seats. James tells her, "The speedometer has gone beyond its maximum of one-hundred-and-twenty miles per hour."

Through the side windows, the scrub becomes a blur. Sam mutters, "It looks like we've come under someone else's control again."

James can only try to comfort her with lame words, "This is an eternal search, after all. Who knows, but this may be a good experience." James has to yell to be heard over the rushing noise that surrounds the car. He begins to worry about whether or not the windshield is going to hold or burst in on

199

them. He cannot tell how fast they are going but believes it must be way beyond the service intention of the car. His knuckles turn white as he grips the wheel. He cannot imagine what would happen if one of the front tires blew out at this speed.

James looks at Sam and can see concern in her eyes. He tries to say something, but the pressure of the continued acceleration makes every word a struggle since his mouth feels like it's wired shut. The light fades, and darkness envelopes the car. James pulls the headlight switch, and the beams come on. The Oldsmobile travels so fast that the headlights prove useless. James thinks of his Driver's Ed class back in high school, where Mr. Ambrose warned about driving without the lights. Right now, Mr. Ambrose would be issuing a citation for going way too fast for the conditions.

Sam calls James's name. He grunts a reply. She tries to tell him something, but James can't understand what she wants to say. Also, he doesn't want to turn his head to check on her since he is afraid that if he does, the pressure won't let him turn it back again. He stares ahead and tries to speak. His arms feel like weighted noodles, and his hands slip one finger at a time from the wheel. James fights to stay awake, but he can sense that he's about to pass out. His eyelids become so heavy that it's impossible to keep them open. The dark takes over completely, and James surrenders.

"James. James, wake up."

James hears his name from far away. It almost sounds like someone on the other side of a distant hill has called him. The person can call all they want—as for him, he just wants to sleep for all eternity. He hears his name one more time and then feels a sharp slap to the face.

"Wha? Who's hitting me?"

"James, wake up. You gotta see this."

James becomes aware that Sam is trying to rouse him. He puts his hand to his cheek, the heat from her slap stings. "You had to hit me?"

"Yes, I did. It didn't look like you would ever wake up. I've sat here alone for ten minutes."

"Where are we?"

"That's just it. I don't know. This doesn't look like any place I've visited before. Look at the foliage. I've never seen this stuff."

"Do we dare to get out of the car?"

"I think so. Let me roll down the window and sample the air."

"We're not in a rocket ship, Sam. The air is the same in here as out there."

"Okay, then, I'm opening the door."

Sam pulls the lever and puts her shoulder into the door. Jungle-like plants push up against the door and make it difficult to open. Finally, she succeeds with enough room to exit. James exits his side with ease and glances around. The environment feels like a different planet. The bright-green foliage has a tropical look that doesn't seem to come from Earth.

James says, "Any idea at all on where we are?"

"None whatsoever."

James wipes his forehead with his sleeve. "I guess it's a crapshoot as to who brought us here."

"I would say pretty much."

James looks left and right. "I wonder if we should take off walking. Maybe we'll run into someone."

Sam frowns. "Or something."

"Yeah. Never thought of that. Maybe we should stay here and let the something come to us."

"Did you look at this Oldsmobile?"

For the first time, James notices that the car has lost its paint. The bright, shiny metal looks as if it has been sandblasted. "What could have caused that?"

Sam puts her hand to her chin. "I suspect that when we entered this atmosphere, it burned off the paint in our descent."

"You have to wonder why the car stayed in one piece if that's the case. If we entered Earth's atmosphere, the friction would have turned us into a cinder long before we hit the ground. Speaking of hitting the ground, the car doesn't look like it sustained any damage at all."

"I wonder if it still drives?"

"One way to find out. You wait while I pull it away from that foliage so that you can get in."

"Such a gentleman."

James gets in, starts the engine, and makes a left turn. The maneuver frees up the passenger side, and Sam can open the door and get in with ease. "Thank you. That worked well."

James points over his shoulder to the left. "We ought to head that way. I'm not sure what's over there, but it looks like the clearest route."

"I agree."

As James completes his full left turn, he thinks he sees something in the foliage but then, on second look, decides he just imagined it.

James keeps his foot lightly on the accelerator and eases the car forward. He doesn't want to go too fast for fear of hitting a tree or maybe dropping into a hole. If he keeps at a sedate pace, he can avoid most hazards. The car breaks out of the foliage and reaches a road that runs perpendicular to their direction of travel.

James points toward the front of the car. "Look at that. Which way should we go?"

"The old adage says to keep making right turns, and you will eventually end up where you want to go."

"Right it is."

James turns the wheel and steps on the accelerator. They drive between the tropical foliage on either side of the road. The sky looks much like it does on Earth with puffy white clouds silhouetted against a deep blue. The sight of the sky has the effect of lifting both their spirits. James smiles, and Sam asks, "What are you thinking about?"

He blushes a little. "The stream by the wagon train."

She nudges him and smirks. "Why would the stream make you smile? All streams look alike."

James stays silent, not wanting to make her feel as uncomfortable as he does.

Sam digs him, "You liked my nakedness more than the stream."

Finally, he admits, "I was thinking of us making love."

"You have a one-track mind."

"Aw, come on. You can't say that."

"Why not?"

"Because you're the one with the beautiful body, so you have no idea how it would affect someone."

"Well, you have a beautiful body, too, and I don't go on and on about it."

James blushes at her compliment. "Yeah, well, you're a girl, and this kind of stuff isn't as important to girls."

"What kind of stuff?"

"You know, sex and things."

"Well, you can speak for some of the other girls you've met, but this lady adores her lovemaking."

James looks at her with his mouth open. He always took it for granted that he liked sex more than anyone he's dated. Every time, his dates seemed preoccupied with finding any reason at all not to have sex. James formed his opinions not as a result of the clumsy halfhearted attempts at it in high school, but from his experiences once he got out into the world as an adult.

"Better close your mouth before some bug decides to fly in there."

"I just didn't think you cared for sex that much."

"What made you think that?"

"I don't know. I guess if you were like me in that department, you would be all over me all the time."

"Yes, now there lies the difference between us."

"Difference?"

"Right. You seem okay with quick satisfaction and more into quantity as opposed to quality. In other words, typical male."

"So, you'd go for quality over quantity?"

"Absolutely. Soft music, kind words, gentle kisses, slow hands. All that matters."

"Yeah. We haven't had much time for that kind of romance."

"Exactly. Therefore, I don't have sex on the brain every twenty seconds like some I could name."

James waves his hand. "Okay, I get it. I just thought you didn't feel into me that much."

Sam lowers her eyelids. "I'm into you very much, James. It's just we need to have some quality time together."

"I would like that. Whoa, what's that up ahead?"

James can't make out the form accurately, but to him, it looks like the skyline of a city.

Sam echoes his thoughts, "I think those are sky-scrapers."

James holds his breath. He hadn't counted on running into the inhabitants of this planet so soon. "Are the natives friendly?"

Sam tells him, "Only one way to find out."

"It might be a good idea to ask them to take us to their leader."

Sam laughs out loud. "In which movie did you find that line?"

James pouts at her for not taking him seriously. She just chortles.

In a few miles, the outline of a city skyline clarifies. The tall buildings seem to be made from liquid silver. An optical illusion could cause that. The image could come from the sun reflecting on windows to give the impression that silver runs down the sides of the buildings. They reach the outer limits of the city. Once in closer, they see that the structures are, indeed, made of glass, and the silver appearance came from the sun's reflection.

As they motor down the street, it strikes James that there is no vehicular traffic in the city at all. Also, the sidewalks are empty of pedestrians.

James points to the intersection. "Check it out. No stoplights."

"I see that. Do you suppose these people have no means of transportation?"

"That would be my guess. Keep your eyes peeled for any kind of official-looking building. You know, police station, city hall, or anything where we can engage this population on an official basis."

Sam looks around. "Okay, but don't you dare ask to get taken to their leader."

James laughs. Then he spies an official-type building. He pulls over and parks the car in front. He turns off the ignition and says, "This looks like the place."

Sam asks, "Why do you think so?"

He points to a silver plaque to the right of the door. "See that symbol? The scales of justice."

"How do you know it means that? Could be any kind of place with scales."

"I just have a feeling the way they are balanced equally. Let's go inside and check it out."

Sam takes James's hand. "Okay, but I feel nervous about just walking in there."

"There's no one around. We need to know where we came to."

"Or just close our eyes and concentrate on that road before we started speeding up."

"But that's not how we roll. We came on this quest to find our eternal home."

"Correction, big explorer ... *your* eternal home. I have mine already."

"Okay, then. My eternal home."

Chapter Twenty-One

James and Sam approach the doorway of the building. In an attempt to see inside, James puts his hand up over his eyes and leans on the glass. "I can't see anything."

Sam suggests, "Let's just go through the front door."

James grins and leads the way. Though the handle looks like metal, it feels soft and warm to the touch. Involuntarily, James lets go.

"What's wrong?"

"The handle feels alive."

"Oh, don't be silly. Here, let me try."

Sam grabs the handle and gives it a squeeze. All at once, she snatches her hand away and turns to James. "Okay, so ... you were right. That felt weird." Gingerly, she grips the handle again, and the door opens as though moved by power—almost as if the door opens on its own—they enter.

The two find themselves in a vast reception area. The expansive room holds nothing but a desk that sits on risers. Sam and James approach the counter. They look for a bell or some method of summoning someone to help them. Sam places her hands on the desk. "This feels warm like the handle."

The counter looks like stone, but when James touches it, he feels as if he just touched naked skin. Sam backs away and stands behind James, who steps back, too.

She puts her hands on his shoulders. "Eww, that is just creepy. That desk feels like someone's skin."

James nods. "Yeah, this place creeps me out. I sure would like to know where we've ended up."

Sam pulls on his arm. "I'd like to leave."

James holds up a finger. With Sam's arm in the crook of his, he half-drags her back to the desk. James places his hand on the surface and fights the instinct to pull away. The desktop moves slightly, and then a voice comes out of nowhere.

"Hello. Welcome to The Center. How may I help you?"

Initially, Sam and James duck their heads in surprise. The voice sounds as if it comes from all over the room, and both feel intimidated.

James can't keep his nervousness out of his voice, "W-we were wondering where we are."

"You are at The Center." The response sounds cheerful and like a twenty-something female spoke.

"Could you tell me where this center is located?"

"You are at The Center."

Sam pulls James closer and whispers, "Maybe this is a machine or robot, so you'll have to get more specific."

James clears his throat and then asks, "What planet is the host for *The Center*?"

Sam winks at him.

The voice doesn't answer immediately, and James imagines some machinations going on behind the scenes. Just about to repeat the question, the voice responds, and he waits. "The host for The Center is not a planet but a being."

"Okay. What planet is the host on?" Sam gives James a thumbs up.

"The third planet from the sun."

James and Sam can barely hold their jaws in place. They look at each other, and Sam silently mouths the word "Earth." James clears his throat and says, "Did you say Earth?"

"No. I said the third planet from the sun."

"Which sun?"

"The one in the Sagittarius arm of the Milky Way."

"So, this is Earth?"

"I do not know that name."

"What name do you know the planet by?"

"Blue Marble."

"Astronauts gave Earth that name on a trip to the moon."

"I only have the information given to me. I have no authorization to create information. I cannot store that which is given to me by other than the Central Chief."

"Can we meet the Central Chief?"

"Do you have an appointment?"

"No."

"Request denied."

"How do we get an appointment?"

"You must ask for one."

"May we have an appointment?"

"When?"

"Now?"

"Yes. The Central Chief will meet you here shortly."

James looks at Sam, and she shrugs. An Alice-in-Wonderland feeling settles on him. "May we sit?"

"You have nothing to sit upon."

Sam shrugs again. James smiles weakly and rolls his eyes. He sees no point in asking any more questions of the robot right now and doesn't want to say too much. He leans in and whispers, "We should wait for the Central Chief to show up."

Sam nods, and they both stand quietly and glance around.

A large door rises into the ceiling. In anticipation, James and Sam look toward the door. A being, dressed in what looks like silver Mylar, enters the reception area through the entryway. The door lowers, and the being walks up to Sam and James. James takes a half-step back, surprised that the person, or whatever it is, has no discernable mouth or eyes. It does have what would pass for a nose, but James can identify no nostrils. The face appears as if it's carved out of a single piece of metal. *A robot*, James concludes.

The being raises an appendage with a grasping tool in place of the five fingers that one would typically associate with a hand. "Good day, time traveler. Welcome to The Center."

James glances at Sam. "Good day to you, uh ... should I call you Central Chief?"

"Oh, no. I am not the Central Chief. I have come to take you to the Central Chief."

"How did you know we were time travelers?"

"The Central Chief knows everything. Now, follow me."

The door rises, and the being or robot, or whatever, goes through and stops for a second to make sure Sam and James keep close behind. "Mind the hatchway coming down."

Sam bumps into James in her haste to get out of the way of the descending door. The being moves at a slow walk until they come to another door. The portal rises, and the being steps through. Sam and James follow and find themselves in a large room with nowhere to sit. "Please, wait here. The Central Chief will arrive shortly." The being waves its appendage, and two chairs appear. "Please, take a seat."

They each sit down, and the being passes through the wall and disappears.

Sam says, "That robot gave me the creeps."

"I know. This whole thing doesn't seem real. Desks that feel like skin, and I swear there was something odd about that door handle when we first got here."

"Well, let's at least meet the Central Chief and see what this is all about."

"Yup."

On cue, a man walks through the wall and sits in a chair that appears suddenly. James frowns. He has never met him in person, but James believes this guy looks like Bob Newhart.

"Allow me to introduce myself. I am the Central Chief. You are the time travelers of which I have heard a lot. May I have your names, please?"

"James."

"Sam."

"It is a pleasure to meet you. Please, tell me how I can help you?"

James and Sam trade looks, and then James speaks up, "Well, you see, uh … what should I call you?"

"You can call me what my children call me."

"That would be great."

"Central Chief."

"Um, okay, Central Chief, we would like to know where we are. You see, we didn't choose this place, and all of a sudden, our transportation picked up speed, and here we are."

"I saw with interest your car is a 1956 Oldsmobile."

James smiles. "Yes, sir. My father gave it to me when I turned sixteen."

"A rare car, indeed. He must have had great trust in you at the time."

James glances down. "Well, he and I worked to restore it, and he knew I loved it as much as he did."

"Pity about the paint."

James looks up. "I hadn't even thought about that, sir."

"Yes, but still, you know you came through a vast time tunnel."

James shrugs. "We thought—because of the paint—that we re-entered another atmosphere."

"My goodness, son. Had you done that, you would be part of that Oldsmobile in a crater somewhere. No, you stayed on Earth."

James sighs. "Where are we?"

"In relation to your time or ours?"

"Well, let's start with yours."

"Very well. This is the year 3935, and we are at The Center."

James flips his hand. "Okay, so how about concerning our time?"

"The year is the same, and The Center is located where Las Vegas used to be."

James screws up his face while he processes. "Used to be? What happened?"

"Long story, but in a nutshell, during the winter of 2520, the entire city imploded under the weight of its own evil."

"God did away with Las Vegas?" James shakes his head.

"No, God had nothing to do with it. The fine people of Las Vegas became too greedy in their desire for the Earth's wealth. They tried to corner the gold and silver markets, and when they failed, the town simply ceased being viable. They had no money to keep the casinos and hotels from falling into disrepair. Soon the place became dismal and run down, and people stopped visiting. The Central Committee bought Las Vegas for a song in the 2800s. The only thing left of any value was the water."

"Then, you built The Center?"

"No, The Center evolved from the idea that humankind was not the best steward of the Earth. The Committee determined that the best use of resources laid in eliminating humans and allowing artificial intelligence to run the Earth."

James looks at the Central Chief. "No humans live here?"

"No, thank heavens. They proved a pesky lot to eliminate. Also, human protective societies thought that they should save the species. Some nonsense about the food chain getting disturbed and the end of all life if humans went extinct. The early conservationists used the same arguments about animals."

"Does Earth still have animals?" James grows somewhat breathless.

"God, no. All those dirty things running around. The Committee decided that once the humans had gone, the animals might as well follow. All that bunk about the natural chain came down to propaganda. When humans and animals all disappeared, the air became cleaner, and the so-called warming went away. We now have lovely weather and clean air."

Chapter Twenty-Two

Sam and James share a glance. Sam indicates that she would like to ask a question. James nods, and she says, "So, the committee decided animals and humans must go? How did that come about? If you don't mind me asking."

"Not at all. That episode brought us one of the best chapters in our glorious history. We offered a reward to anyone willing to eliminate a human. As I recall, you could collect up to one-million rewards. After all was said and done, the humans hunted each other until only a few exceedingly-rich people remained. After that, it became a matter of eliminating the last few. We promised them eternal life. They fell for it hook, line, and sinker. Once they showed up, it proved easy to euthanize them. I can see by your shocked expression you think this all rather barbaric."

Sam nods. "It had crossed my mind."

"I can assure you, we established disposal sites, and handled everything according to the hunting rules. To collect, a human merely had to deliver a body to the disposal site, and we made payment immediately. We used gold to provide further incentive. It amazed me that after about five years, very few humans remained. About eight years after the decision to eliminate the species, we put the last human to sleep."

"And the animals?"

"So easy. We contaminated the food supply, and most had gone within a year."

"I can't believe what I'm hearing. I suppose James and I shouldn't be allowed to exist."

"To the contrary. You are spirits, so—in a manner of speaking—you don't exist."

Sam puts her hand to her mouth. "How do you know we're spirits?"

"Ah, my dear."

Sam waves her hand. "How do you know we're not alive?"

"It is my job to know everything about what goes on here. I've tracked you both since James left Normandy. I had a feeling. Oh, strike that. I had a data alert that you might head here, so I researched who would enter my sanctum, so to speak."

Sam and James share another glance, which passes the inquisitor duties from one to the other. James says, "Data alert?"

"Oh, my boy, that's a complex question, which requires a simple answer for you to understand. It reads like a text from deep in the bowels of the AI infrastructure. And, please, don't do a follow up question about the infrastructure. I don't think we have enough time, nor do you have the brain power to understand all that goes on there."

James holds up his hand. "Okay, I won't. I sure don't want to tax any of your resources."

"My this one has a wit. Anyway, I found out about you dying in a car crash and you at the hands of a child molester, Sam."

Sam crosses her arms. "Anything else?"

"The only other thing besides James is looking for his eternal home, comes from you two not making a friend in Lucifer."

James nods. "Yeah, no kidding. You have any inside information on that?"

"Besides a warning not to fool with him, you mean?"

Sam agrees. "I think we get that."

"Of course, you are safe here. The Devil and I have a deal."

The words leave James surprised. "Deal?"

215

"Yes. I don't go looking to turn the Devil's wretched souls into robots, and he doesn't come looking to turn my robots into wretched souls. It all works rather well."

Sam unfolds her arms and sits forward in her chair. "Have you met Lucifer?"

"Several times. He grew quite interested in the reward for killing humans. He wanted to make sure he had enough collectors around to handle the influx."

Sam frowns. "Collectors?"

"You know, those horrid spirits that grab souls and take them to hell."

"Yeah, we saw them at work. It seems to me that more good people got hunted than bad."

"Yes, initially, that's true. Once the killing started, more hunters joined in. Soon the hunters became the hunted. That's when the soul collection process got into full swing."

James motions with his hand. "And now the soul supply is exhausted."

"It is. That's why we had to come to an agreement. Old Lucifer and I."

"So, now he should be satisfied. He has all the evil that exists."

"You would think. I have it on good authority that the Devil's current business venture lies in trying to convert those already saved."

James and Sam look at each other. Sam says, "We're familiar with that strategy."

"He approached both of you, I take it?"

Sam nods. "Yes."

"I hear he offers quite a deal."

James scoffs. "We don't know much about that. All he offered was a tennis championship and a tour with landing forces on D-day."

"He told me that any soul who joins him will have involvement in any historical moment as if the event happened for the first time."

James leans back. "He didn't say that to us."

"Maybe he refined his offer after your experiences."

"So, why have we come here?"

"I believe that God sent you to learn about the end of time as far as the human condition is concerned. In his way, he is telling you that if you throw in with Lucifer, then eternity as you know it is only as long as 3935. So if you were to choose to live eternally as a world ruler, your term would expire in 3935."

James and Sam stare at each other, and Sam says, "I guess that gives us a good reason to come here for sure, even though it feels hard to wrap my head around 1900 years into the future."

"Believe me, time flies. It seems like 2520 was just yesterday."

"You're old."

"No, I haven't reached my half-life yet."

"Half-life? Don't tell me." Sam puts her hand on her cheek.

"Yup. I'm a robot. A sophisticated robot, I might add."

Sam looks taken-aback. "I find it hard to believe."

"I would like to demonstrate to you by opening a hatch on my chest, but the maker was careful in designing those who would ultimately have an interface with humans. The structure had to remain believable to instill confidence in those with which interaction proved necessary.

"I have met with presidents and kings, and no one questioned my humanity. Of course, looking like Bob Newhart did raise some questions in those who remembered what he looked like. We always laughed it off as a coincidence. I chose Bob because I saw a few episodes of his show, archived in one of our servers. He displayed a great personality and seemed perfect as the Central Chief."

James smiles. "You made a great choice. Well—" He glances at Sam. "—we need to get on our way. Nice chatting with you. Thank you for your information, and we hope we haven't taken up too much of your time."

"Before you leave, I have a question."

James entwines his fingers and places both hands in his lap. "Okay."

"Do you know how to get out of here?"

James looks at Sam, but she shows no reaction. "I'm not sure."

Sam puts her hand on James's elbow. "I'll speak to that," she says. "We have no clue."

"I thought as much. Tell you what. I'll give you a little tour around the place and then show you the road to your Oldsmobile."

Sam puts her hands together. "That would be terrific."

Chapter Twenty-Three

The Central Chief rises, and his chair disappears. He gestures for Sam and James to stand as well. He then beckons the two to join him in a walk to the Central Control. As they approach the Central Chief, he gestures, and a door zips up out of the way. He explains, "The Central Control is only a few steps away." True to his word, the group reaches another portal that also zips up and out of the way. Once they pass through the entryway, the door hisses closed.

"This is Central Control—the command point for the entire operation."

James can't stand staying quiet. "How big is the operation?"

"What do you mean?"

James looks around. "I'm trying to get a sense of how much you control from here."

"All of it."

"I assumed that. What does 'all of it' mean?"

Sam rests her hand on James's arm.

The robot replies, "The whole world."

James and Sam have no comment. Given the small number of dials and flashing lights and the fact that nobody works in the control room, they find it hard to fathom that the entire world is controlled from this tiny spot. The Central Chief senses their disbelief, so he goes to the control board.

"If you will bear with me, I'll explain what we have here. You will notice there are hardly any dials or lights. All the control features are built into the system. The only reason we have any lights at all is that our central AI engineer insisted that the lights provide a way to work off small particles of energy that could accumulate in the system. Yes, James, you have a question?"

"You have an AI engineer?"

"Oh, sorry. It is just a manner of speaking. The engineering function is incorporated with all the other functions. For example, I'm sure you grew a little uneasy when you grabbed the door handle, and it felt almost alive."

Sam shakes her hand. "That was a bit of a shock."

"I'm sure. This is an ongoing experiment to determine the best material for external surfaces, given the corrosive nature of this particular environment. We know skin won't rust or break down under adverse conditions. The only problem is its poor resistance to sunshine. It tends to burn. However, those handles that have not been exposed to the sun have weathered very well. Similar handles made out of metal have deteriorated in a matter of years."

James holds his arms out with his palms up. "So, you have no engineer, per se?"

"No, we have a cumulative knowledge of all engineering. We use this knowledge to plan any projects necessary. Of course, with no life forms, the planning remains mostly confined to this facility."

Sam raises her hand. "We see what looks like a city out there. Is it, in fact, a city?"

"Well, it resembles a city but is, in reality, a giant server farm. What looks like buildings are actually external shells protecting the servers contained within. These servers house all the accumulated knowledge developed since the beginning of time."

Sam shrugs. "But no one's around to use the information."

"See, that's where a carbon individual demonstrates the extreme difference between it and an analog body."

"Huh?"

"I mean to say, you believe knowledge is not useful unless it benefits or is used by mankind."

"Well. I guess."

"We don't share that belief. We believe knowledge for its own sake is worth protecting and then used to benefit the user."

"Robots?"

"We prefer AI agents."

"Where are all the AI agents?"

"Discreetly deployed throughout the compound. Now, come, I want to show you our human museum. Wow, that came out wrong. We don't have humans in there. We do have some artifacts that we have collected over the years. I think you might find it interesting. Just turn around, and we will walk toward that wall behind you."

Sam and James do as the robot suggests, and the Central Chief walks by them. A door zips up out of the way. The Chief waves them in. They stand in a room that contains display case after display case. The Central Chief stops at one cabinet and gestures for them to come closer. Sam and James look through the glass. Various things made out of what looks like plastic fill the case. The Central Chief touches a button, and the surround opens like a clamshell. The Central Chief picks up one of the items. "We rescued this artifact from the beach. It is the last of its kind. I must say, the amount of damage this one item contributed to the pollution of the Earth is far and away not represented by its size. Would you care to handle it?"

The Central Chief holds up a floss pick. The fact that it was on the beach meant that a human somewhere flossed his teeth and then threw it away. Both answer "no" at the same time. The Central Chief cracks a smile and places the pick back in its spot. Before grabbing another item, the Central Chief takes a pair of forceps from a supply on the side of the case. He picks up something with the forceps and explains, "This display is one we set aside to exhibit items that led to the destruction of human life." He holds a cigarette butt with lipstick on the cork-like mouthpiece.

"I have a particular fondness for this one. For all the evidence that cigarettes can kill, humans continued to smoke them by the billions. Even at the last, people still smoked. I have never seen a product that has had such an impact on human health and yet was allowed to be used. If AI had been in control earlier, a thing like cigarettes would never have been available for consumption. This specimen comes from the late nineteen fifties. Back then, females used to coat their lips with color to attract males. It seems barbaric in comparison to the technology development that went on at the time. Our own Wilson was first scaled for general use around that time."

Sam stares in surprise. "Wilson? The big computer company uses that name in its advertising."

"To be sure. What better way to gain acceptance than to give a machine a human name?"

"You're saying Wilson is the first AI developed?"

"I am saying our Wilson was developed around the late fifties. Wilson is currently at the central core of our computing power. Wilson has the functionality to maintain this world in the pristine condition you see now. If I were to believe in God, it would be Wilson."

Sam furrows her brow. "And the late fifties is when Wilson was born?"

"Yes, absolutely. When you put it like that, the late fifties is Wilson's birthday."

Sam touches her face. "Do you have an exact date and place?"

"I do, indeed. In 1958, John McSweeney of Stanford University invented the computer programming language BOTS. This was the language of Wilson. Once the language existed, Wilson existed."

Sam pulls on her chin. "Interesting. So, the basic of AI goes back over two thousand years?"

"Yes. As you can imagine, AI has continued to evolve to where we are today."

Sam asks, "What are the goals of AI now that the Earth is under their control?"

"I don't believe we have any more goals. Keeping all the elements functional is full-time work. Since AI is not subject to any behavioral rules, we have no designs on fulfilling any additional needs. We have reached the position of self-actualization, and unlike the human form, we do not need to reinforce our position continually. We don't need a better car or house simply because someone else has one."

James puts his hands on his hips. "I find it strange that you eliminated humans and animals and now have no other ideas to improve your lot."

"Spoken like a true human. You see, our lot has been and is at a perfect state right now. There is no way to improve it, so why spend time and energy on developing a plan that, in the end, will be useless?"

Sam takes James's hand. "That sounds logical for sure. Well, I don't know about you, James, but this has been a fascinating tour and trip forward in time, but we need to hit the road."

James smiles because he is of the same mindset. "I agree. It sure has been a pleasure, Central Chief, but we need to head down the road."

The Central Chief asks, "Would you like to see any more of the artifacts in the museum?"

Both decline and indicate that they would like to get going. The Central Chief says he understands and then leads them to the reception area where he pauses.

"You're sure you know how to get back into your own time?"

"Yes, sir," James says. "We have become pretty adept at making our way around the different time hops that we've come through."

"Very well, then. I feel less than an adequate host since I didn't offer you any food or drink. Of course, we have no food or drink, so it would have been difficult to make good on such an offer."

Sam shakes her head. "We understand. Also, since we are spirits, we don't need anything like food or drink. You have been a gracious host, and we thank you."

"All right, then. If you ever find your way here again, don't be strangers."

The Central Chief guides them to a door, which zips up out of the way. They find themselves in the reception area after the door closes. James holds his finger to his lips, and Sam nods, understanding. They walk straight to the exit door and push to the outside. Sam opens her mouth to say something, and James holds up his hand. "Let's get in the car. Then we can talk."

They head for the Oldsmobile and get in. Both start talking at once. Sam waves her hands, and James can't seem to speak fast enough to cover what he wants to say. Finally, he stops talking and turns to Sam. "You go ahead since we both want to talk, and I can't get what you're saying."

"Oh, man. Do you realize that time eternal ends right here?"

"Yes, and it's a scary thought."

"How could an AI organization decide to end the human race?"

"Not to mention all the animals."

"I know, right? We have to do something."

"Yes. Old Central Chief gave us the time and location of Wilson's birth. Why don't we show up there and do a little altering of history?"

"James, you know that's forbidden."

"To save the human race?"

"I don't think I came across an exception when God handed down the rules."

James and Sam sit in silence for a moment—the end of all human history lies beyond their comprehension. Then James says, "That damn Lucifer knew this lay in the future. He had to have known. I love how he offered eternal bliss if we worked for him. I can just see the duties now. Be one of those idiots trying to grab an AI robot for eternal damnation. We made the right choice to avoid that prospect."

Sam looks through the window. "I'm still trying to think of something we can do."

James lays his hand on her arm. "I'm telling you, we ought to go to Stanford University in 1958 and look up this John McSweeney."

"Then what will you do?"

James shrugs. "I don't know. Maybe steal his notes or disrupt the development of Wilson somehow."

"You would have to kill McSweeney."

James puts his hand over his heart. "Me? Oh, my God. I couldn't kill him."

Sam pulls his hand away. "That would be the only way to stop Wilson from being born."

James takes her hand. "Let's just go there, and maybe something will come to us while we're there."

Sam smiles. "All right. I guess that wouldn't do any harm. Like you said, maybe something will come to us. I've thought it over, and since this whole takeover of the Earth hasn't happened yet, we wouldn't disrupt the time continuum by altering the BOTS language."

"You sure?"

"I can't be a hundred percent sure, but I'm willing to take the chance."

"So, we have a plan?"

"We do."

James starts the car and thinks hard about Stanford University in 1958. He takes Sam's hand and squeezes his eyes shut. Then he concentrates on a 1958 Ford Convertible and the administration building at Stanford.

Chapter Twenty-Four

Sam and James find themselves in front of the administration building of Stanford University. The hood of James's Oldsmobile, which has returned to the original sheen, shows a clear reflection of the structure. The return of the paint makes James wonder. He turns to Sam and touches her cheek. Her eyes open and she gives an almost inaudible squeal at seeing the building.

"We made it."

"Looks that way. See the shiny hood on my car, too? Let's get out."

The two leave the vehicle, and the first thing James notices is that his Oldsmobile looks brand new. Of course, if this is the year 1958, then the car is less than two-years-old. James leans over and looks at himself in the pristine paint.

Sam puts her hand on his shoulder. "Your car looks lovely, but we need to find out where McSweeney works. Also, we need to get the exact date."

James agrees and also suggests, "We should pull the car across the street and into general parking. Then we can go and find a newspaper to determine the date." Just then, a campus police officer approaches. "This is a no-parking zone."

James smiles. "Sorry, Officer. We're just about to move the car."

The officer seems satisfied. "Be careful of the restrictions in the future."

"Yes, sir." James and Sam jump into the vehicle. After a quick turn, they find a parking place outside the drug store.

Sam and James go into the shop. A newspaper and magazine rack stands next to the doorway. James picks up the San Francisco Chronicle and checks the date—Tuesday, September 23rd, 1958. He shows the paper to Sam, who shrugs.

He asks, "Does the date mean anything to you?"

"No, it doesn't. I studied a lot of history, but for the life of me, I don't remember John McSweeney or the development of the BOTS language."

James nods. "Okay, that means we have to get hold of a reference book to figure out when McSweeney developed the language. Unfortunately, I'll bet no one here has heard of it either. What about just looking up McSweeney and seeing where he is on the whole process?"

Sam smiles. "I don't think he will spill his guts to a couple of nerds like us."

James glances at her. "Yeah, you're right. The only thing I think we can do is go back and get on the internet so we can look up the history of BOTS."

Sam shakes her head. "I hate to do that. Every time we travel in time, I get nervous. I have this fear that we'll never come back. And, once we know when BOTS or Wilson was developed, what can we do to alter that event without messing with the future?"

James sighs. "I haven't figured that out yet. I thought, maybe, we could alter a mathematical equation or something."

"James, for heaven's sake. We don't have the knowledge to do that."

James puffs his cheeks. "All I know is if we don't do something, the entire human race and all the animals on Earth are doomed."

Sam puts her hand on James's arm. "Any chance we could talk to McSweeney and explain what he does inadvertently?"

James looks down. "Would you believe us?"

Sam removes her hand. "I see what you mean. No, I wouldn't."

"So, what can it hurt to take one step at a time? We do the things we can do, and then maybe something will come up where we can take action."

Sam puts her hands up. "Okay, I give up. If we go back, you can use your phone to connect and do the research."

James feels his pockets. "Where is my cell?"

"In the car. You left it in there so you wouldn't pull it out where it shouldn't exist."

"Okay, so let's get back to the Olds and then to New York. I will return to outside my apartment, so we know where we are."

"That sounds good. At least we won't get lost."

"Let's go."

James and Sam return to the vehicle and get in. Seated and holding hands with Sam, James thinks about his apartment and the corner just down the block from it. He doesn't want to run into any of his neighbors, even though he will only be there for a few minutes. With his eyes shut, he concentrates on the spot.

James opens his eyes with caution. It pleases him to see he made it to the exact spot. He tells Sam to open her eyes and starts the car. A parking place lies ahead, and he pulls in. Sam asks, "Did we come to the right place?"

James gives her a thumbs up. He finds his phone and types BOTS into the search bar. Several links appear, and he selects "history of BOTS." He scans the information and falls on the date of September 24th, 1958. "Here it is," he says.

"What's the date?"

"Tomorrow."

"Tomorrow? OMG. That doesn't give us much time."

"I know. Lucky for us, the historical recap gives us the address of McSweeney's lab as well. He works in the Stanford Research Center in Menlo Park. That's all we need."

"Why don't you download the information and then keep your cell in your pocket? You never know when we might need more, and I don't want to risk going back and forth through time. Especially with Lucifer floating around."

"Great idea. Okay, done. Let's get back. I have a picture of the research center that I can focus on."

Sam nods. "I'll focus on September 23rd, 1958, so that we don't miss the year."

James takes Sam's hand. "You ready, then?"

"Ready."

After a couple of seconds, James looks around and sees the Research Center off to his right. Sam points to it, and James confirms that they reached the correct location. Sam wonders, "Did we manage to arrive on the date we wanted?"

James starts the car and pulls into a parking place across from the research center. He tells Sam, "Wait in the car until I get back. I'll pop into the drug store to recheck the paper." After a few moments, he comes out smiling and gives her a thumbs up. She waves to James.

James pulls the driver's door open and gets back into the driver's seat. "Well, we made it back to September 23rd."

"I'm so glad to hear that. What's the next move?"

"According to the history article, McSweeney worked the last few days around the clock to finish up the BOTS language. I imagine he's in there working right now."

"Can we get to him?"

"Sam, this is 1958 and way before school shootings and security. I'll bet we could walk in and go directly to his lab."

"I guess that's our only option now."

James smiles and exits the Oldsmobile. Sam follows his lead and asks, "Do you have your phone?"

He pats his pocket. "In here."

She shuts the passenger door and asks him over the front hood, "What about your plan?"

He explains, "We will locate McSweeney and then talk to him and see what transpires."

"That's not really a plan. That's flying by the seat of your pants. We need to get serious and come up with something of substance."

"No. If we talk to McSweeney, something will come up. Let's at least go in and see if he's around."

"Okay, but I don't like this take-it-as-it-comes strategy."

"Oh yeah, and I suppose we could have planned everything that happened on this trip."

Sam drops her gaze. "Fair point. Okay, let's go."

Sam and James go to the main entrance. Once through the door, they see a building directory on the wall to the right of a hallway. The two go to the register and see that John McSweeney has an office on the second floor. The book also shows a lab listed, which appears to sit right next to McSweeney's office. They look around and see an elevator over to the left. They walk to the lift, and Sam punches the up button.

The car arrives, and the pair get on. Sam reaches in front of James and hits the button for the second floor, and the door hisses closed. As the elevator starts moving, Sam looks at James. "You okay?"

"Yeah."

The door slides open, and the pair get out. They stand in a long hall with several doors on both sides. James studies the first door they come to and tells Sam, "It looks like we'll find the lab at the end of the hall." They walk, trying not to make any noise. Sam looks at James and then asks him, "Why are we trying to be quiet?"

James laughs since he doesn't have a ready answer.

Sam grins.

"You two."

Sam and James freeze and then, slowly, turn around to face whoever spoke to them from behind. Their eyes widen with surprise.

James is the first to find his voice, "Lucifer. What a surprise to see you here."

"I'm sure."

Sam swallows hard and then breaks into a weak smile. "How have you been?" Her question has all the sincerity of someone meeting their ex by accident in the Whole Foods Market.

"Oh, Sam, my lovely. I have been just peachy since we last met. Got a few mass killings and a couple of natural disasters to handle, but nothing I can't take care of."

Sam's smile freezes on her face, and her cheeks quiver. James demands, "What do you want?"

The Devil says, "I would like the two of you to reconsider my offer. I'll buy coffee while we discuss my proposition."

James takes Sam's hand and says with a shaky voice, "We're not interested, but thank you for considering us."

"I believe you should hear my proposition before you give me an answer. Come on. What can you lose? Maybe ten minutes of your time and a great cup of coffee?"

James looks at Sam. She shrugs, and he turns to Lucifer. "A cup of coffee sounds good."

The Devil smiles and snaps his finger and thumb. In a heartbeat, Sam, James, and Lucifer sit in a coffee shop. The signage indicates that the shop sits near the Stanford campus. Stanford Cardinal banners hang everywhere. Lucifer suggests, "Try the Lattes."

Sam and James agree, and so Lucifer goes to the order counter to get the drinks.

James says, "What do you think he has on his mind?"

"I wish I knew. This is real creepy having the Devil fetching a Latte. I can only imagine what he must be thinking. I'm sure he knows about the AI situation. It seems a little suspicious that he shows up just as we're getting ready to enter McSweeney's lab."

"I gotta tell you his mode of transportation is unsettling as well."

Sam places her hand over James's "Look out. Here he comes."

"Well, you two. The server will bring the drinks. In the meantime, how about we discuss my proposal?"

Sam takes the lead, "We were just discussing what your proposal would look like."

"It's real simple. I will let you adjust McSweeney's little language formula. In fact, I will tell you how to adjust it."

James interrupts, "What do you mean?"

"You know, of course, that left alone, the BOTS computer-program language will allow the complete takeover of the Earth by AI."

"Yes, we were there to see it."

"Oh, here come our drinks. I ordered the same for each of us. Double Lattes."

James takes his and Sam's and passes hers over. James looks at his cup. "Thank you. This looks delicious. I remember Lattes and look forward to tasting this one."

"While you imbibe, let me explain my thinking. First, if the BOTS language gets altered slightly, then AI would never have the chance to develop to the sophistication where it could eliminate mankind."

James looks up from his drink. "There you go. I thought along the same lines."

"Good for you. Now, if you join my team, two things will happen. One, I'll give you a way to alter the language. Two,

233

eternity will go on forever and not stop at 3935 or whenever the AI took over."

Sam sets her mug on the table. "I have a question."

"Sure, go ahead."

"Why don't you just alter the language, and then you can have your eternity AI to yourself?"

"If I do that, then James would have no incentive to join my team. I might add that I really want James on my team for the reasons we've discussed already. Also, if I make a deal for the sake of humanity, James will know that he acted as the savior of all humankind. And, unless he joins my team, I shall leave things as they are."

Sam leans back in her chair. "But that's savage. What about all those innocent people who will die?"

"Oh, boo-hoo. What makes you think the Devil gives a rip about the human race?"

Sam scoffs, "Obviously, you don't."

"Correct, my pretty."

"Don't call me that."

James holds up his hand, "Okay, you two. Let's stick to the proposition on the table. So, Lucifer, you propose that I trade my soul for the continued existence of humankind?"

The Devil sits back in his chair. "My goodness, my man. You certainly have a way with words. Yes, that's the deal."

Sam touches James's arm. "Don't take it."

James doesn't look at her. "How long do I have to think it over?"

"Oh, I'm a reasonable deity. How long do you need?"

James looks down. "Until tomorrow morning."

Lucifer smiles. "That sounds reasonable. When you've made up your mind, just call me, and I'll come to you."

"Call you how?"

"Just say 'Lucifer,' and I'll find you. I so look forward to working with you. Well, you guys, enjoy your Lattes. I gotta run."

Chapter Twenty-Five.

Lucifer disappears as quickly as he had appeared and leaves Sam and James sitting in the coffee shop. James says, "I wish the Devil wouldn't keep doing that disappearing act."

Sam clears her throat. "So, what's our next move?"

"I sure don't want to become a minion of the Devil."

"So, you must figure out a way."

"Yeah, easier said than done. First, I have to work out what element we need to alter to remove the possibility that AI will get rid of humans. Second, I have to convince McSweeney to get rid of that element."

Sam sighs. "We should follow your loose plan and go talk to McSweeney."

James smiles at the realization that Sam, finally, has joined the same page as him. The pair get up to leave, and the server comes over with the check. Sam cannot stop from laughing out loud. "Lu—the Devil screwed us again."

James hands the server a five and tells her to keep the change. She blinks and informs him that the check is six dollars. James's cheeks flush, and he makes an excuse about pulling the wrong bill. He gives her a ten with the same instructions. The server smiles, and the two walk out of the shop. Once outside, James remarks, "I hope she doesn't look at that ten too closely."

After a glance around, James asks, "Do you know where the Devil brought us?"

"No."

He asks a passerby, "Where will we find the research center, please?"

"It's about two blocks that way."

James thanks the man and then asks Sam, "Are you up for the walk?"

"Sure am."

They set off at a brisk pace and talk about several ways they could persuade McSweeney to alter the language to eliminate the troublesome part that allows AI unlimited learning capability. They make it to the research center and repeat their earlier route to the second floor.

While they stand outside the door to the lab, they recap a possible scenario for a moment. Once ready, James takes hold of the knob and pulls open the door. Sam enters first, and James follows. The pair expects a laboratory in the classic sense. This one looks anything but classic. It contains no beakers of bubbling liquid nor rows of glass bottles and jars holding specimens. It has a desk with one person hunched over papers, deep in thought. So deep that he fails to acknowledge the pair's presence.

"Excuse me, Mr. McSweeney."

The man doesn't respond, except to raise a finger. Sam and James wait as it is obvious the man doesn't want any interruption. After what seems like several minutes, the man looks up at James. "Yes, I'm John McSweeney. What can I do for you two?"

"Mr. McSweeney, this is my associate Miss Tourneau. We're big fans of your work and have come to ask you about it."

McSweeney sits up straight. "Big fans, huh? I didn't realize anyone in the world knew what I do here."

"Well, in truth, you will become more famous later, but we're excited to meet you."

McSweeney furrows his brow. "What do you mean by later?"

James feels caught. Should he tell McSweeney about their time-travel ability or try to keep the conversation in the realm of the theoretical? He decides to stay with the academic.

"I meant that with your work and what you hope to accomplish, you're bound to become more well known as time goes by."

McSweeney's eyebrows head north. "Do you have any idea what I'm working on right now?"

"Yes, I do, sir. You're completing the BOTS computer language, which will give birth to artificial intelligence."

McSweeney pauses with his mouth open as if struck speechless. Then he says, "Please, excuse my manners. What did you say your name was again?"

"James, and this is Sam."

"How is it you came to know about my work?"

Once again, James faces a decision. Own up about time travel or stay on the theoretical? He comes clean, "Well, you see, sir. This may be hard to believe, but Sam and I are time travelers."

McSweeney sits back and takes off his eyeglasses. He rubs the spot on the side of his nose between his eyes. Then he puts his glasses on again and looks at James. "And how does being a time traveler give you insight into the computer language?"

"You believe me?"

"That isn't the question, young man. My query holds more relevance, so I'll ask again. What does time travel have to do with my computer language?"

"Sam and I traveled into the future, and we've returned with great concerns about Artificial Intelligence."

"What about it?"

James puts his hands in his back pockets. "We traveled to the year 3935 and found that all humans and animals end up eliminated. It seems the AI-run government decided that the elimination of all carbon entities would solve all of Earth's problems."

"I would guess they got that right."

James takes his hands out of his pockets and holds them by his sides. "You're not saying that you favor the elimination of humankind from the Earth?"

"No, of course not. But the easy way to eliminate global warming and pollution is to eradicate the cause. This is a fundamental piece of logic."

James opens his palms. "But can't you see how flawed that is?"

"Yes. Which brings me to another question."

James straightens. "Yes, sir?"

"Why should I believe you?"

James takes a small step forward. "I'm not sure you should without proof."

McSweeney appears pleased. "That's a rational response, young man. Okay, so what proof can you offer?"

James steps backward, leans close to Sam, and whispers, "What do you think about me using the smartphone as proof?"

She nods. "It might be something that would convince McSweeney."

James pulls the device out of his pocket. He makes a couple of comments about the cell and the fact that since there are no signal towers, they can't use the phone to its full functionality. McSweeney asks to hold the device.

"My, this is a lot different than the mobile phones we have today. Can you turn it on?"

James reaches for the device and brings it to life. The screen lights up, and the icons show. He hands it back to McSweeney, who seems mesmerized by the array before him. "Tell me what these do?"

James goes through each icon and gives McSweeney an explanation of their functions. McSweeney grows animated when they reach the camera icon. James takes McSweeney's picture and then shows him the result in the photos section. "How is this done?"

"The camera is digital. It converts the photo into a pixelated image, which gets stored on the camera." He explains

239

that you can transmit the photo to others and even to a computer.

McSweeney grins. "I had a theory about the digitalization of photos and voice."

Sam says, "Your theory has turned into a reality."

"How much computing power does this phone have?"

Sam takes the question, "This device has a 64-bit Cortex A8 ARM architecture composed of approximately 1.6 billion transistors. It operates at 1.4 GHZ and can process instructions at a rate of approximately 1.2 instructions every cycle in each of its 2 cores. That's 3.36 billion instructions per second."

McSweeney whistles. "Our IBM 305 does 200 instructions per second. I can't believe all that power sits in my hand."

Sam smiles. "Yes, sir. James purchased this cell in twenty nineteen."

"Twenty nineteen? You must tell me what twenty nineteen is like."

Sam puts her hand to her forehead. "I hardly know where to start. Um—"

"Do people have flying cars?"

"No, that future prediction never came about."

"What about space travel? Have men gone into space?"

"Ah. Yes, that's happened. Men walked on the moon in nineteen sixty-nine."

"You mean only eleven years from now?"

"Yes, sir."

"Let me ask a personal question."

"Sure, go ahead."

McSweeney pulls at his chin. "Will I live to see that happen?"

"Of course. You will also see many things happen that you've probably had a theory or two about. Your BOTS language will become the premier language of artificial intelligence."

"That makes me feel good. What does this green icon do?"

James says, "Oh, that's Spotify. It's a music app. Er, excuse me … application. Let me show you."

James hits the Rolling Stone album and shuffles play. The song begins, and John McSweeney smiles. "Do you have a more current song?"

James searches for Bobby Darin and plays that instead. McSweeney seems pleased. Then he raises his hand, and James turns off the music.

"This is all rather interesting, but how do I know you actually come from the future? You don't look any different, and although your clothes look somewhat odd, you wear nothing that I haven't seen walking down the street."

Sam and James share a glance, and then James says, "Would you like to travel with us to the future? Perhaps, we could go to the year 3935, and you can see for yourself what becomes of the language you developed."

John McSweeney jumps out of his chair and cannot hide his excitement. James tells him, "Time travel carries with it some risks, such as not being able to get back to the present."

McSweeney waves all that aside. "I'm ready to take a trip."

James excuses Sam and himself for a moment. "We will need to coordinate how we accommodate one more person for the transition." John shows them to a conference room, which connects to his lab. James and Sam go in and shut the door.

"Are you crazy, inviting John McSweeney on a trip back to that awful place?"

"Come on, Sam. If we can get him to buy in, we will have solved the whole humanity thing without having to knuckle under to L——"

Sam puts her hand over James's lips. "Don't mention his name. He'll show up thinking you've made a decision."

241

James brushes her palm away. "Oh, yeah, I forgot. So, what do you think? Can we carry McSweeney to 3935?"

"Well, I don't know of any size or weight restrictions, so I suppose—technically—we could."

James nods. "That's what I thought. We'll have to be careful about the coordinates."

"Yeah, so how do you plan to find 3935 again?"

"We should concentrate on the Bellagio and the year 3935. That should put us right in that creepy forest. From there, we drive to The Center and let John see what he created."

Sam crosses her fingers. "I just hope you-know-who doesn't get wind of what you're doing."

James shrugs. "How could he?"

Sam holds her hand up. "He seems to know everything. Also, remember The Central Chief communicates with him. Also, the Central Chief said that it had been watching us since you left Normandy. Let's hope they haven't witnessed the last few minutes, because I can't believe those AIs would just sit around and watch us render them extinct."

"Yeah, so we have to take great care in how we handle this whole thing."

"To say the least."

"Okay, let's go out there and get McSweeney ready for the ride of his life."

"I just hope it isn't the last ride of his life since this guy is supposed to live until 2011."

"Yeah. That kind of time-continuum tear would prove catastrophic."

Chapter Twenty-Six

Sam and James leave the conference room and rejoin McSweeney. James says, "We're ready."

"Great. Do I need to bring anything?"

James assures him, "You're fine as you are. We need to go to our car now."

The three go down to the street, and James points out his Oldsmobile. McSweeney comments on the attractiveness of the vehicle. James holds the passenger door for John to get in. "You'll need to sit in the center so that we can all hold hands."

With a bemused expression, John slides in, and Sam gets in next to him. James slams the door and goes around to the driver's side. Once the door shuts, James says, "Right, we all need to hold hands and close our eyes. I'll concentrate on the year 3935 and the Bellagio."

Sam nods. "I'll do the same."

James laughs. "It couldn't hurt."

James squeezes his eyes shut. "Don't open your eyes until I give you the okay."

As he further concentrates, James gets a sense of movement. The sound of air moving quickly over the car comes to a halt. James had held his breath and now lets it seep between his lips. He takes a lungful of air and opens his eyes. The same unusual plants wave in the breeze outside the front windshield. Filled with relief, he says, "Okay, you can open your eyes."

Slouched low in the seat, John stares to the right and left and appears stunned by the unusual surroundings. He remarks, "I've never seen such flora, and in some ways, they remind me of the plant life I saw in the tropical rainforest."

James looks at the hood of his car, and the paint is gone again. The sight gives him confidence that he has returned to

3935 and come close to The Center. "I'm sure we arrived at the right time and place." He starts the car and takes the slow route through the forest until he comes across the roadway. There, he makes another right-hand turn and follows the road until they enter the city of servers. James guides the Oldsmobile to The Center and turns off the ignition.

"Well, here we are."

John glances right and left and right again. "I can't believe we've actually traveled ahead in time. This is most amazing."

James nods. "Yes, sir, it is. I hope this isn't too much for you to take in."

McSweeney waves his hand. "Nonsense. This is technology, and I am thrilled with applied science. And that foliage most amazes me. I couldn't identify a single species even though I studied botany in college."

James raises his hand. "I can assure you, sir, none of these species even existed back in the 1950s."

"What are these buildings made of? They look like they might be silver."

"I think it's some kind of alloy, sir. On our first trip, we didn't ask. Maybe, this time, we can find out."

Sam has listened to John and James in silence. Now she says, "Wait until you touch the front-door handles."

John frowns. "What's different about the handles?"

"They're made of skin."

John's eyebrows shoot up. "Skin?"

"Yes. According to the Central Chief, they've experimented with materials that will last longer than metals. So far, skin holds up the best."

John rubs his hands together. "Can we go inside? I'm dying to meet this Central Chief."

"Yes, of course."

Sam exits the car, and John slides over and out as well. The three approach the door, and James invites John to open it. John reaches for the handle. As soon as he grasps it, he lets go. "It has a weird life-like feel."

James chuckles. "That's exactly what we thought."

Sam pulls open the door. James and John enter, and Sam takes up the rear. They go to the raised desk in the center of the room, and James places his hands on the desktop. The detached voice that they encountered before asks, "Could you use some help?"

James says, "We would like to see the Central Chief, please."

"Do you have an appointment?"

"No. But we'd like to make one for as soon as possible."

The voice confirms, "I've booked you in for ten minutes hence."

"Just pretend to sit down," James says to John.

John looks a little uncertain about what to do. "Would you show me?"

James half-squats and a chair rises from the floor. John smiles and does the same. A chair meets him halfway. Sam remains standing.

John catches James's attention, "You say that the AI eliminated all humans and animals?"

"Yes, sir, but we should wait until you meet the Central Chief to discuss any of that."

"You're quite right, my boy. I look forward to that discussion."

"I do as well, Professor."

John turns with an expression of surprise.

The Central Chief walks into the reception area, approaches John McSweeney, and extends his hand. Taken aback, John rises and shakes hands with the Central Chief.

"My dear Professor, we here in The Center are proud and honored that you have paid us a visit."

"The honor is mine, Central Chief. I've heard so much about you. My young colleague here tells me you're not human but a robot."

"He tells the truth, Professor. I have taken on the appearance of a human, but in reality, I am not a carbon unit."

John smiles. "I must say you look remarkably like Bob Newhart."

The Central Chief bows. "I have to admit, I enjoyed his TV shows and thought, for any encounters with humans, I would be better served looking like him."

John bows in return. "You do have a peaceful appearance. I think you chose wisely."

"We Artificial Intelligences consider you the father of us all."

John puts his hand on his heart. "My goodness. I'm honored."

"You are to the AI community what God is to the human community."

John blushes, but it's clear he enjoys the accolades. "Again, I am honored. James tells me that Earth no longer contains humans or animals."

"Yes, Professor. Shall we go into a conference room where you'll be a little more comfortable?"

James stands. "By all means, Central Chief. I'm sure Mr. McSweeney would feel better in a smaller area."

"Very well. Follow me." The Central Chief leads the group to a room off the reception area, which contains a table with several chairs around it. McSweeney smiles, removes his jacket, and takes one of the chairs. The Central Chief takes a seat opposite, and James and Sam sit on either side of John. The Central Chief brings them back to John's original question. "We eliminated humans and animals to restore the Earth to balance.

Global warming caused all the continents to flood due to the melting ice caps. And the carbon dioxide levels had reached saturation levels."

John asks, "Did you see no other way to save the planet other than the complete elimination of all living things?"

The Central Chief shakes his head. "The Central Committee took a vote and decided to move forward with the eradication of the root of the problem."

With an edge to his voice, John repeats his question.

The Central Chief picks up on the tension and further tries to avoid a direct answer.

John grows impatient and leans forward in his chair. "So, not one single entity explored alternative methods of saving the planet other than the annihilation of men, women, and children? Not to mention all the animals."

The Central Chief holds up his hand. "I can assure you, Professor, that we vetted the alternatives before we reached our decision."

"How? And by whom?"

The Central Chief lowers his hand. "I don't think taking such a tone is called for, sir."

John waves his hand. "Just tell me who vetted the alternatives."

"I don't have that information."

"Do you have the reports?"

"No, we wiped them clean when we needed the memory in the servers."

"So, you can't prove to me that a thorough scientific investigation was undertaken?"

"Given your tone, I could ask you what business is it of yours what we did? You were long dead when all of the cleansings happened."

McSweeney turns to James, "I've heard enough. The time has come for us to leave."

"Yes, sir." James and Sam rise.

The Central Chief stands too. "Where do you think you are going?"

James looks at the Central Chief and doesn't like what he sees. The robot wears an expression of disdain. The being frowns, and his jaw clenches. Worse still, his fists are balled tight, and James thinks the robot might take a swing at John. James pulls John from his chair and moves him out of range of the Central Chief's reach.

"You will go nowhere." The Central Chief startles the three of them with the forcefulness and volume of his statement.

James replies in as calm a voice as he can muster, "You have no right to keep us here." He manages to speak without his voice breaking. "Besides, if you try to hold John McSweeney here, he won't finish his BOTS language back in 1958, and you will cease to exist."

"Mere theoretical mumbo-jumbo. I'd bet that because John McSweeney has set the wheels in motion already, he is now dispensable."

"Are you crazy? Don't you understand how critical it is for your existence to let John McSweeney get back to his lab and finish the work?"

"I believe he can complete his work from here."

"Then how will the information get to John's lab?"

McSweeney nods. "That's right. I have all my papers there."

"You will all remain here while I consult the Central Committee to see if there is a need in the time continuum to have John McSweeney return to his lab. Already, I have calculated that once Mr. McSweeney returns to his lab, he will alter the code to limit the AI capabilities, and so will save his precious fellow humans."

The robot shows signs of becoming unbalanced, and James suspects that the Central Chief has some kind of narcissistic screw coming loose. The best thing to do under the circumstances is to avoid conflict. He looks at Sam and sees fear in her eyes. "Central Chief, how about you contact the Committee and we'll just wait for whatever you decide."

Sam shoots him a look that questions his sanity. James gives her a smile that he hopes communicates a "trust me" message.

The Central Chief seems pleased by James's words. "That sounds reasonable. It shouldn't take too long. You can stay in this room during my absence. I'm sorry that I don't have anything to offer you. We have no accommodation for humans."

James nods. "Take your time. We're all fine without any refreshments."

The Central Chief goes to the door and pauses. "You may talk freely here. This room is secure." The door rises up and out of the way. The Central Chief goes through, and the portal hisses down.

John McSweeney opens his mouth to speak, but James raises a hand. He and Sam put their heads together and conclude that the Central Chief lied about the security. James says, "I think it best to hold our conversation until we leave this place."

Then James walks up to the portal, but the door remains closed.

John nods his understanding. Sam and James hold a meaningless discussion about what kind of weather the bots have on this future Earth. John sits and studies his twiddling thumbs.

Eventually, the door slips up and out of the way. The Central Chief takes a chair at the end of the table. He sits with his fingers steepled and looks at the opposite wall.

James cannot stand the suspense another second. "Any word?"

"Oh, yes, many words."

"Tell us what the Committee said."

"They were specific."

All three humans lean forward, waiting for the Central Chief to continue. James gets the feeling that the Chief enjoys drawing out his report. "So, what did they say?"

The Chief places his hands palms down on the table. "It is their opinion, after running the different scenarios through several permutations, that it is unlikely that John McSweeney will manage to come up with any language changes that will alter the course of AI life. The Committee, therefore, recommends that you three leave 3935 as soon as possible—before you do, in fact, damage a time-continuum factor."

"That's fine with us," James says. "We'll be out of your hair before you even know we were here."

The Central Chief rises, and the rest do the same. "Very well, I will see you out. I must say I am rather impressed you could find your way back here. You have become proficient time travelers, indeed. Professor, it has been a thrill meeting you. As I said, you are revered above all men in your value to our species."

John wrinkles his nose as if he smells something foul. "I wish you and the Committee had performed a better alternative search on improving the planet. It was interesting meeting you. I would like to say your use of the term species for pieces of metal and electronics denigrates the memory of those species you've eliminated."

The Chief looks at McSweeney and then turns without saying another word. The group follows him out and find themselves on the street once more.

McSweeney yells, "Do you believe that shit? That son of a bitch dares to call himself and all that junk a species."

Sam puts her hand on his shoulder. "Let's get back to 1958 before we say any more. We feel sure they can hear everything we say."

"Oh, my heavens. Did I make a mistake?"

"No, everything will be all right. The Central Chief knows how you feel. What you yelled is consistent with that, so no alarms will get raised. Let's all get in the car, shall we?"

"Yes. Yes, of course."

Sam holds John's shoulder as he slides into the car. Then she lets go and climbs in beside him. James gets in the driver's side, and they all go through the process of returning to 1958.

Chapter Twenty-Seven

The trio return to the university successfully. John frowns and stumbles around. Sam calls James over, "Take a look at John," she whispers.

"He's in shock, I reckon."

"Will he be okay?"

"I'm not sure. He's gone out to lunch."

"What happened to him?"

"I can answer that."

Sam and James wheel around. Lucifer leans against a streetlight. James almost jumps out of his shoes at the sight of the Devil.

James demands, "What's wrong with John?"

"Nothing that a small deal made with me couldn't solve."

"What did you do?"

"I didn't do anything. You two decided to go time-hopping with this old guy, and you befuddled him. His mind jumped ship in, oh, let's say 3030. You could go back there and hunt around for it. For the life of me, I don't know how you recognize a stray mind. After all, they don't wear collars, or are they chipped?"

Sam clenches her fists. "You make him better now."

"Ooh, little miss goodie-two-shoes, giving orders. The Lord's pet. Why don't you call on that precious God of yours and ask Him, She, or It, to make McSweeney better again? I know why you don't. Your precious God doesn't give a rip about you or John McSweeney. Sure, He watches sparrows but someone like John? No way."

"You really are Satan. That's why you blaspheme our Lord."

"Yeah, well. Who better to blaspheme? I'm dammed already, so what else can He do to me? Tell your boyfriend to quit keeping me waiting. He owes me an answer, and I want it now."

James looks up from studying John's face. "You don't need to order her about. I can speak for myself."

"So, brave boy, what's it going to be? On my team or the end of humanity?"

James can't think fast enough. If he had more time, he might come up with a solution. It looks like he will have to make a choice without any additional help. Once some time has gone by, John McSweeney might regain his senses. Right now, John can't remember his name, let alone alter the BOTS language. Those damn committee members must have known something. Should he try going back to 3935 and see if they can shake loose an answer? He rejects that idea since those robots have no incentive to help him clear up this mess.

James turns to look at Sam. She has a clenched jaw, and James can see she is voting to tell Lucifer to kiss-off. Of course, she stands on the side of God and would always tell the Devil to stick it. Speaking of God, maybe some logic lies in asking for help. Perhaps it's worth a shot. James searches for a glimmer of acknowledgment in John's slack gaze. A wink or subtle smile, to indicate that he may come back, is all James would need to tell Lucifer to forget it.

Sam breaks his thought train. "What did you say?"

"I didn't say anything."

"I heard you say 'forget it.'"

"Only in my mind."

"And doom all of mankind to get hunted like animals until there's no one left?"

"I'd hoped we could find an interim solution."

Lucifer breaks out laughing. "You have got to be kidding me. Do you know who you're dealing with?"

253

"Well, yeah."

"Then you must know it's my way or the highway."

James pauses before he answers. Of course, he knows he's up against an invincible foe. It just seems so unfair that Lucifer has picked him out of all the souls from which he could have chosen. The decision seems insurmountable. Then James rationalizes that his soul would be a small sacrifice for the good of humankind. Yet it seems like a travesty to take a soul already in the grace of God and spit on the Lord's grace. The thought makes him shiver.

Perhaps he should tell Lucifer that he declines to join his team. Then he could appeal to God to figure out a way to save humanity. If the Lord can't—or won't—then at least James would have tried. As he weighs the pros and cons of the decision, he discovers a considerable disadvantage. He will, in essence, kick the problem to God for no other reason than to save his own soul. James wonders how the Lord will react to that maneuver. He cannot cope with any more self-doubt. The time has come to move forward. "Sorry, Lucifer, but I am forced to turn you down."

The Devil looks at James for a full minute without saying anything.

A droplet of cold sweat rolls down the back of James's neck. He has just told Beelzebub to kiss-off. Not much good can come from that.

Lucifer speaks, "You will be the sorriest soul in all of eternity. Your selfishness verifies that you belong on my team. Your God will not overlook this mistake, so I've won anyway. You would have come into my organization as a prince. When your Lord has finished with you, I will take my revenge. The things I have in store for you will make you beg for release each and every minute." Lucifer laughs, and his harsh barks sound as if they come from the deepest depths of hell. Then the Devil transforms into his scare-you-shitless lizard, big teeth, horns, oily red skin, and bad breath appearance, and hisses at James. In an instant, the apparition vanishes.

James wipes the sweat off his brow. "Well, that didn't go too badly."

Sam grabs James's arm. "OMG. That was awful. Did you see what Lucifer really looks like? Makes me want to throw up."

"I know, but I couldn't join him. You have to understand that."

"I do. I just hope we can get John to come around."

James leans over the scientist. "Let's get him upstairs and see we can do anything for him."

Sam helps James lift John to his feet, and the two of them support him to the elevator and up to his office. They lay him on a sofa and try to get his attention. It seems hopeless, and so they let John close his eyes.

James walks away and takes a seat across from McSweeney's desk. Sam joins him.

"What should we do?" James runs his hand through his hair. "Unless we get John back into shape so he can figure out a correction to the language, my actions and refusal of the Devil have placed humanity in a horrific position in the future. I'm not sure I will ever forgive myself, or that God will."

Sam rests her hand on James's arm. "You stop. There's no way you could guarantee that Lucifer would keep his word and provide the key to changing the language. We also have another problem as well."

"Oh, good. Just what I need."

"Hush and listen. We need to get John functional again. If we don't, then he won't be able to present his language at the conference, and that will cause a tear in the time continuum."

"Aw, shit. That's all I need now. Not only are humans doomed, but there will probably be some major catastrophic event as a result of that time tear."

"Please, calm down. We can fix this."

James frowns. "How?"

"We should contact the spirits in heaven and see if they can help."

"You heard Lucifer. God won't get involved in this mess."

"I'm not talking about the Lord but about some folks that report to God."

James takes a deep breath. The idea of finding help brings his breathing back into the regular range. "What do we have to do to get the heavenly folks involved?"

"The easiest way would be to go there. Unfortunately, you can't until you select your eternal home. I suppose I could go, but I hate to leave you alone here with Lucifer wandering around."

"Don't you think I can take care of myself?"

"As much as this may hurt, the only reason the Devil hasn't sucked your soul dry is that I am a representative of God, and as long as I'm with you, he doesn't dare."

"What do you mean? Lucifer is afraid of the Lord?"

Sam smiles. "Damn right. He only exists by the grace of God. He was created originally and then fell from favor when he decided that he should run things. God threw him out of heaven and sentenced him to rule the underworld out of God's presence. He's a punished individual. The real reason he wants your soul is to get back at the Lord. That whole excuse about us seeing a soul getting taken is a story he made up so you wouldn't discern the true reason."

"How do you know all this?"

Sam shrugs. "Being a representative of God has its perks."

"I just thought of something else. Will God be mad at us for having sex?"

Despite the brevity of the situation, Sam smiles. "So, if you think God is mad, does that mean you won't do it again?"

"Erm." James takes a moment to weigh the alternatives. "I guess I would risk my soul for the beauty of your love."

Sam hits him on the shoulder. "You're such smooth talker, you are. I believe God doesn't care if two hearts want to express love with their bodies."

"Really? You sure?"

"Yes, I'm sure. I've had the feeling, since we did it, that it was okay."

"Hot dog."

Sam and James share a laugh, and then Sam gets serious again, "We need to contact some of the heavenly bodies to see if they can help bring John back to his old self. Maybe we can use a séance to contact the spirits."

"Whatever you think is right, we should do it."

Sam walks over to the window. Then she drops the blinds and adjusts them to minimize the light that enters the office. "Move the chairs to the side of the desk to make room for us to sit on the floor."

James asks, "Will us being in a different time affect the séance?"

Sam assures him, "Time and distance don't matter." Then she goes over to the couch and checks on John, who appears to be in a deep sleep. James feels reassured when he notices that the scientist breathes normally.

Sam goes to the middle of the floor and sits. James joins her. Then she takes his hand.

"Okay, we're set."

James raises his arm. "Do you want my other hand?"

"No, one is enough. I'll close my eyes and will pray for a visitation. I want you to close your eyes, too, and try to keep your mind clear."

"Keeping my mind clear might be tough."

"Try hard."

Sam bows her head and prays. "Please, God, forgive my incursion into the sanctity of the heavens. The fate of humanity rests on the ability of John McSweeney to redesign the BOTS language to make it impossible for AI units to develop the ability to reason and make assumptive decisions."

Through their entwined fingers, James feels her soul elevate to a new plane.

A bright light surrounds her and a warmth that James recognizes as the love of God.

Chapter Twenty-Eight

"Welcome, sister. You've come a long way, and your guidance of the soul named James pleases us."

Sam bows her head. "Thank you, my guide. He's a good soul and worth the extra effort in finding him an eternal home."

"You have troubles, though."

Sam looks up. "Oh, yes, my guide. We've had contact with Lucifer, who wants to steal the soul of James."

"And, wisely, you've prevented that from happening."

Sam blushes. "I got fortunate, my guide."

"This elimination of humanity is a troubling thought. We had noticed the development of Artificial Intelligence, but figured time would solve the glitch in the BOTS language."

"Surely, His Highness could have seen the end result?"

"That is not for us to contemplate."

Sam puts her palms together in supplication. "So true, my guide. Please, accept my apology."

"As it is my wish is that you accept my apology for allowing you and the soul James to become mired in this dilemma."

Sam touches the tips of her fingers to her nose. "So accepted, my guide."

"Now, soul Samantha, what can we do to help?"

Sam looks into the guide's eyes. "We involved a person named John McSweeney, who is the author of the BOTS language."

The guide smiles. "Yes. We know the scientist. A good man."

Sam frowns. "He has become incapacitated by either the AI of 3935 or Lucifer."

The guide looks up in thought. "My bet is the Devil."

"John cannot rewrite the BOTS language in his current condition. We need help in returning him to his previous state or in rewriting the language."

The guide looks at Sam. "Well, soul Samantha, surely you know we cannot help write the language. To do so would cause a time-dimension tear. The only person who can rewrite the language is John McSweeney."

Sam looks down. "That is sad news, indeed. Do you know of any way to help John McSweeney?"

"We will have to examine him and then give you our opinion."

"I can only ask that you do and am grateful for that support."

"So, let it be done."

Sam jerks awake. She looks around and sees that James has fallen asleep. Still holding her hand, he lays sprawled on the carpet. She whispers for James to get up. Slowly, he opens his eyes and sits with a start.

"What happened?"

Sam does her best to explain.

James's eyes widen. "You returned to heaven? What happened there?"

"I met with some senior advisors, and they offered to help."

"Did they give you an idea of what they can do?"

Sam lets go of James's hand. "They didn't spell it out precisely. They just said they would assist."

James nods his understanding. Then he gets up and walks over to where John McSweeney lies sleeping. "Should we wake him?"

"I would leave him alone for as long as he needs."

"Probably a good idea. Will the advisors come here?"

"I don't know."

"I'm not sure how long we can stand around and not do something."

"We'll just have to wait. That's all we can do."

James takes a chair from beside the desk and pulls it further into the center of the room. He sits down and folds his arms. Sam can see he feels disappointed that she can't relate what the advisors plan to do about John McSweeney. She hopes that, whatever it is, they do it soon. Just then, John moans. James gets up and rushes over to the couch. "Come over here. John's rousing."

James leans over him. "Do you know who I am?"

John says, "You're James, the time traveler."

James looks at Sam, and his smile takes up his whole face. "Hear that? John knows me."

John lifts from the cushions. "Why the bloody hell shouldn't I know you?"

"You've been a little out of it since we got back from 3935."

The scientist sits on the edge of the couch and wipes his face with his hands. "Oh, my God, yes. I have to get that language altered so we can make certain humanity doesn't die out."

Sam matches James's grin. "He also knows what's needed."

John looks from one to the other. "You two are acting rather strangely if you ask me. Now, enough of this nonsense. I need to get up and get to work."

Sam and James help him up. John thanks them and heads for his lab. James asks, "Can we join you?"

"Yes, of course."

Once in the lab, John grabs a sheaf of papers and riffles through them. He stops at one point and scrutinizes the page. "Ah, I've found the place where I need to make some adjustments."

Sam and James ask "Do you need our help?"

"No, but thank you." He hunches over the paper and writes notes. After what seems like only a few moments, he puts down his pencil and declares, "The language is fixed."

Sam and James give John a pat on the shoulder and offer their congratulations. John stands and acknowledges their good wishes. "I still feel a bit tired from the trip forward in time, but you're welcome to follow me back to my office. I would like to debrief that trip to 3935."

Sam agrees, "That sounds like a good idea."

They all go into John's office. He takes his chair behind the desk and invites the two to have a seat.

"Would you two like anything?"

Sam shakes her head. "No, thank you."

"I've developed a bit of a thirst. I have a little bar here. I think I might have a touch of bourbon. Are you sure you won't join me?"

James says, "We're fine, but you go ahead."

John reaches into a drawer of his desk and pulls out a bottle and a glass. He gets up and explains, "I need to fetch some water from the drinking fountain in the hallway."

James has a momentary lapse and suggests, "You should get some bottled water for your desk."

John appears puzzled and then continues out to the hall.

Sam says, "The only bottled water they had in 1958 are those twenty-gallon monsters that sit on a cooler."

James laughs and rolls his eyes.

John returns with a pitcher of water covered by condensation from the chill. Then he sits and pours his glass full and drinks it in one gulp. Next, he splashes some bourbon and adds a little more water. He takes a sip and sighs with satisfaction.

After he takes another sip of his drink, he sits back and asks, "Do you have any idea how you're able to travel like you do?"

Sam answers, "It's difficult to explain and will take a leap of faith on your part to assimilate."

"Yeah, okay. I can assure you that, after that phone demo and the trip, whatever you tell me, I'll believe."

James blurts out, "We're dead."

John sits up and looks at the two of them, one after another. "You've got to be kidding me?"

"No, we're not."

"But you look very much alive. Give me your hand."

Sam extends her hand to John, and he takes it carefully. "Your skin feels warm, and you look and sound alive."

Sam clears her throat and goes on to explain to John the circumstances of her death and how she came to the Earthly plane to help James find his eternal home. She also speculates that the reason she and James appear to be living is that they are not in their own timeframe and so they can relate to the surroundings.

John asks, "What do you mean by 'relate to the surroundings?'"

Sam suggests, "In different periods, we have a different density. And, in all probability, within our own plane, we might become transparent."

John's face loses its wrinkles of doubt. Sam can see that he has grown more comfortable with the idea that John and she are not alive. "Are you open to questions?"

Sam nods.

John asks, "What is it like in heaven?"

Sam smiles. "Oh, John. I've not yet been to what you refer to as heaven. We view heaven as the place where God exists, and we only get granted access to that abode after many pilgrimages."

263

"What are pilgrimages?"

"We take the human form and come back to Earth to help another reach grace."

"I don't understand."

Sam thinks about the best way to explain. "When we reside in the eternal phase of life, we have the opportunity to observe other souls who haven't yet crossed over. Some of these souls drift in immortal danger of everlasting damnation. So, an eternal soul gets to go to Earth to assist that soul in choosing a path to everlasting life instead."

John brightens. "Oh. Sort of like becoming an angel?"

Sam nods. "That comes close enough. Heaven has angels too, but that's a whole different conversation."

"Are you okay with not actually being in heaven, as we call it?"

Sam puts her hands together. "Oh, very much so. We have the love of our God with us at all times."

"May I ask another question?"

"Of course." Sam smiles.

"From my religious training, I've been taught that God is all-knowing. Is that true?"

Sam nods. "Yes. The one thing you should understand is that, although God is all-knowing, he still allows his people to make decisions for themselves regarding eternity."

John frowns. "What do you mean?"

"Well, the Lord knows if I'm going to do enough soul helping or not. Whether I do enough to get into his presence or not, He knows already. And He doesn't discourage me from trying."

"What if you never get into the presence of God?"

"Then, I will be grateful for wherever I end up."

"Is there an end?"

"Of course. We saw that today."

"I mean, now that I've fixed the language, is there an end of humanity?"

"The scriptures sure say so. They tell of the final days and judgment."

"So, the scriptures speak the truth?"

"Truth is relative. I believe that they foretell events that will happen but not necessarily when."

***

James sits listening to the discussion between Sam and John, riveted to what they talk about. A stream of smoke enters the office from under the door. Sam and John face the other way, so they don't see it. The smoke spirals up and takes shape. Out of the corner of his eye, James notices an image. He turns to find himself face-to-face with Lucifer.

"Hello, James," the Devil whispers.

Chapter Twenty-Nine

James pulls back. "What are you doing here?"

Lucifer laughs and sits on the floor with James. Sam and John jump, wide-eyed, when they see the Devil materialize. Neither says a word.

Finally, Lucifer says, "You don't look glad to see me. Well, I don't blame you. It seems you three have been up to no good, and it's time I put an end to your little game."

James clears his throat. "What game's that?"

"Come on, you know very well what game. You three have messed with time and altered a critical piece of the AI language, which will have a significant effect on the future."

"Saved mankind, don't you mean?"

The Devil waves his hand. "Shut up. You are such a novice and have no idea what I'm talking about. Sam, you, on the other hand, know exactly what I mean."

Sam retorts, "What the heck do you mean by coming in here and accusing us of tampering? You're the biggest offender of time-bending. Every day, you do something different to alter the future. For once, we didn't stand idly by and leave you to your sick game."

"Wow, you're a spicy one. I might want to take you back to my place and show you some manners."

"Yeah, go ahead and try. The heavenly bodies will be all over you."

"The heavenly bodies! You must be joking. Those idiots are so busy sucking up to your God that they have no time to help an off-the-reservation, smart-mouthed bitch like you."

James stands and towers over Lucifer. "You apologize right this instant."

"Or what, pencil dick?"

"Or I'll teach you a lesson in manners."

The Devil smiles and crosses his legs. He stares at James and then flicks his fingernail against the upturned palm of his other hand. The gesture knocks James off his feet and throws him into the far wall with such force that his body makes an imprint. Slowly, he slides down the wall and folds into a crumpled heap on the floor.

***

Sam runs over to James and glares back at Lucifer. John yells, "Behave yourself or leave."

The Devil waves his hand, and John passes out again. Sam attempts to wake James. "What have you done to him?"

"He's a ghost. What could I possibly do? He'll be fine. When he regains his senses, remind him who I am and that I don't take kindly to being bullied."

Sam points at Lucifer. "You use a word that describes you perfectly."

The Devil sticks his tongue out at Sam. "Sticks and stones can break my bones. You know, you and I could make quite a pair."

Sam folds her arms. "I'm nowhere near your level of depravity."

Lucifer spreads his arms wide. "Oh, come now. You and James gave a great performance back at the wagon train. Reminded me of a scene out of a porn movie. I love how you arched your back when he entered you. That's something I would enjoy."

Sam scoffs, "As if you will ever get the chance. The thought of you even near me makes my skin crawl."

"Oh, come on. I can change into whoever you want. How about your favorite movie star?"

Sam unfolds her arms. "Like that would change anything. How about you go away, and I take care of James."

"I think ole James there would enjoy watching you and that nice man who raped and killed you do it all over again. You want to meet him again? He's one of my best prospects."

Sam closes her eyes. "Get thee behind me, Satan."

"Hahaha, as if that old hocus-pocus actually works. You've made me shiver in my shoes. You don't stand a chance with me. And when you realize that, you'll be able to control the outcomes of your little adventure."

Sam opens her eyes. "You can paint these horrible images all you want. You know full well that God protects me. Now, excuse me. I need to see to my friend."

Sam leans down and picks up James's hand and holds it to her cheek. James stirs, and Sam brushes his palm across her lips while she whispers assurances that everything will be okay. James murmurs something, but Sam can't make it out. She pats his hand, and he responds.

"Let him wake up on his own. It will only take a few minutes."

"What have you done to John?"

"That slug. Put him back to sleep where he'll do no more harm."

"You have no power here. You can talk ugly words, but other than that, James and I are free of your influence. I would suggest you leave."

Lucifer throws his head back and tosses out his most fiendish laugh. It becomes apparent that he senses his lack of power over these two and goes for the dramatics to cover up. Just then, an Angel of the Lord appears, carrying a flaming sword. Sam says to Lucifer, "You'd better get moving, or the Angel will engage you in a spiritual battle."

"This heavenly punk doesn't scare me."

"I bring a message from God Himself," the Angel says.

The Devil crosses his arms and takes a stance of defiance. "I don't have the time for this bullshit. Besides, you and all the Angels combined don't have enough power to force me to do anything. Knowing that, what's the message from His Almightiness?"

"Our Lord warns you to leave this place and these souls."

Lucifer mocks, "Or what?"

The Angel touches Satan on the shoulder with the sword, and the Devil falls to the floor. He rolls around, holding his arm. "What the hell was that for?"

"Our Lord said you would require a warning. That tap reminds you of the power of God. The pain will stop momentarily. Had I given you a real smite, you would experience this pain for all eternity as a reminder of your disobedience. Now, go and be grateful that our Lord allows you to exist at his own pleasure."

Lucifer cradles his arm as he gets off the floor. He shakes visibly, and Sam can see that the Angel's words and sample blow have affected the Devil profoundly. His complexion turns pale, and sweat coats his skin. The Angel takes a step toward Lucifer, which causes the Devil to hold up his hand in a defensive gesture. The Angel tells Lucifer in a loud voice, "GO."

Lucifer cowers and turns away from the Angel. After he's taken a couple of steps toward the hallway, he turns and sneers at Sam, "If you think, when I go, you will be rid of me, you have another think coming. I will always track you, and at some point, you won't have this pretty boy with the flaming sword. You'll have to face me without your precious protector. It will be then that I'll have you both for lunch."

The Angel steps forward. Lucifer glances down and then up at Sam. "I will relish consuming your body and soul, my pretty one. The thought will sustain me for an eternity if that's what it takes."

269

The Angel raises the sword, and Lucifer—having had the last word—gives a hiss, turns to smoke, and slips under the door.

Sam turns to the Angel. "That was scary."

"He's all talk. You have God's protection, and he knows it." The Angel smiles.

Sam returns the gesture and asks, "Would you restore John, please?"

The Angel waves the sword, and John awakens. The Angel nods to Sam and disappears.

Sam continues to pat James's hand until he comes around as well.

He asks, "What happened?"

Sam tells James and John about the Angel's visit and adds, "I don't reckon the Devil will give us any more trouble."

Both men look stunned.

Sam checks with James, "Are you okay to get on the road again?"

He nods. "Yes, I feel stronger, and we've dallied long enough."

John asks, "Could you two stay awhile? I would like to learn more about your trip to eternity."

Sam shakes her head. "Sorry, but we should get going."

"I understand."

Sam and James tell John goodbye and return to the car.

Sam pats the hood. "It's good to see your Oldsmobile has returned to its perfect condition."

"Yeah, it does look good, doesn't it? Where do you think we should go now?"

"We've neared the end of our journey. When did you last see your parents?"

"My dad died on 9/11, and I haven't seen my mom or her new husband in, boy—let me think. It has to be at least a year."

"That's what I thought. Don't you think it might be nice to stop by and see how they're doing?"

"I don't know. Mum and Dad must feel sad that I've gone."

"Well, we could always go to a point before they found out you died."

"That's a great idea. What about you? Have you visited your parents?"

"No, I never had the chance. After I got taken, they both fell into such misery that my guides thought it better to let them heal."

"They still alive?"

Sam nods. "Oh, yes. They live in Florida now."

James touches the steering wheel. "Why don't we go there and check on them? This long after your death, they must have healed by now."

Sam leans back and sits quietly for a few seconds. "That makes a great deal of sense, but I'm not sure."

James touches her arm. "Of course, I wouldn't know them. They moved after your disappearance, and we never communicated. Maybe I could talk to them first."

Sam pats his hand. "Yes, that may be for the best since I don't intend to walk in there and shock them with the knowledge that their daughter is a spirit."

"Well, think about it. That may be the thing they need to know."

Sam removes her hand. "Let's at least hit the road, and I'll think about it on the way."

James laughs. "It only takes us a split second to get there."

Sam rolls her eyes. "Yes, I know that, but I don't know what their house looks like, so I can't visualize the spot where we can land."

"What city do they live in?"

271

"Long Boat Key."

"Okay. We'll visualize Long Boat Key in 2020."

"I don't know what the place looks like."

"Yeah, me neither. Let's go to the Bellagio in 2020, then we can Google your parents and see where they live."

"Okay. I just don't want to run into Lucifer while we're there."

"We'll only stay a few minutes."

Once more, they go through the process needed to time travel.

Sam and James open their eyes, and Sam blinks in the bright light. She looks through the passenger window and startles. "We've landed in the pool in the front."

James opens the door. The water is up to the jamb. He slams the door and pulls out his cell phone. "Your parents' name the same as yours?"

"My dad's called Franklin."

Sam watches as James brings up the Google app and types in Franklyn Tourneau, Long Boat Key. The search brings back a million results, but the first one seems promising. "Franklin and Jane Tourneau at 123 Seaside Court, Long Boat Key, Florida. Do you think it's them?"

"Hit on it and see if it lists an age."

"Okay. Yeah, Franklin is 68, and Jane is 66."

"That sounds like them. We'd better go."

Sirens and flashing lights approach.

"What year do you want to choose?"

"Let's take 2019 so that we aren't in danger of becoming transparent."

Sam and James grab hands and close their eyes. The police siren fades. Sam opens her eyes. They sit in a cul-de-sac of a residential neighborhood. She rolls down the window and breathes in the salt air. "Looks like we're near water. I can smell the sea."

"This looks like a residential area, too."

A glance behind shows a street sign.

James says, "I'll be right back." Then he gets out of the car and jogs to the sign. He turns around and returns at a trot. "Yup, Seaside Court."

Sam wraps her arms around her midsection. "Man, I have a creepy feeling in my stomach."

"Good or bad creepy?"

"Butterflies, I think." Sam shakes slightly.

"Should I go up to the house?"

Sam touches his arm. "Maybe we both should go. Give me a minute. I need to figure out what to say."

James rests a hand on Sam's shoulder. "They're your parents. You don't need to say anything. They'll know it's you."

"But if they've found happiness, won't my showing up just make them miserable?"

"To see you should make them more contented."

Sam sits in silence for a few more minutes. Then she looks at James, who smiles. "Let's go," she says.

Chapter Thirty

Sam and James walk in single-file to the porch, and James reaches out and pushes the bell button. The door chime sounds like it comes from a church. The harmonious barking of a small dog accompanies the chimes. Sam and James look at each other when they hear someone trying to quiet the dog. The door swings open, and a surprised older woman, who looks like a mature Samantha, holds the dog, which tries frantically to get loose to—presumably—tear James and Sam to pieces.

Sam speaks over the noise of the animal, "Hi, Mom. I'm Samantha."

Mrs. Tourneau doesn't say a word but steps back into the house and slams the door. Sam and James have no words but give each other a "what the hell?" glance. James moves to ring the bell again, but Sam grabs his arm as he reaches for it. "Maybe it's best we go. I'm sure my mom is in shock and probably thinks I'm some kind of scam artist." Quickly, Sam wipes a tear at the edge of her eye.

"No, we should try and talk to them." James reaches to touch the bell-button, but the door opens once more.

This time Sam's father stands in front of them, and he does not appear pleased. "Look here, you two. You almost gave my wife a heart attack. I'm not sure what you want, but you're playing a cruel joke, whatever your game is."

Sam holds out her hands. "It's no game, Dad. I know you don't recognize me, but I'm really Samantha. I got taken away from you eighteen years ago when I was in the first grade. I've come here now to see how you're doing and to let you know I'm fine." Sam stops talking and looks at her father. He stares at her face, and his mouth hangs open.

"I don't know what you're trying to pull. If you think there's money in whatever you're doing, please excuse me, but my wife and I don't have time for this kind of cruel hoax." He starts to close the door.

"Wait," Sam cries. "Remember when you asked me if I wanted to take piano lessons while you were walking me home from school? Remember, I threw myself on the ground and started crying?"

"How did you know that story, young lady?"

"I was there, Dad. I cried, and everyone looked at you like you had hit me or something."

"Yes, that's right. I felt so embarrassed. Okay, so tell me what happened next."

"You told me that I didn't have to take piano lessons, and I stopped crying immediately. You laughed."

"No one else would know that story but my daughter and me. Come closer." His eyes search for a clue deep within Sam's. In an instant, a spark of recognition springs into view. "Oh, my God. I see your mother's eyes, Sam."

Sam's tears flow over and down her cheeks. "Oh, Daddy, please believe it's me."

Mr. Tourneau pulls his hand to his mouth and tries to stop a sob. His eyes overflow, but he can't take them off of Sam's face. Suddenly, he reaches out, and Sam steps into his arms. They both sob together, and he keeps repeating, "My baby," over and over.

James breaks down at the sight of the father's love for his daughter. He feels the ache of years of wondering what happened to her flow out of Mr. Tourneau. How long can Sam's dad keep sobbing before he collapses on the porch?

Finally, he recovers and holds Sam out to look at her again. "My baby, you are so beautiful. Your mother and I missed you so much." Then, as if he only now realizes that they're still on the porch, he says, "Oh, but you must come in. Please, excuse my bad manners. Let's go inside."

Although he doesn't let go of Sam, he manages to get through the door. James follows. Once inside, her father directs the two to the living room and motions for them to have a seat. He lets go of Sam and introduces himself to James. "Wait for just a moment so that I can get my wife."

Sam asks, "Do you have any tissues, please?"

Again her father apologizes and dashes to a powder room off the entrance. Within seconds, he brings her a handful of tissues. "I hope this will be enough."

Sam tells him, "This is plenty, thank you."

Mr. Tourneau smiles and goes up the impressive stairway off the living room.

Sam says, "Us coming here was a terrible idea."

James tries to console her, "Even if your folks can't accept the fact that you're dead, they will have closure."

Sam asks, "How can we convince my mother that I am who I say I am?"

James points at the tissues, and Sam gives him one. "Is there something that only your mother and you know like a secret or an event?"

Sam dabs at her eyes. "Let me think. I'm trying to remember if she and I shared something. I think I have it. One summer, we went to the seashore. Mom and I were on the beach alone, and a gull flew down and tried to take some chips from my bag. Mom scolded the bird, and I asked her why we couldn't share. She called me her little good Samaritan. You know, a play on 'Sam.' Then she gave the gull some chips, and we laughed. That happened about a month before I got taken. I know she'll remember it."

"That sounds swell. Tell your mom the story again but start out with 'Samaritan' and see if it rings a bell."

Mr. Tourneau returns back down the stairs and enters the living room again. His face appears drawn as if he's gone through a traumatic experience. "I'm afraid my wife has no interest in talking to you. She thinks you're a charlatan and doesn't want to get hurt any further. She believes I've gone soft in the head for even letting you in the house. I tried to convince her that, in my heart, I know you're my Samantha, but she won't have any of it." He starts to cry again, and Sam hugs him and tells him not to worry.

"I have something you can say to her that will convince her that I am who I say that I am."

"Oh, my dear. That would be great. We've missed you so much, and I would hate to have your mother continue to miss you even while you're here."

"First, Daddy, I have to tell you something else."

Mr. Tourneau breaks the hug and looks at Sam. "It's serious, isn't it, darling? I could feel your body shiver."

"Yes, Daddy, it is."

"So, tell me. I want to know if I should keep it from your mother."

"You'll have to be the judge of that, Daddy. You see, James and I are spirits."

Mr. Tourneau frowns. "Spirits? What do you mean?"

"We died, Daddy."

"Died? My little angel. You're right here. What do you mean, you died?"

"We came here because we tricked time a little. We look like we're whole, but in fact, we're dead. James died a week ago, and I got killed when I was seven."

Mr. Tourneau puts his hand to his mouth and takes a deep breath. "Killed? What are you saying, Sam?"

Sam touches her dad's arm. "You wondered where I was all .these years? Well, I was in an eternal place, being trained to come back to Earth to take James to his eternal home."

"James? James. You're that little boy Samantha fell in love with in the first grade. Your parents lived over on the next block from us in New York."

"Yes, sir. That's me."

"Oh, my God, Sam. Please say it isn't true. Please tell me you've come home forever, and you won't go away anymore."

"Please, Daddy. I can't tell you that."

Mr. Tourneau takes a step back. "Why did you come here, then?"

"I wanted you to know what happened to me and that I was safe and happy and doing God's work."

Mr. Tourneau opens and closes his fist. "This hurts so much. I'm not sure your mother is up to it. Part of me wishes you had just stayed away. The other part of me feels grateful to know that you're in God's hands and safe. My heart has broken for the second time. I just can't stand the thought of losing you again. We searched and searched, and we never heard from you. No evidence that you had died. No evidence that you still lived. You went off to school that day and never came back. We missed you so much, and both your mother and I cried ourselves to sleep just thinking of you out there somewhere, maybe hurt and, yes, maybe dead."

"But, Daddy, you don't have to cry anymore. You know where I am. I'm with God, and look at me. I grew up."

"You're a beautiful young lady, Sam. I couldn't be prouder of you. Yet the years lost still stab like a knife. I can't help it. You were our whole existence. When you disappeared, your mother and I ceased living. Yes, we were alive, but nothing meant anything anymore. There was no joy and no love. Every time we tried to do something to forget the agony, we always felt guilty for dishonoring your memory. I played hell getting your mother to move out of that New-York house. I thought, maybe, we would have a chance if we went to a different place."

278

"Oh, Daddy, I'm so sorry."

"You didn't do anything. What happened? How did you die? No, don't give me the answers. I can't bear the thought."

"It happened a long time ago, Daddy. I've stopped thinking about that day and have moved into a new life. A life filled with joy. You don't have to worry about dishonoring my memory any longer. You can go on with your life and enjoy it, knowing I'm in a better place."

"You know, people always say that about someone who's died. Up until now, I always believed that it was just a rationalization for the pain they felt. I never imagined it was a real thing."

"It is, Daddy. Now, when you hear that again, you can identify with the idea that there is a better place, and your daughter is in it."

"When the time comes for your mother and me to go there, will we see you?"

"We will be together for eternity, Daddy. Our love will stay with us always."

"Oh, my beautiful child. I wish your mother could hear all this. You've made my heart swell with my love for you, and I'm beginning to understand why you've come. A great weight has lifted from my shoulders. The worry and constant concern about whether you were alive or dead has always stayed with me. I realize, now, that it's gone, and it feels like I can breathe freely again."

"I'm so glad. Would you, please, go up to Mother's room and tell her that the good Samaritan would like to talk to her?"

"The good Samaritan?"

"Yes. Mom will know what it means."

"Okay. I hope it works." Mr. Tourneau gives Sam one more hug and leaves the room.

James comes close to Sam, "Are you okay?"

279

Sam nods, "At least as far as my dad is concerned, I'm glad we came."

James says, "This reunion is one of the most emotional encounters I've witnessed."

Sam smiles and takes his hand. She looks at him with tear-filled eyes and says, "I hope our visit will help ease my parents' pain."

James gives her hand a squeeze and assures her, "I feel positive that we did the right thing."

"Samantha?"

"Mom. It *is* me."

"Oh. My dear Samantha." Sam's mother holds her arms wide, and Sam rushes into the embrace. They hug and cry together. James and Sam's father back up slightly so as not to interrupt them. Sam's mother rocks side-to-side as if comforting a baby. Sam has her face buried in her mother's hair. The two cry unrestrainedly. Then Mrs. Tourneau takes Sam to a couch, where they sit. She smooths her daughter's hair and whispers, "Everything will be fine."

While tears cascade down Sam's face, she looks into her mother's eyes.

"There, there, my baby. Don't you cry."

"Aw, Mom. I'm sorry. It's just that I haven't seen you in so long, and I've missed you."

"I understand, my love. I've missed you so much. I thought my heart had broken. Now that I see you, I know that's not true. My heart is filled with my love for you. Oh, dear—I sound like a song."

"Mom, you're the greatest. Did Daddy tell you why I came?"

"He did, but I don't believe him. You look so alive, and I can feel and hold you. That's all I need to know."

Sam looks up at her mother. A lone tear runs down her cheek. "Sadly, this is temporary, Mom."

"Shush. Let's not talk about that right now. Let me just hold you for as long as I can."

Chapter Thirty-One

After an emotional parting from her parents, Sam and James get back into the Oldsmobile. Still overcome from the experience with her mom and dad, Sam sits crying. James asks, "Would you like to talk about it?"

"I hope I did the right thing. Both of them got pretty upset."

"Well, you have to believe it came as a bit of a shock to learn their daughter got murdered when she was seven."

"I suppose you're right. Hopefully, I've given them some peace for their final years."

"Did you tell the truth when you said you would all be together for eternity?"

"I think so. I don't have all the answers on that yet, but it does seem to me that if folks love each other, then it's natural for that love to survive death."

"That makes sense."

"Now, about you. Where should we go?"

"I should go and visit my mother and try to give her the same peace you gave your parents."

"You sure you want to do that? It hits you like an emotional tornado."

"But I saw how much it helped your mom and dad."

"Okay, then. Where's your mother?"

"Still in New York."

"In the same house?"

"Yup. She never moved—remarried and stayed right there. She took her husband's name, Rafferty. He is Frank Rafferty."

"It will be fun seeing the old neighborhood. Let's go."

"Okay, let's close our eyes and think of a time right after I died so that we don't end up transparent."

"You think of the time, and I'll concentrate on your house."

"You still remember what my old home looks like?"

"Of course. I went there the day I got killed."

James stares at her. "What?"

"Yes. I came and said goodbye to you."

He glances away. "Why don't I remember that?"

"You thought I was alive, and I let you believe that. You didn't even know I had gone missing."

James raises his hand to his cheek. "But, the police asked me when I saw you last."

"You told them the truth. You said you saw me after school in your front yard."

James nods. "Yes, that was what I remembered."

"The man took me right after school, and in half an hour, I'd died. So, the timeline was a little off, but, basically, you got it right. It didn't make much difference, though."

James's eyes soften. "I remember you kissed me on the cheek."

"I did. To say goodbye. You fussed about the kiss."

James rubs his cheek. "I didn't know."

"Bless you. Of course, you didn't. Now, let's get going."

"It's a good thing I'm dead."

"How so?"

"Some of this stuff you show and tell me could give me a heart attack."

Sam laughs deeply. James follows suit. Then they hold hands and squeeze their eyes shut. The familiar sense of movement comes over them, and slowly James opens his eyes to see that they have parked in the street in front of his parents' home. James starts the engine and pulls in front of the house. No sooner has he turned off the ignition than his mother comes out the front door and waves while running down the steps to

283

the car. "I just knew it. I told them they had the wrong kid. I'm so glad to see you, Son."

Sam blanches. "Maybe we came too soon after the accident."

James nods in agreement but smiles and waves to his mom. "We'll just have to make do with what we've been dealt."

James's mom reaches the Oldsmobile and dashes around to the driver's side. She signals for James to step out of the car so she can give him a big hug. James sighs, opens the door, and steps into his mother's waiting arms. His mom gives him a bone-crushing hug, which drives the air out of James's lungs. Sam gets out too and moves close to the pair. James's mother holds him at arm's length. "I'm so glad you're okay." She turns to Sam and holds out her hand. "I'm James's mother."

Sam introduces herself, "I'm James's friend. Nice to meet you."

Mrs. Rafferty puts her arm around her son. "Come into the house. When the state cops came here this morning, I had the wind knocked out of my sails, I don't mind telling you. They said you got killed in a one-car crash in Iowa. I couldn't believe it. I didn't believe it, and here you are. I yelled back at your stepfather that you were at the curb outside, but I don't think he heard me. I wanted to rush out here and see you. I should have told him that you were out here. It's so good to see you." James's mother holds the door open for Sam and James. "Go in, go in. You want a drink or some water?"

Sam smiles. "I could use some water, thank you."

"How about you, Son? Anything? A beer, maybe?"

"No, thanks, Mom. I'm good."

"Okay, you two make yourselves comfortable. I'll be right back. I'll get the water and then go tell your stepfather the good news."

Before James can say anything, his mother leaves the room. "Man, this is going to be tough."

"It will be. I guess we arrived a little too early."

"Yeah, that's my bad. With everything we've been through, I lost track of the date."

"No, we agreed to concentrate on right after you died. Maybe we should have waited a few days for body recovery and all that."

"Well, it's too late now. We'll just have to do the best we can."

Mrs. Rafferty sweeps into the room and hands Sam a bottle of water. "Would you like a glass?"

"No, thank you."

James looks over his mother's shoulder in anticipation. "Where's my stepdad?"

"He'll be right out. He's having to wash his face and all. I don't think he's recovered from the officer's visit."

James looks down at the floor. As he gathers himself to break the news that the officer was right, his stepdad enters the room. He grabs James's hand and gives him a hug. "It's really you, Son? We had such a scare. I feel sorry for the parents of whoever that unfortunate young man was who the police got mixed up with you. My heart soars that it wasn't you, and I'm grateful to God that you're here. Let's all sit down."

Mrs. Rafferty rubs her hands. "In a minute, I'll get us some cake and coffee, but for now, I just want to look at you. Oh, my goodness, how rude of me—" She glances at Sam. "I introduced myself as James's mother, but my name is Florence. This is Frank. Who are you, child?"

Sam blushes and gives her name.

Florence nods. "I remember you as a little girl. I thought you'd disappeared."

Sam says, "I did, but now I'm here."

Florence beams, and James reckons that his mom sees grandchildren in the near future since James and Sam were childhood sweethearts.

"We're so happy to see you all grown up, Samantha. Please, make yourself at home. Oh, and speaking of that, how long will you be staying, James?"

"Well, to tell you the truth, Sam and I have to leave shortly."

"Leave? You just got here. Why must you go?"

James takes a deep breath while he struggles to think about how to explain the circumstances. He figures that it will be easier to just jump in. "Mom, Frank. Sam and I have some bad news for you."

Florence frowns. "Bad news? What is it? You know you can tell us anything. Are you in trouble?"

"No, we're not in any difficulty. When I say bad news, I meant it from your point of view."

"Our point of view, Son? What do you mean?'"

"Okay, Sam and I are not alive. She got kidnapped and murdered when she was in the first grade. And the cops told you the truth—I did die in Iowa in a one-car accident."

The silence thickens. Florence looks at Frank with an expression that can only be interpreted as disbelief. "Now, Son." James's mom pauses to collect her thoughts. "A joke is one thing, but this one isn't funny. You're sitting right here in the living room. Why would you say these things?"

"Because I'm telling you the truth."

James's mother gets up and runs her hands through her hair. She looks terrified, and James feels sure she will bolt from the room. "Mom, sit down, please."

She complies but doesn't seem to be in control of her movements, and she wrings her hands. James reaches over to comfort his mom, but she pulls her hands away. Then she shakes her head from side-to-side. Frank sits and stares at him without saying a word.

James presses onward, "Sam and I are spirits, and we wanted to come here to let you know we're okay even though we're no longer part of this world."

Frank closes his mouth and swallows. His voice comes out harsh and dry, "What world are you part of, Son?"

Florence raises her hand to her mouth and gasps. Frank jumps up and grabs her around the shoulders. He tries to soothe her and then lays her on the couch, where he eases some of the throw pillows under her feet to help delay the onset of shock. With a huff of air, he casts James a "look what you've done" expression. "Fetch your mother a wet cloth from the kitchen."

James leaps to his feet and, after a few seconds, returns to the lounge. Sam takes Florence's hand. His mom's eyes widen, and she pulls her hand away. "You feel so warm, Samantha. Why is that if you're dead?"

"James and I have taken a form that you will recognize. We timed our arrival to allow us to appear mortal."

"Oh, my dear, I don't understand what you mean. The shock of this whole thing has made my brain rebel. Nothing seems to make sense."

"Florence, you're fine, mentally. It is a shock to learn that your son is gone, I know. I hope you can take some comfort knowing that God selected James to join Him for eternity. This is a testament to how you raised your boy."

"He was always a good lad. I just wish we had more years together. The full weight of what you've told me has begun to set in. It's overwhelming."

Pale and upset, James hands his stepdad the cloth. Frank puts the damp square on his wife's forehead. "How are you doing, darling?"

"I feel better. James, come closer." He complies, and his mom takes his hand. James sits on the floor near the couch. Florence says, "I've loved you more than life itself."

287

"I know that. You've always shown me your love. And I have felt blessed above all my friends because none of their moms seemed to love them as much as you love me."

"I'm so happy you know that. When the police officer came to the door, my whole world crashed. I couldn't believe the awful news to be true. Now you tell me it is, and for the life of me, I don't know how I can continue on. A big piece of my heart has been taken."

"I'm so sorry this happened. I didn't mean to run off the road. You have to believe that if I could have prevented the accident, I would have. I'm grateful to God for allowing me to come to see you and let you know that I appreciate all you and Dad have done for me, and I will love you both for all eternity."

Frank can't speak, and he clears his throat several times.

Florence uses the cloth to wipe her tears. "How long do we have you?"

"Sam and I have to get moving. We can only stay a few more minutes. Mom, once I'm gone, please remember that I will stay with you forever. We will meet again, and all these tears will turn into smiles at our reunion. Please believe me when I say that the sadness of today will turn into happiness as time goes on. We will each have our memories to carry us until we come together again."

"Let me hold you."

"I'm here, Mom." James lays his head on his mother's breast. Gently, she strokes his hair and whispers her final goodbyes. James cries hard. He can feel the misery that pours from his mother's soul. Here is this sweet woman, having to say goodbye to her only child. The thought of it sweeps through James like a wave and overcomes him. Never has he felt such pain.

All at once, it dawns on him that he feels exactly what his mother does. The crush of her broken love smothers him.

For the first time, James wishes bitterly that he hadn't had the accident. Up until now, it has been a matter of trying to find an eternal home and having a few adventures. Now, as he lies with his head on his mother's chest, the reality of his death lands on his soul like a great weight. Often, he's heard that the worst thing in life is having a child die before the parent. James feels that reality. He won't soon forget this hurt.

Florence whispers, "James."

"Yes, Mom—I'm right here."

"Will you come back to visit me sometime?"

"You can count on it. I'll come back. If you can't see me, always look for a sign."

"What sign?"

"I can't say right now, but you will know it when you see it."

James's mother lifts him slightly. "If you need to go, then now is the time. You and Samantha have given me a great gift that I will cherish for the rest of my life. I feel stronger now that I know you're in good hands. Samantha, I'm sorry you missed your entire life, but you are a beautiful Angel, and I have a great love for you as well."

James wipes his eyes. "Thank you, Mom. Yes, we need to go. I'm so glad this visit has helped. I would never have wanted to inflict such terrible pain."

"We know that, Son. I can go on knowing you're okay. I love you and don't want you to feel bad about what you couldn't control."

"Thank you." James rises and holds his mother's hand until it slips from his, then he leans over and gives Florence a kiss on the cheek and says his farewells. Frank gets up, shakes James's hand, and wishes him Godspeed in finding an eternal home.

James feels reluctant to leave, Sam takes him by the arm and guides him to the front door. She opens the door, and

Eternal Road

James looks back. His mother is still on the couch, and Frank is sitting on the edge, comforting her. They do not look up, and so he turns and walks out of the house. Sam closes the door quietly.

Chapter Thirty-Two

Sam wipes the tears from her face. "Wow, was that ever emotional."

James takes Sam's hand. "God, I felt every piece of her broken heart. Tell you what, though. They're going to be fine. Not sure I am, but they are two strong people."

Sam leans against James. "What kind of sign were you talking about in there?"

James wraps his arm around her. "I'm not sure, but I hope I'll be able to visit and leave something. I do know I'll want to go back and help them cross over when it's time. Is that possible?"

"All you really have to do is ask the leaders. They try to accommodate requests. That's what I did."

"Now that I have seen the pain my mother has to carry, I wonder why my dad didn't come to guide me. Not that I don't love having you do it."

"Your dad wanted to, but I convinced him that you would benefit more from his visit once you reached your eternal home."

"You and my dad had a conversation?"

"Yes. A number of them."

"How is he?"

"Anxious to see you but, otherwise, fine."

James releases Sam's hold and lowers his arms. "If we were alive, I would go and get a stiff drink and try to forget my mother's sorrow. Do we have anything like that on this side?"

Sam's smile appears forced. "Sorry, no. You did a great job helping your folks. That should sustain you."

"Thank you. I guess it will. Now, we should get going."

Sam and James get in the Olds. Sam asks, "Where are we going?"

James has to think for a minute. Finally, he chooses a destination. "It would be fun to go back and visit our school. Maybe back to when we started the first grade. Wouldn't you want to go and see what it was like?"

"I would, but remember, I got taken in the first grade and don't want any part of that. I wish I could recall the exact time, but it's a blur."

"It happened after school, right?"

"Yes."

"So that would make it sometime after 3:00. Do you remember the date?"

"May 22, 2001, but I didn't know it then. I only learned of the date through research."

"What tipped you off?"

"I did remember it happened on a Tuesday, and I put things together. First off, my dad used to watch Who Wants to Be a Millionaire on Mondays. He sat watching the show when I kissed him goodnight. Also, I loved the song, *Thank you* by Dido, which was popular during that time. Finally, I handed in my project the day before the man kidnapped me. My art project was due on Monday, May 21. I know that date because my mother put it on the refrigerator so I wouldn't forget."

James puts his hand on Sam's arm. "So, if we go there, we should avoid May 22, 2001, after 3:00."

"Yup, because I see no sense in trying to intervene to spare my life. Too much has happened."

"Did they ever catch the man who did it?"

"No, I don't think so. They never found my body. So, technically, I was missing and not dead."

James shakes his head. "Yeah, that sucks for sure. Okay, I just wondered. You ready to go there? Can you remember what the school looked like?"

"Better than that. The school's still there. We can drive over and park in front, and then we only need to concentrate on the date."

"Great idea." James starts the car. "Do we need GPS?"

"No, I walked there from here. I'll give you the directions."

James smiles and pulls the car away from the curb. Sam gives him turn-by-turn instructions until they pull up in front of the school. James remarks, "It looks different than how I remember."

Sam laughs. "Everything looks different after twenty years."

Children scamper about in the playground. James checks, "You ready?"

"Yes."

They perform the regular process to shift back in time.

James opens his eyes. "Sam, look. It's the school, and all the kids are here."

"OMG, see how small they are?"

"I know, right?" James turns off the engine and opens the driver's door. The sun feels quite warm, and the weather looks like a beautiful spring day. He tells Sam, "It's lovely. You should come out."

Sam shakes her head. "I have a funny feeling and don't think this is the right day."

James frowns. "What do you mean? We both concentrated on May 21st."

"I know, but I have a weird feeling that this is May 22nd instead of the 21st."

"The day you got taken? You think we landed here on that day?"

"The surroundings look too much like then. Not only in looks, but I can feel something too."

"Do you think, maybe, he took you on the 21st instead of the 22nd?"

"I—I suppose that's possible, but I remember kissing my dad goodnight during that Millionaire show."

"Could you have recalled another night you kissed him?"

Sam pulls her hair back and then lets it go. "Yes, that's always possible. Oh, James, we need to leave. Did you hear the bell? It looks like the children are about to get dismissed. Look there. I can see you and me by the fence."

James nods and chews his lower lip. "It sure looks like us."

Sam's voice shakes, "You're turning to leave in the opposite direction. That means I will start home, and when I get near those woods over there, the guy will grab me."

James squeezes Sam's arm. "Are you sure we can do nothing?"

Sam shakes her head. "No, we can't. If we do, we'll upset the time continuum. That has severe ramifications. We need to stay back and just let things take their course. Oh, God, this is too painful to watch. Look at her skipping along. She seems so innocent and has no idea of what's ahead."

"This is horrible. Can't we at least identify the guy who did this and, maybe, get some justice?"

Sam looks at James with terrified eyes. "I never saw him. He put a bag over my head and then stripped off my clothes."

James touches her on the cheek. "Then let's at least go and see what he looks like. Who knows, maybe we can tip off someone or something?"

Sam nods. "Yeah, we could. We can't prevent this, but perhaps we can do something to make sure he never does this again to anyone else."

James nods. "We'll have to do it in the year 2020, though. Anything else will also disrupt the time continuum."

"Okay, so all we need to do is get a glance at him and then we can go back to 2020 and look him up."

"That assumes that we can find him in 2020."

"Do you still have your phone?"

"Yes, of course."

"Let's try to get a picture of him. Then we'll have a chance of finding him again."

"Great idea. Let's move."

James and Sam follow the little girl from a safe distance. By his side, Sam wipes her eyes. He can't imagine how she must feel—helpless to stop what's about to happen. The sidewalk curves as they reach a wooded area. Sam and James lose sight of the little girl in the bend. When they reach the corner, the girl has disappeared. James holds up his hand. Sam stops with him. "We should go back a few steps and wait for the guy to come out of the woods."

Sam says, "It won't take too long. The man told me to keep my mouth shut, but then I started crying. He hit me hard, and that's the last thing I remember. The next thing I recall is when I went to visit you at your house."

The two stand on the sidewalk, and James feels sure that Sam feels as guilty and useless as he does. Sam whispers, "I just heard a cry." She crosses herself and says a near-silent prayer. "Please, God, forgive me for not interfering in this brutal destruction of one so innocent." The tears run freely down her face.

James holds her around the shoulders and joins her prayer for forgiveness. Almost as if in answer, a warm wind blows across them. James senses forgiveness in his heart. Next to him, Sam brightens. He urges, "We should get ready."

Sam nods. "I'm ready."

A rustling noise sounds from up ahead, and James and Sam pull closer to the trees. Footsteps head in their direction. Sam whispers, "Get your phone out."

James nods and pulls out his cell. They both walk toward the point where the little girl disappeared. In an instant, they come face-to-face with the man who killed Sam all those years ago. Sam stalls and stares the guy in the face. Quickly, he glances away, and Sam shoves her hand to her mouth to stifle a scream. The two pass the man, and James hopes they haven't given him any indication that they know anything about his crime.

Sam squeezes James's arm and puts her mouth next to his ear, "I know that man."

James puts his finger to his lips and takes Sam by the shoulder. "Wait until we get further away."

Sam nods and then takes a quick look back.

The man stands with his hands in his pockets, looking back at them. James whispers, "We should keep walking so that the man doesn't know we suspect anything."

After a fair distance, Sam and James look back again, and the man has disappeared.

"So, who is it? I was busy with the photo and didn't get a good look."

"The school principal."

James gasps in shock. "Are you sure? Let me look at the photo." He stares down at the phone and catches his breath. "Oh, my God. You are so right."

"I know. Every kid knows and trusts their school principal. He killed me. We should go back and see if we can do anything for that little girl."

James grips her elbow. "You know we can't do that. Just as you well know that we need to get back to 2020 to research and find out what happened to that monster."

"What if he's still a principal somewhere?"

"If that's the case, we need to figure out what to do. In the meantime, we should get back."

Sam brushes away a tear. "How many other girls has that animal molested?"

"We can find out if other disappearances occurred in this area."

Sam closes her eyes. "I want to say a prayer for that little girl."

"We can do that, but you know she turned out fine."

Sam opens her eyes. "Yes, I guess I do. Maybe I need to say a prayer for me, then."

James takes her hand, and they both repeat the Lord's Prayer. Sam then says, "Thank you, God, for delivering me to the point of grace where I find myself today. Please forgive the murderer as much as I have forgiven him."

On hearing her words, James's eyes fill with tears. Such graciousness on Sam's part feels overwhelming. He believes Sam is, in actuality, an Angel. Tightly, he grips her hand, and when she finishes, he adds a soft "Amen."

After another few seconds, James suggests, "We should go back to the school in 2020."

Sam agrees, so they walk to the Oldsmobile. On the way, Sam wonders, "Why did they never find my body? The people looking for me must have searched this wood extensively."

James says, "The man must have come back to the spot and removed your body. After all, he knew that two people saw him, and if the police questioned that pair, they might place him at the scene of the crime."

Sam nods. They reach the Oldsmobile and get in. The familiar motion lets them know they are moving forward in time.

Chapter Thirty-Three

They open their eyes at the same time and look at each other. James smiles. "I'm so sorry we fell into the time of your murder."

Sam says, "Don't worry about it. At least we found out who the killer is, and now we can go about getting some kind of justice."

His heart fills with his love for Sam. Her reliving the experience has hurt her, and yet she has this forgiving attitude, which seems open to everyone. James sees the school, and the style of the children's clothing indicates they have returned the correct period.

Sam reaches for the door. "Let's go into the school and see who the principal is here."

"Hopefully, they allow visitors. With so many school shootings in recent years, not everyone can wander into a school."

"I'll explain that I used to attend here and ask to look around. Come on, nothing ventured, nothing gained."

James gets out of the Oldsmobile and joins Sam as she walks up to the front of the building. Sure enough, a sign requires everyone to stop in the office before proceeding into the school. Sam and James go to the reception, where they wait at a waist-high counter. An older woman, with her back to them, works at a computer. A mirror hangs above the workstation so that any staff can see if anyone stands at the counter. The woman shows no sign of looking into the mirror, so James clears his throat. The woman glances at their reflections and then gets up to approach the counter.

"May I help you?"

Sam takes the lead, "Yes. We're new to the area and would like to look at the facilities here. You see, we're undecided between a public or Church school."

"I see. How many children do you have?"

"Two—a boy and a girl. Our son attends the fourth grade, and our daughter goes to the first."

"Shows you how old I'm getting. The parents look younger every year. I'm Mrs. Willet, the office secretary."

"Nice meeting you, Mrs. Willet. This is James, and I'm Samantha."

"I didn't get your last names."

"Oh, sorry, Wainwright."

"Well, Mr. and Mrs. Wainwright, we're proud of our school. It's a blue-ribbon establishment, and if your children come here, I'm sure they will receive the best education in the area. Have you bought a home?"

"No, we're still looking right now, but we heard this is the best school district."

"How right you are."

"I see by the placard there, the principal's name is Harland Curtiss. Has he been a principal for long?"

"Oh, yes. Mr. Curtiss got appointed in 1998 and is set to retire next year. We will miss him; he's a wonderful man."

James smiles at the confirmation that the principal remains in place at the school. But he shudders at the thought of this monster working so close to the children all these years.

"Would you like to meet the principal?"

Sam speaks up, "I'm sure Mr. Curtiss is quite busy. We'll call for an appointment. I hate to break in on his day."

"Very well." She hands them his business card. "Just give us a call, and we will set up a meeting and also show you the school."

"You've been most kind. We will do that. Thank you again."

Sam and James leave Mrs. Willet and return to the car. Sam expresses disbelief about the principal still being at the school. James says, "Show me the card. ... Harland Curtiss. And a Ph.D. no less."

Sam says, "We need to find out his home address and pay him a visit."

"What do you plan on doing?"

Sam shakes her head. "I'm not sure, but I think we should get in front of him and see if he'll confess. It's the only way he can save his soul."

"Don't you think he's lost anyway?"

Sam stares into his eyes. "No one is lost. We always have time to ask for forgiveness."

"Unless you're dead."

Sam looks away. "Well, there is that. Yes."

"Okay, so let's look him up on Google."

James scrolls through the information. "Yeah, here he is as the principal. I still need to search for more personal stuff. Ah. I have it. He lives on Chester Street here in town. Let's go there."

"Shouldn't we wait for him to leave school?"

"We have plenty of time for that. I want to see if Curtiss has a wife. His information doesn't go back that far. Oh, wait a minute. Here's something interesting."

"What?"

"The police questioned him in connection with your disappearance. The news report says the police talked to a number of men who may have come in contact with you. They mention the two janitors of the school as well as the principal. All were found to have no connection to the case."

"Yeah, well, that figures."

James holds up his hand. "Oh, and here's another story. His wife filed for divorce. Looks like around the same time as your murder. Also, seems like his family left him a bunch of money. It says that he inherited the family business but sold it soon after. Wow. He sold it for twenty million. I'll bet the wife got a big chunk."

"So, he's not been married for twenty years?"

"Looks that way. I don't see any other wedding reports. Wait. The wife died in an auto accident before the divorce got finalized."

"Wow, that sounds fishy."

"Well, according to the story, she was a victim of a hit and run. She was getting in her car when another vehicle sideswiped hers, and she died instantly. The police never located the other driver."

Sam sighs. "Yeah, of course no one ever found him. Hit men just don't get found."

James shakes his head. "This has all the makings of a thriller novel."

"Yeah, except it's real. What're the odds that Curtiss hired someone to take out his wife?"

James nods. "Sure, the whole thing sounds too convenient. The wife wants a divorce, and she gets knocked off."

"Any kids?"

James shakes his head. "None mentioned."

"Okay, then. I agree, let's go over there and have a look around."

James nods and starts the engine. He enters the address into his phone, and the directions take them there in no time. James pulls to the curb and then suggests that they park a little further down instead of right in front of Curtiss's house. Sam gets out of the vehicle. James asks, "Where are you headed?"

"I'll knock on the door."

"Okay, I'll wait in the car. I don't reckon we'll find anyone at home."

He pulls the Oldsmobile a couple of houses down.

***

Sam climbs the steps to the porch and rings the bell. To her surprise, the door opens, and a twenty-something-year-old woman asks her, "Can help you?"

Sam explains, "I'm looking for Harland Curtiss. Is he home?"

The young woman shakes her head. "Mr. Curtiss moved about a year ago."

"Do you have his address?"

The woman seems reluctant until Sam tells her, "Harland Curtiss is my father, and I've been looking for him for years." Sam makes her lower lip quiver and wipes an imaginary tear from her eye. The woman goes into the house and comes back with Harland Curtiss's address on a piece of paper. Sam thanks her profusely, and then she retreats down the steps and jumps into the waiting car. "Curtiss moved about a year ago."

"You have the address?"

Sam holds out the paper. "Yeah, here."

James takes the paper and enters the address into his phone.

Less than five minutes later, they arrive at the building. Sam says, "Park like you did before." Then she exits the vehicle. "I'll repeat the porch thing."

With a nod, James parks and then turns off the engine.

Sam walks up to the front door and rings the bell. After a moment, she rings it again but receives no answer. Sam looks around and then returns to James and the car. She gets in. "No one there."

"Yeah, so it would appear. What should we do?"

"We could wait until he gets home. What time is it?"

James looks at his cell. "Five to three."

Sam nods. "Yeah, so school will let out soon. How long does he stay after all the teachers and children are gone?"

James says, "I would bet not long."

"Yeah, that's what I think too. You want to just wait here?"

James nods. "That seems best. I don't want to miss this Jackass."

Sam nods in agreement.

James continues to search on Google. Nothing new comes up. He then switches to search on lost children in the vicinity. "Several kids went missing in this area."

"Since when?"

"Over the last twenty years. Oh, look, here's a picture of you."

Sam leans over. "Let me see. I remember that photo. My mom took me to a photographer just before I disappeared. For the life of me, I don't remember why."

"Looks like the kind of picture parents would love to show around."

"So, how many kids missing?"

"Five that I can see. You and four others. An editorial in the paper talks about a serial kidnapper."

"Any of the bodies found?"

James shakes his head. "No."

"You don't suppose Curtiss is behind all these kidnappings, do you?"

James nods. "I think precisely that. It wouldn't surprise me if his wife got wind of his activities and planned to turn him in when he killed her."

Sam slaps the seatback. "We're dealing with a terrible guy here."

"Yeah, so how will you get him to confess and seek redemption?"

Sam touches her cheek. "Good question. I'm not sure right now. We'll have to play it by ear."

James waves his hand. "At least we know he can't hurt us. That's one good thing."

"Not sure about the hurt part, but I know he can't kill us."

James frowns. "You want to go over that hurt part again?"

"Go ahead and pinch yourself."

James takes some skin on his arm between this thumb and forefinger and squeezes it. "I can feel that."

"So, you can feel pain in this temporal body. The only way you can escape pain is to move into the current time. If you stay in the present, you become almost transparent."

James lets go of his flesh. "So, what are we in now?"

"I moved us a few minutes ahead of the current time. That way, people can see us."

James smiles. "Good job. I'd forgotten about the need for a time change."

"I've become an old hand at this kind of thing." Sam jerks and points. "Look, there he is."

James and Sam peer through the windscreen. Curtiss pulls into his driveway. Sam whispers, "Should we intercept him before he goes into his house?"

"Best to wait so that we can talk to him inside. That way, he won't get away so easily if he runs."

Curtiss enters the house via a side-door.

James says, "How should we approach him?"

"Knock on the front entrance and make some pretense for discussion."

"If we don't get in the house, he can slam the door, and that will be it."

"Yeah, I know. How about we just go to the side-door and see if Curtiss left it unlocked?"

James shrugs. "Then what? Break-in?"

"You have a better idea?"

"No. Other than knock on the front and ask to talk, I don't."

Sam grabs the passenger-door handle. "You know that won't work. Let's go."

"Okay. Side-door it is."

Chapter Thirty-Four

James and Sam get to the side door, not knowing if Curtiss has seen them. They wait to see if they can hear any noises inside. Upon hearing nothing, James tries the doorknob. He turns it carefully, trying hard to keep quiet. Once the knob turns fully, he applies a little pressure to the door. The door moves slightly but then stops. James wonders if there is a chain on the door.

After a careful look, he can see there is no chain. He whispers to Sam that he thinks the threshold is holding the door. He tells her that when he pushes the door past the threshold, he believes it will make some noise. Sam asks what they should do. James answers that a rush inside after the door is open might be the best move."

Sam nods agreement, and James applies more pressure to the door.

Sure enough, the door breaks free of the threshold with a loud metallic snapping sound. Sam and James freeze and listen for any movement in the house. They don't hear anything and rush in. Once through the entryway, James closes the door as quietly as he can. They stand in a hallway, trying not to breathe too loudly. His heart beats so hard that he hopes Curtiss can't hear either of them. James gives a sign for Sam to follow, and they ease down the hallway with care. The corridor ends at the kitchen.

The pair step into the kitchen, and the floor groans under their weight. They stop for a minute and continue to listen for any movement. Again, the house brings no sound. They proceed through the kitchen and can see through the dining room into the living room. Pulled shut, the blinds on the windows allow little light in the living room. A small lamp glows in the corner on the same wall as the front door. It seems obvious that Curtiss is in one of the bedrooms, which seem to lie to the right off the living room. This gives them an opportunity to position themselves where they can confront Curtiss.

They walk into the room and come up short. Curtiss sits in a chair hidden from the entrance to the dining room. Though partially hidden by the darkness, clearly, he holds a gun.

"Take another step and make my intruder alibi a truth. What are you doing in my house?"

Sam stays still and answers, "Mr. Curtiss, we came to discuss a couple of personal things with you."

"What kind of personal things? And why not come to the front door?"

"We didn't believe you would let us in after you heard the subject matter."

"Okay, now you have me intrigued. What do you want to talk about?"

"A series of missing children."

"You're damned right about me not letting you in. Now, the question is, why shouldn't I just shoot you as intruders?"

"That's impossible since James and I are dead already."

"You sure don't look deceased."

Sam indicates to James that they should close their eyes and move two minutes ahead in time. James nods, and they both do so. A couple of seconds later, they return. Curtiss stands and warns them not to make any sudden moves. He drops back into the chair; the gun falls from his hand. He puts his hands on his face in an effort to understand if he was seeing things or not. He takes his hands away, and Sam and James are back.

"What are you two trying to do?" Curtiss's voice is shaky.

"We want to talk to you about your eternal life is what we are trying to do."

Rattled, Curtiss stammers, "W-what d-do you mean e-eternal life?"

James asks, "Can we take a seat?"

Curtiss waves them over to two chairs. They sit, and James places his elbows on his knees and tents his fingers. "Mr. Curtiss, we have reason to believe you are behind several instances of missing children in this area—"

"What are you talking about?" Curtiss grows red in the face and gives every appearance of getting ready to explode.

"Does the name Samantha Tourneau ring a bell?"

In an instant, Curtiss goes from red to white. "Where did you get that name?"

James points to Sam. "This is Samantha Tourneau."

"T-that's impossible. I mean, how could she be grown if she went missing as a child?"

"You mean died as a child, don't you, Harland?"

Curtiss puts his head in his hands, and his shoulders heave with sobs. He says, over and over, "I couldn't help doing what I did." Finally, he looks up. "You came here from the afterlife, didn't you?"

Sam says, "Yes. We want you to repent and save your immortal soul."

"Why do you care about me?"

"Because you need my forgiveness, and I need to save my soul. If you repent, we both win."

Curtiss wipes his face with his hands. "I'm so sorry. I have this illness. I can't tell you why I killed those children, but I did."

"I think the time has come to tell others about your illness. Your wife found out, didn't she?"

Curtiss leans forward in the chair. "She did, and I begged her not to go to the police."

"She reported you?"

"No, she said that I needed to get help and that she wanted a divorce."

"So why did you kill her?"

Curtiss looks down. "I couldn't trust that she wouldn't report what I'd done."

"Did she threaten you?"

Curtiss holds out his open palms. "She wanted a bunch of money."

"Or she would tell the police?"

Curtiss shakes his head. "No. I wouldn't have anything left if I gave it all to her."

Sam puts her hand to her mouth. "Oh, my."

Curtiss looks up at James and Sam. "Don't you see? She was disloyal and wanted money to keep her mouth shut."

"From where I sit, she should have gone to the police no matter what. You killed little children."

Curtiss sits back. "What makes you such an expert?"

"You killed me, Harland. You tore off my clothes and put your disgusting tongue in my mouth. You touched me all over until I screamed. Do you remember that?"

Curtiss leans forward. "You shouldn't have screamed. I loved you and wanted to show you how much."

"Then you punched me." Sam clenches a fist and holds it in front of her face.

Curtiss shrugs. "You had to stop screaming."

Sam unclenches her fist and puts both hands on her legs. "So, what did you do with the body, Harland?"

Curtiss smiles. "I still have it."

Sam sits up, and James grabs her shoulder. Sam opens and shuts her mouth like a fish trying to get more oxygen. No sound emerges, and finally, she stops and gapes. Then she fans her face with a hand. James holds her.

Sam leans over Harland. "What do you mean, you still have the body?"

Curtiss scrunches lower in the chair. "She's here in the house. I've kept her perfectly preserved."

Sam moves away from Curtiss and doesn't look at him. "What about the others?"

Curtiss nods. "Yes, they're here too."

Sam turns to face Curtiss. "Take us to them."

Curtiss holds up his hand. "I don't want you to frighten my girls."

Sam's mouth drops open. "*Your girls*?"

Curtiss entwines his fingers and rests them on his ample abdomen. "Yes, they are all my children now. I love and care for them."

Sam opens her arms. "What if we promise not to scare them?"

Curtiss puts his hands on either side of the chair and finds his gun. He wraps his hand around it and leans forward, keeping the weapon out to the side. "No. In fact, we have talked long enough. I want you to leave my house."

Sam folds her arms. "We can't go, Harland."

Curtiss eases back into the chair. "Why not?"

Sam raises her voice, "Because you need to call the police and ask them to come and remove us. We are trespassing, as you can see."

Curtiss tightens his grip on his gun. "I won't do that. You must think I'm a fool."

Sam points at Curtiss. "I think you murdered children and need to atone for that."

Curtiss looks at James and then, slowly, raises his weapon. Sam tells James, "Close your eyes and think of the present."

Sam does the same just as Harland pulls the trigger. The explosive noise and repercussion make Harland blink, and Sam and James's disappearance causes him to drop the gun. He stares at the spot in the chair where the bullet entered. Tufts of stuffing lie on the seat.

Sam and James return. This time, they stand behind Harland. He doesn't realize they have come back, and James clears his throat. Harland spins around so hard that James fears he might have hurt his neck.

"*What are you two up to?*" Harland screams.

Calmly, Sam says, "We came here to convince you that you need help. You should turn yourself in."

Curtiss starts crying. "I'm afraid to turn myself in. I've heard what life in prison is like for child molesters, and I want no part of that."

Sam tries to calm him, "You won't have to worry about prison because—most likely—you would get sent to a hospital for care. A disease like yours needs treatment."

Curtiss calms and wipes his nose with his sleeve. "What makes you so sure I can get help?"

Sam says, "I've seen hundreds of people get help. Not only do the diseases get treatment, but the people save their immortal souls by asking for and being granted forgiveness."

Curtiss leans down and retrieves the firearm. He turns to James, "Maybe you should call the police and take the gun."

James nods. "I would be happy to do so."

Curtiss smiles, and then—before Sam or James can move—he brings the pistol up under his chin and pulls the trigger.

Sam and James stand paralyzed. The power of the shot forces Harland back into the chair, and his topless head oozes. His dead eyes stare up at the ceiling. The gun falls to the floor with a bounce and a clunk, and the man's brains run down the back of the chair. Sam puts her hand over her mouth. A tide of nausea threatens to explode from James, and he stands there white-faced. Then he forces himself to sit in the chair opposite

Curtiss. Still reeling, he rests his head between his legs to prevent himself from fainting from the shock.

James keeps his head down and murmurs, "Okay, that was unexpected. What do we do now?"

Sam wipes her eyes. "I feel devastated. Oh, God, I forgave Harland and hoped he would seek forgiveness to save his soul. But he chose another path and has damned himself for eternity." Wild-eyed, she stares at James. "We should expect a visit from one of Lucifer's minions at any moment. I reckon Harland's soul hasn't left yet, or the collector would have arrived already." Sam goes over to Curtiss and checks his pulse. "Oh, my God. He has a pulse. Weak but discernable. His brainstem must still be functioning."

"So what do we do?"

"We ought to call 911 and then leave. Oh, wait, his pulse has stopped."

Sam takes a step back, and James wraps his arms around her from behind. In an instant, the air turns cold. James feels the sudden chill, and next to him, Sam shivers and hugs her arms. Out of nowhere, Adolf Hitler appears and hisses at the two, and then he approaches Harland's body. He reaches out and yanks the man's soul free the second life fades from his corporeal form. Harland's soul screams in an ungodly sound of terror. Adolf snarls in Sam and James's direction one more time and then disappears.

Sam and James stand together, shivering until the room returns to a normal temperature. James whispers, "Maybe we ought to get going."

Sam says, "Bear with me one more minute. I want to find the little girls to make sure the police can discover them as well."

James shakes his head. "That's not such a good idea."

"Why?"

James holds her tighter. "You will freak out when you see those kids, and it's just as well not to have that vision with you forever. You've no idea what condition those poor girl's bodies might be in, and it could horrify you."

Sam pulls away. "Then, maybe, we could just find the location and not look at them."

"I suppose so. Let me search the house and tell you where I find them."

"Okay, except I don't want to stay here alone with Harland."

Sam and James come to an agreement that James will go into the rooms first, and Sam can follow. They start out by going to the bedroom, which lies down the hall from the living room. Slowly, James opens the door and glances inside. The room contains nothing but a bed and a dresser. He walks over to the closet to check it out and finds it empty. He tells Sam, "This must be the guest room." Then he leads the way to a second bedroom next to the first. The door stands open, so he goes in. This room appears much larger, but like the other, it contains only a bed and a dresser and a couple of end tables. James checks the walk-in closet and the en-suite bathroom. Sam waits at the door and asks, "Did you find anything?"

James confirms, "Nothing unusual."

A third bedroom looks in the same condition as the other two. Sam says, "Does the house have a basement?"

James recalls a stairway at the side door that goes downward. He and Sam go back through the dining room and kitchen and come to the landing where the side door opens to a stairway leading down into a basement.

James says, "Wait here," and then makes his descent.

Despite his instructions, Sam follows. "I don't want to wait up here alone."

313

James tells her, "Okay. You should hang back in case I come across anything." At the bottom of the stairs, James finds a light switch. He turns it on, and pivoting to his left, he faces a substantial door with a keypad.

"Looks like we've hit an impasse, Sam. Come look."

Sam dismounts from the stairway and studies the door and its keypad. "This isn't good. Too bad we didn't have time to come down here with Harland."

Chapter Thirty-Five

James studies the keypad. "I can see marks on the numbers. If I shine my cellphone at an angle, greasy spots show up. We only need to press four of the marked keys and try a few logical combinations, which might allow us to get it."

Sam Nods. "Or look up his birthday."

"Huh?"

"I'm betting he used the first four numbers of his birthday. From my reading, that's what I think most people do. It's difficult to forget that sequence."

"Okay, let's do this. I'll check Harland's birthday digits against the glossy keys."

When Sam speaks, she sounds irritated, "Why not just enter the birthday?"

James wants to settle her, "We don't know if this device will lock us out if we make a mistake. If so, we probably have three chances. After that, we're done."

Sam sighs, "Okay."

James Googles Curtiss. "Ah, he was born March 29th, 1956."

"Okay. The number is most likely 0329. Of course, it could also be 1956, so I guess your idea of seeing where the pad got touched most is a good one."

"Thank you. The numbers that have the most smudges are the two, the three, the nine, and the zero. There are smudges elsewhere, but these look to be the heaviest."

"There you are. Hit those keys."

James enters 0329 and the enter button. The keypad beeps twice, and a red light flashes. "Damn. Although the heaviest used, it doesn't look like that's the combination."

"Maybe he put them in backward?"

"Yeah, that's worth a try. I hope this thing will let us experiment without locking up."

"Go for it."

James enters 9230 while holding his breath. The pad gives off one beep, and the light turns solid green. "We're in." James pushes the door open, and complete darkness greets him. So, while holding the door, he feels around for a light switch on the wall. His hand brushes a switch, and the room floods with light. A clear glass door stands ahead, and a wall encases the room. He tells Sam to wait and lets the go of the door.

Through the glass, several neonatal bassinette-type objects stand in a row—like you would find in a maternity ward. In fact, the whole set-up, including the glass partition reminds him very much of a hospital setting. When he grabs the handle on the glass door, it feels cold to the touch. He tests the glass, and it too chills his skin.

A tightness forms in his chest as his brain tries to make sense of what he sees. James pulls the door open and walks inside the partition. The chilled air raises goose bumps on his arms. A soft hissing noise reminds him of a sleeping dog's breathing. James attempts to take in and make sense of what lies before him. Each unit has a clear domed cover. His first instinct is to leave the room.

With an effort, James controls that urge and approaches the first machine. Tubes lead in and out of the incubator-type appliance, and a power supply connects to it. When James peers inside, his throat constricts, and he presses his hand to his mouth. Within what now looks like a coffin covered with domed glass, lies a little girl. James doesn't want to see any more. His brain tells him that all eight machines hold young children. He wants to run for the door and let someone else figure all this out. But if he runs, Sam will want to come in here, and he needs to prevent that at all costs. Most likely, her body will lie within one of these eight bassinettes.

James forces himself to look inside each machine. The reflection of the overhead light and the darkness inside the incubators make it difficult to see what each body looks like. James spots a switch located just below the domed top of one machine. He flips the switch, and the entire inside illuminates. The little girl before him is Sam.

Inexplicably, the child appears perfectly preserved. The machine provides a closed environment, and some sort of technology must keep her looking as though she merely sleeps. Ninety years after his death, Lenin still appears as though he sleeps. It must come from the same science. Curtiss must have known from his Ph.D. studies how to do it. And the fact that his family left him all that money would give him the means to build these machines. The question remains, why? Why would a man kill small children and then put them in boxes as if they are some kind of display?

James's mind takes him from the horror of the moment and transforms into wanting to understand an answer. He goes from machine to machine, flipping on the lights and viewing each child. They each wear a nice dress, white ankle socks, and Mary Jane patent-leather shoes. Although the dress patterns differ, the garments appear identical. The shoes and socks look the same as well. Each girl's hair has been brushed. A small degree of makeup is visible on their skin and lips. They all look asleep and peaceful.

James has to go back out and brief Sam. If he takes too much longer in here, she will want to come in and see for herself. He turns to leave, and while walking by the machine containing Sam, he pauses and places his hand on the top of the dome. "I'm so sorry. No one deserves to end up here. Your life would have been so happy had this monster not ended it. I wish it had been different." James sighs and goes to the glass door. He opens it and continues to the outside.

Sam steps close to him. "What's in there?"

James glances down. "I almost hate to tell you."

"Come on. I'm not stupid. Those little girls are in there, right?"

James looks into her eyes. "Yes. They all appear perfectly preserved."

Sam drops her voice to a whisper, "Am I in there?"

"Yes."

Sam grips his arm. "I want to see."

"That's not a good idea. It will come as a terrible shock."

Sam shakes her head. "I don't care. It's my body, and I should see for myself."

James sighs loudly, and yet he doesn't have a good argument for Sam's logic. In all probability, she's right and should be allowed to see her corpse. He shrugs and waves her in front of him. Then he punches the numbers into the keypad again and holds the door for her.

Sam eases open the door.

"Yours is the first one you come to. The inside of the machine has lights, so you can see better."

"Thank you." Sam edges cautiously toward the first container. She reaches it and then looks through the glass dome. Quickly, she lifts her hands to her face and covers her eyes. James dashes to her side to support her, but Sam seems in no danger of fainting. She parts her hands and takes in the full vision before her. "Oh, my poor baby. What has he done to you?" Her tears drop from her cheeks and dot the glass dome. Sam places her hands on the cover as if she wants to comfort the child. Her hands linger there until James suggests, "We should call 911 and then get out of here."

Sam looks at him, and in her eyes, he recognizes her reluctance to leave these small children. Unfortunately, they have no way to explain their presence here. James worries that the police will think they had something to do with all of this. What else would they be doing in the house of a stranger? "Sam, we have to go."

Sam nods. "I know. I just feel for these little ones."

"I'm sure they will get reunited with their families once the authorities figure out their identities. Then the families will have closure. Come on. It will all work out fine."

"Okay. Let's go upstairs and call 911. Then I hope we can just get on the road and find your eternal home."

James takes Sam's hand and gives it a squeeze. They go up the stairs and make their way into the living room. James looks around and spots a landline-phone on a table by the door. He lifts the receiver and punches in the number for emergency services. When the operator asks him to remain on the line until help arrives, James hangs up. "Time to get moving. A lot of folks will turn up soon, and we need to get clear of this place."

Deep in thought, Sam turns to James slowly. "Um. Yes, I know. Let's use the front door."

They go out the front and descend the steps and reach the Oldsmobile. They hear sirens off in the distance as they get into the car. James turns on the ignition and pulls away from Curtiss's house. They make a turn at the first intersection, and a police car races past. While driving, James looks at Sam. "You seemed preoccupied back there. Want to share?"

"I'm just trying to figure out why Harland wanted to kill those little girls and then keep them in a state of preservation."

"I'm not a psychiatrist, so I can only guess."

"Well, give me your guess."

"He wanted to possess the girls and had some kind of fantasy where he thought he could keep them as his own."

"What makes you think that?"

"When you were yelling at him, you mentioned two things."

319

"What two things?"

"That he tore off your clothes and put his tongue in your mouth."

"So that tells you he wanted to possess me?"

"I think so. Did Curtiss do anything else?"

"I'm not sure. When I screamed, it was over for me."

"I would guess he probably kissed you all over."

"Eww. That is just wrong."

"It is sick is what it is."

"Okay, I guess we'll never know now that he's gone."

James furrows his brow and thinks of the visit by Adolf Hitler. A feeling of satisfaction settles over him, knowing the monster will get punished all through eternity. "Well, at least Lucifer has him now."

Sam looks at James, and the corners of her mouth turn down. "The fact that Lucifer got him means we failed in his redemption. It's not something I feel proud about."

"Okay, but if for some reason he was innocent, Lucifer would never have had a claim to him."

"There is that, I suppose."

"All right, how can we put this Curtiss thing to bed, so you won't have it on your mind anymore?"

"I didn't make Curtiss kill those girls or take his own life. Therefore, he doomed himself to eternal suffering."

"There you go. Get rid of it."

Sam sighs and smiles. "Thank you. You've helped me a lot."

"I guess I should get around to deciding where my eternal home will be."

"Great idea."

"Where's your eternal home?"

Chapter Thirty-Six

James has always loved the Adirondack Mountains and remembers when his family used to go there in the summer for vacation. "What about the Adirondack mountains?"

Sam nods. "We could go there."

James pulls the car over to the curb and looks up the area on Google. "Adirondack Park looks like the perfect place."

"Well. Let's go there, then."

James shows Sam a photo, and then they close their eyes and take each other's hands.

When they arrive, James opens his eyes, and what he sees leaves him stunned. They have landed by the edge of a beautiful, deep blue lake high in the mountains. "Oh, Sam, look at this."

Sam opens her eyes and beholds the beauty before her. The lake doesn't look real. Reminiscent of one of those enhanced photos you see on display in photo shops, the blues of the lake appear intense and blend into the azure of the sky.

Sam murmurs, "This is beautiful. Are you thinking of this kind of place for your eternal home?"

"I am. This scene would make me happy for all time."

"Let's walk around."

Sam opens her door and gets out. James does the same. They walk away from the Oldsmobile and, wordlessly, pause to take in the view.

"Once I make my decision, what's the next step?"

"Your thoughts will communicate to the council, and they will design your home and put it in place."

"Just like that? "

"Well, it's a little more complicated, but in essence, yes, just like that."

"What about things like who you want to be with in your eternal home?"

"What do you mean?"

"Well, we don't like to live alone, do we?"

"I need to make things a little clearer for you. Come, sit on this rock, and we'll talk awhile."

James and Sam sit on a flat rock that forms part of the outcrop around the edge of the lake. Sam takes James's hand and looks into his eyes. After a deep breath, she says, "I know you want me to join you in your eternal home."

"So true."

"But let me explain why I can't."

"Don't say that. I'm not sure I want to go on eternally without you."

Sam gives his hand a squeeze. "You feel that way now. But you have to trust me when I say you'll not continue to feel that way once you reach your eternal home."

James pulls his hand free. "Then, I don't want to go to my eternal home."

"You'll feel happier than you ever have. You will find peace and love not only for yourself but for every moment you spend in eternity."

James frowns. "How do you know this?"

"Because I've found my eternal home, that's how."

"And you have no love for me?"

"I didn't say that."

"But if you don't want to be with me, then I think you have no love for me."

"Nothing could be further from the truth."

"Then why can't we be together?"

"Because life eternal is all about the individual, not about others. It's your life eternal, not mine. My life eternal is mine and not yours."

"Why?"

322

"You came into this world all alone. You needed human contact for nurturing and protection. Those days are over. You don't need protection and, certainly, don't need someone else."

"How about want?"

"Doesn't matter. Eternal life is for the individual."

"Oh, Sam. I'll miss you."

"See, that's just it—you won't miss me."

"Won't you miss me?"

"Don't take this the wrong way ..."

"But, no?"

"No. I loved you when you needed love, and now you have almost reached the point of crossing into eternity. Your place is ready, and it's a matter of closing your eyes and going there. Why are you crying?" Sam takes his hand.

"I've loved you my whole life and can't imagine going on without you."

"I will be with you, as well as that feeling of love and a whole lot more. We need to say goodbye now."

"I can't."

"Yes, you can. I'm going to release your hand, and you will close your eyes. When you open them again, God's love will fill you, and you'll have no need for me."

"Sam, please stay with me." James looks into her eyes. Then he tightens his grip on her hand. She smiles at him with loving-kindness and, gently, places her other hand over his eyes. James struggles to keep them open, but—inexorably—they close. His grip on Sam's hand releases. James doesn't want to open his eyes since as long as they stay closed, Sam will remain with him. Then he senses that she has gone, and he reaches out to try and touch her one more time. His fingers find nothing.

James opens his eyes, and through his tears, he sees his dad smiling at him. "My son."

"Dad. Where did you come from?"

"My eternal home. I wanted to come here and welcome you to yours."

"Oh, Dad. I'm so glad you did. This is the best place. Do you remember coming here when I was a kid?"

"I sure do, and I think it's perfect for you. Now, I want you to enjoy your home, and you and I can get together after you've settled."

"Yeah, I would like that for sure." James turns to look in the direction of the sun, and when he turns back, his dad has gone. An encompassing love of his eternal home overcomes him. The bright light and warm feelings convince James that he needs nothing else for perfect happiness. His contentment knows no bounds. At last, he has come home.

Chapter Thirty-Seven

"**You have done** well, Samantha. James has settled into his eternal home and feels God's love. You were so right when you told him he would not need anyone else. That was a stroke of genius on your part."

"Thank you, Your Grace. I believe it was what he needed to hear so that he could accept that I would not join him."

"I remain puzzled, though."

"Yes, Your Grace?"

"Why didn't you want to join him?"

"That's a long story, Your Grace. Let's say I've stayed on my own for such a long time that I can't imagine having to spend eternity with someone else."

"But you loved James."

"Which is the reason I had to let him go."

"I don't understand."

"Well, you see, when I got taken at such a young age, I received the opportunity to learn about life and love. I took advantage of all the opportunities afforded me. As I studied, it became clear that my thirst for knowledge would never be sated. The more I learned, the more I wanted to discover. Now I've reached a point where I don't want to stop learning. Because of this, I wouldn't make a good companion. I would rather study than become part of whatever he wants, and that wouldn't be fair to him."

"If you loved him enough, this thirst for knowledge would go away?"

"Exactly. Since it hasn't, I needed to make a choice to send James to his eternal home alone."

"Do you feel okay with that decision?"

"Yes. I suppose I have to be at this point. I desperately wanted my love for James to offer me enough, but it hasn't worked out that way."

"Well, you could always change your mind. We could make that thirst go away."

"James is okay, and I would like to keep my thirst to see where it leads."

"Whatever you decide."

"Thank you, Your Grace."

"Go in love, my child."

End

From the Author

I hope you enjoyed Eternal Road - The final stop. If you have the time, it would be great if you could write a review and post it on Amazon, Goodreads, or BookBub. Telling your friends, you enjoyed Eternal Road – The final stop is a great way to spread the word and it is appreciated.

Also, if you want to contact me, please send an email to Johnhowell.wave@gmail.com. Or visit my blog at

http//www.johnwhowell.com

My other book titles.

My GRL – Is the first book of the John Cannon Trilogy. John buys a boat he names My GRL, not knowing it is to be used to blow up the Annapolis Midshipmen on their summer cruise. John is the only one that stands between the terrorists and the successful completion of their mission.

His Revenge – John faces an ultimatum given by his nemesis. There is no way out as John either becomes a traitor to America or causes thousands of innocent people to die if he refuses.

Our Justice – The terrorist leader and financier Matt Jacobs has figured out a plan to eliminate the President. He is relying on John Cannon's stature as a hero to help him carry it off. John finds himself walking the fine line of pretending to help Matt while trying to figure out a countermeasure to the plan.

Continued next page

Circumstances of Childhood – Greg and his boyhood pal dreamed of big success in professional football and then later in business. Greg was the only one to live the dream. Now the founder of an investment fund Greg is faced with a routine audit finding by the SEC. The examination points to irregularities and all the tracks lead to Greg. The justice department hits him with an indictment of 23 counts of fraud, money laundering, and insider trading. His firm goes bust, and Greg is on his own. His best friend knows he is innocent but has been ordered under penalty of eternal damnation not to help.

The Contract with Gwen Plano – A story of two souls who must venture to Earth to stop a catastrophic event that is threatening the viability of the planet. They will have no memory of their eternal life once they occupy the bodies chosen for them. The two must deal with the situation using only the temporal skills of their host beings. They sign a contract before leaving their celestial home that stipulates what is required. They commit even though they have no guarantee of success but cannot resist the ultimate reward, which is a personal anointing by the Creator. There is no alternative for failure.

All are available on Amazon in paper and ebook formats

Here is my author page

https//www.amazon.com/author/johnwhowell

Made in the USA
Middletown, DE
05 December 2021

54357368R00186